Shelter at the Moorcroft

By

Ken Gorman

 New Generation **Publishing**

CHAPTER ONE

The entrance porch to The Moorcroft Residential Hotel was three steps up from the pavement. It was a stone pillared canopy open to the wind. There was just enough light in the porch to see by but the light beyond the half glazed door inside was bright and welcoming. Denzil Elliott was impressed by the many detached houses in the neighbourhood. He liked solid houses in large gardens with trees and bushes. He liked their space and he liked the play of light and shade along their paths, particularly the shade. This was the best side of the town, settled, spacious and comfortable. This was his first visit to Maskerley and he had taken time to have a good look round. He had not thought of staying in this particular vicinity until he had turned the corner and had become aware that the house ahead of him street was a superior lodging house. It would serve him well for a few weeks if he could afford it. He rang the bell confidently, then, emboldened by a wild gust of October wind, he stepped inside.

Immediately he was confronted by a small dark haired woman in her fifties. Her sharp eye and her businesslike manner established her as the proprietress.

"Can I help you?"

"I've just arrived in town and was looking for somewhere to stay. Have you any vacancies?"

He was aware of the woman's eyes examining him carefully and wondered if his shabby suit would disqualify him.

"How long would you be wanting to stay, Mr....er?"

"Elliott, Denzil Elliott. It will be for at least a month, maybe more. I have some holiday to take and I'm using it to look for a new job...."

"Here are my terms, Mr.Elliott," the woman picked up

3

a leaflet from the hall table and handed it to him, "Bed, breakfast and evening meal, weekly in advance, laundry extra as you can see. I have only the one room at present, you are welcome to it if you like it but I shall want a decision straight away, I can't be holding it open. You are wanting it straight away?"

"Oh yes, I would just need to fetch my case. I left it at the station."

"How did you come to hear of this hotel, Mr.Elliott?"

"I didn't. I've just been walking through this part of town and I turned the corner and found it. I felt that it would suit me as soon as I saw it.

The proprietress looked at him steadily.

"Right, I'll show you the room and you can make your mind up. It's on the top floor but you can manage that can't you?" She gave him another penetrating look and led the way.

The room was surprisingly big and solidly furnished. Elliott gently tested the bed. It had just the right firmness and its coverings were soft and generous enough. The walls looked as though they had been freshly painted in a light cream colour. The carpet showed little wear and tear. He strode to the window and peered out through the gathering gloom.

"It has a good view over the next street, then?"

"Yes, it catches the sun in the mornings. The bathroom is the floor below, the toilet is next to it and the fire escape is at the end of the corridor. Well now....?"

"I'll be happy to take it, Mrs?"

"Ridgeway. Terms in advance, Mr.Elliott. You can see me downstairs when you bring your belongings. There's a bell to my door if I'm not about. I'll let you have the keys then. The evening meal is at 6.30. You'll find the other residents quiet but friendly."

"That would suit me very well."

"Yes, they tend to keep themselves to themselves."

Half way down the stairs they met someone coming

up. Mrs.Ridgeway paused to introduce her new resident.

"Miss Catesby, this is Mr.Elliott coming to join us. He's on your floor."

The newcomer was a thin lady with a distracted air. Elliott took her to be about sixty. She was dressed rather strangely in a mismatch of expensive clothes. A small black felt hat leaning to the right lent an air of frivolity out of keeping with the serious face with its nervous grey eyes and its layer of powder. The lady extended her hand rather doubtfully.

"Oh yes. Yes. Well, we must talk later, young man. Where did you say you were from?"

"Mr.Elliott has to go to the station, Miss Catesby." Mrs.Ridgeway proceeded downstairs. Miss Catesby continued to climb but her voice boomed on.

"The station? Leaving already? Nobody has time to talk these days....."

On Denzil Elliott's return he encountered a tall, heavily built man on the first landing. Intent on being sociable, he held out his hand. To his surprise, the other withdrew slightly before reaching to take it.

"My name's Elliott, Denzil Elliott. I've just arrived. Pleased to meet you, Mr...?"

"Oh, ah, yes. Allingham, Henry Allingham. Mmm...I hope...you...er will like it here...er...excuse me." With that he was gone.

Denzil Elliott stared after him. He hoped that the other residents were not like him. What a stuffed shirt! He resented what he took for disapproval in the big man's downward glance. What had he got to be so superior about? He snorted and carried on his way until he found his room. It didn't take long to sort out his few belongings. That left him plenty of time to explore, he had quite a few things to find out before he could settle.

At 6.15, Denzil Elliott was careful to present himself in the sitting room. He had calculated that he would meet most of his fellow residents there before the meal. He was right insofar as three of them had gathered there and were watching the news on television. He made himself known to them and they responded warmly enough. One was Ernie Baxter, a genial, square built man in his early sixties who said he was in the watch-smith and jewellery trade. The sociable Mr.Elliott expressed great interest and warmed to his new acquaintance. Mr.Baxter beamed and jovially promised the new resident a discount of 10% on anything he chose from his shop but laid down the condition that it would only be if he, himself, served his customer. They laughed and were joined by a thin, pale faced young man with sleek blond hair. He introduced himself as Walter Jackson who worked for Ingoldsby's the agricultural engineers. He proposed that the three of them go out for a drink that evening but Elliott claimed that he had some urgent business to attend to. The vagueness of this excuse seemed to switch off Jackson's interest immediately.

The third person present was a lady in her forties with lustrous light brown hair and a gentle, sympathetic manner. She rose with an easy dignity to greet the newcomer and introduced herself as Elisabeth Elmwood. They exchanged a few vague pleasantries before they were joined by another lady.

"Christine, this is Mr. Elliott, just arrived. This is Mrs.Jervis. How long have you been with us, Christine?"

"It was September 10th, I remember it most distinctly. That means that I have been here almost seven weeks. My word, it doesn't seem so long."

The tall and rather formidable lady gave a little laugh. Denzil Elliott made a mental note to be wary of this lady. She was just a little too overwhelming for him. Mrs.Elmwood passed her hand lightly over her hair and resumed her seat Mrs.Jervis sat next to her and launched into a conversation about the history of the town. Elliott felt excluded and looked round to see where he might sit. The other men had resumed their casual observation of the news. There was a noise from the dining room behind him and everyone rose and moved towards the door.

"Oh, I should explain. There isn't a gong or anything. Mrs.Ridgeway is very good. She allows us to come down to dinner when we like so long as it's between 6.30 and 7.30. We sit anywhere we like though some of our habits have become fixed."Mrs.Elmwood took a kindly interest in the new man for which he was very grateful. "This is Mr.Allingham," she pointed to the tall, weighty man whom Eliot had met on the stairs. He was sitting at a small table near the far door and appeared to be half way through his meal. As before, this solitary man bridled then nodded stiffly, only briefly looking up. Elliott, determined to make the best possible impression, said "We've met already," and smiled sweetly.

Baxter and Jackson sat together at a table for two, their habit was clearly established. To prevent unnecessary embarrassment, Mrs.Elmwood invited Elliott to join her and Mrs. Jervis and while they ate he entertained them most politely. The ladies were delighted. By the time they had finished their soup, Mr.Allingham had gone and an amiable young man had entered. He was the same size as Jackson but he had frizzy brown hair and a thin moustache and his comparatively ruddy face had a generous spread of freckles. He greeted everyone with good humour. He was introduced as Mr. Frimton who worked for Tremlow's. He seemed to get along with the others without saying very much. Finally, Miss Catesby arrived with another lady. This time she was dressed in a long crepe dress with white crocheted collar and lapels. Her companion, a short, round lady, was relatively dowdy in a tweed jacket and skirt. She was introduced as Miss Edith Havers, a retired music teacher. They sat together and talked rather loudly about mutual acquaintances from the past.

By the time he had finished drinking his coffee and was ready to leave the dining room, Denzil Elliott felt that he had the measure of his fellow residents and that he had made a good choice in staying at The Moorcroft Hotel.

CHAPTER TWO

As the days went by, it was generally agreed among the ladies that Denzil was a modest, charming, sensitive young man who was an asset to the little community. He may be thin and shabbily dressed but he was scrupulously clean, gracious and smiling. They vied with each other in establishing his age, his occupation and his general circumstances. So charming was he that none of them realised how little information he vouchsafed. He fielded their questions like a professional cricketer. His manners were irreproachable and his modesty was remarkable. It was a joy to converse with him, however briefly. He appeared to be interested in everyone. He knew when to incline his ear and when to offer sympathy or general advice. He knew when a little joke or story was called for and his sense of humour was much appreciated. In short, he seemed to be the very paragon of a lodger.

It was not the case with Henry Allingham. Henry was somewhat alarmed at the new lodger's conviviality. Henry did not welcome attention of any kind. He was not curious about others and did not feel that others should be curious about him. He lacked a sense of humour and was not equipped to appreciate it in others. He disliked the fuss this newcomer seemed to generate. When Denzil was sufficiently ill-advised as to try to engage him in general conversation, he coldly excused himself and moved on. Not unnaturally, this did not endear Henry to the new man and it was not too long before the paragon began to mock Henry, at first, secretly then later, more openly.

Henry Allingham had been a resident of The Moorcroft for a number of years. He was a fussy senior clerk in a provincial branch of a big national company of some importance. His major problem was not that he was balding and running to fat but that he felt he was as important as the company he worked for. He equated his length of service with the company with indispensability. He really believed that the company could not do without him. Naturally he had acquired valuable experience in the work and, most certainly, he was extremely reliable. He had two other Christian names not known to his fellow workers except for their initials **C.W.** and this had led to his nickname "Clockwork". He became known as C.W. and in his ignorance he believed it to be a mark of respect or even affection. Sadly, he was not much liked. At work he was fussy and overbearing and not very sensitive of others' feelings. In allocating work rotas he gave little thought to individuals and their needs. Although he took pride in his work, there was something mechanical about his thoughts and actions and this affected his relations with everyone both in the office and outside.

His world outside the office was very limited. He had blundered into matrimony very young. He could hardly remember taking the initiative in this venture and, perhaps, he hadn't. His wife had been pretty as a teenager, but, as often happens, pretty plumpness had given place, all too quickly, to plain fat. He was always tidy and methodical, she had become slovenly and idle. One day, only two years into the marriage, he had returned home, punctual to the minute, to find her gone. A message in her undoubted scrawl indicated that she had had enough of him and that she would not return. He had found himself shocked but also, surprisingly, relieved. He discovered a new satisfaction in conducting his day in an even more orderly fashion unobstructed by considerations for another human being with uncomfortably close ties. It would seem that whatever affection or desire had been involved at the beginning of the marriage no longer existed. Never again was he troubled by thoughts of matrimony or emotional involvement. There were no known relations on either side. He made no attempts to trace his wife. After a few months, he sold their modest house, banked what was left from the sale and the settlement of the mortgage and took to living in homely lodgings. From then on, his satisfactions lay in the regularity of his life. He comforted himself with the thought that all was as well ordered as could be and that he was the successful and undeviating centre of that order.

From time to time he had had to move from one lodging to another. This had always been a dreadful upheaval for him, however, in many ways he was an ideal lodger and he had never had any difficulty finding another lodging quickly.

At first, his latest lodging proved to be rather irksome. There were more comforts and better food than he had to settle for in the past, but counterbalancing these was the disturbing fact that there more human beings than he had been used to dealing with. He wasn't sure that he wanted to adjust to their company. He swung between intense dislike of the occasional familiarity and the sudden warm glow he experienced after an unexpected kindness on the part of one or another of them. Most of the time he was distant. When he did speak for any length of time, he was prone to adopt his office manner, which scarcely endeared him to anyone. As time went by, he became aware that his fellow lodgers tended to avoid him as much as he avoided them. This was a welcome accommodation as far as he was concerned which had helped him to accept his present boarding establishment.

One of the inevitable problems was the sharing of the bathrooms and the hot water supply. Henry was very particular about having sufficient hot water for all his ablutions and he thought he was most reasonable in requiring a spotless bath or washbasin when it was his turn in the bathroom. Another thing was that as he did not linger in the bathroom, he found it inexcusable that anyone else should. This was a cause of some testiness on his part and amusement on the part of his fellow residents.

He failed to understand any attitude that did not accord with his own reasonable logic.

When Henry had cause to complain, he preferred to make such complaint to the landlady rather than to a particular person. This satisfied his sense of order and helped to keep a distance between him and the others. He liked to think that they were people who were only temporarily housed alongside him. He was the one certain, permanent resident. As he fortified himself with this thought he was able to summon brief smiles of condescension as he passed anyone on the stairs or in the dining room. At mealtimes he was the first to present himself and the first to be served. He ate quickly, occupying himself with a newspaper or a book so as to avoid conversation if at all possible. Inevitably he was the first to leave, which he did without flourish or signal. The words 'excuse me' lingered almost unspoken on his breath as a token of good manners should anyone seem to require it. No one did. His unsociable nature had quickly established a norm in which communication was avoided. It says much for the sensitivity of all occupants of The Moorcroft that Henry was left alone to behave as he wished with the minimum of comment and, seemingly little resentment.

This was not a situation that Denzil Elliott was inclined to accept. He had been offended by Henry's frosty reception of his friendly approaches. He mistook Henry's shyness for disdain and assumed that Henry disapproved of him for one reason or another. He was not one to take a rebuff lightly.

There were two bathrooms, one on the first floor and one on the third. There was no ruling as to the sharing of their use but it was accepted that the occupants of the first and second floors should use the bathroom on the first floor and the occupants of the third floor and the attics should use the bathroom on the third floor. The bathroom on the first floor was superior only in that it had a shower over the bath with a curtain at the side. The use of this shower was the common excuse for the residents 'from above' to use the first floor from time to time. Henry, as a first floor resident, disapproved of this practice on principle. His habits were fixed. No one interrupted his morning routine as he was an early riser. It was his evening bath that was liable to be delayed or disturbed. Until the arrival of Denzil Elliott, no one had given Henry any real trouble in this respect. Henry's regularity had identified his bathroom times very clearly and he was left largely undisturbed

Having been kept waiting twice in succession by the new resident and twice having been asked by him to hurry up, Henry decided that he must complain to Mrs.Ridgeway. After all, Elliott was an occupant of the third floor and had no real excuse for disturbing Henry's strict regimen. Mrs.Ridgeway was very sympathetic and spoke to the new man about the matter. With all the charm he could muster, Denzil pointed out that he only sought to use the shower but he assured her that he would not disturb Mr.Allingham again. Mrs.Ridgeway was reassured by Denzil's manner and wondered, not for the first time, why Henry was so intolerant.

Denzil's assurance was a smoke screen. For no other reason than to amuse himself, he became determined to be as big a nuisance to Henry as possible. He would have some sport as his expense but he would set about it carefully. If he created too much of a stir, he might be asked to leave which didn't suit his plans at all. Henry being a very senior resident had a major advantage in that respect. Denzil would proceed slowly and cautiously so that no one would suspect him.

CHAPTER THREE

Mrs.Ridgeway's establishment was well known and well recommended. She rarely had any of her bedrooms unoccupied for long. Business acquaintances often telephoned her to ask when she might have a vacancy so that they might house an employee, however temporarily.

A few days after the arrival of Denzil Elliott, Miss Havers was summoned to look after an aged relative in Scotland. She had lived at The Moorcroft for almost three years and she was quite distressed to leave. She and Miss Catesby had been close companions for most of that time and both of them took badly to the separation. While they shed genteel tears in the porch, Mrs.Ridgeway was on the telephone informing one of her acquaintances that the room she had spoken of was now vacant. By five o'clock, it was re-occupied.

The new resident was a bright young woman in her early twenties. She radiated good humour and high spirits. The fact that she was the youngest member of a rather quiet group did not trouble her in the least. Her modesty and charm were lighter and a great deal more natural than Denzil Elliott's. Immediately she became the focus of attention from the younger male residents. Walter Jackson pressed for attention but it was Gerald Frimton who was favoured with her company at meals. She was a newcomer to the town and had found work with a local estate agent. She was very outgoing and eager to have an active life within her new environment. Within the first week she had joined the town's amateur dramatic group, the Maskerley Players, and the Maskerley Choral Society. She was not given to spending time in front of the television or lingering in her room.

Henry, from his solitary corner of the dining room, found her personality quite endearing and thought it unlikely that she would stay long. Even her name had a pleasant ring to it - old fashioned, light and musical, but with depth, he thought. Sadly, he did not find her any more at ease to speak to than the others. Lucy Oxbury enjoyed everyone's company it seemed. She never lingered long in conversation with anyone but she made a point of speaking to everyone, including Walter Jackson who had been rather too eager to further his acquaintance with her. She would spend a few minutes in the sitting room most nights to get to know her fellow residents and she did this with grace and understanding. If Denzil Elliott was a paragon in his way, Lucy Oxbury was certainly a paragon in her's.

Denzil Elliott faded a little in her light but he was not put off his stride as far as his personal plans were concerned. After a suitable time had elapsed and the order of things had settled, he was ready to amuse himself at Henry Allingham's expense. His first trick was to disturb Henry's evening bathtime with a rattling of the doorknob. He made sure that nobody saw him and he made no reply to Henry's pompous growl from inside. After three such disturbances, Henry reported the matter to Mrs.Ridgeway who felt obliged to request that whoever was disturbing Mr.Allingham's bath time should desist. There was a shaking of heads and a sympathetic murmur at this, a look of astonished innocence on the face of Mr.Elliott and a general glance towards Miss Oxley. Lucy coloured and hastened to declare her innocence. She had never used or tried to use the first floor bathroom at any time.

The second trick was to unscrew the bathroom doorknob so that it came off in Henry's hand, making it difficult for him to get out. This did not worry Henry unduly. He had long experience of boarding houses and was given to expecting minor mishaps of this nature. He simply mentioned the matter to Mrs.Ridgeway. When it happened again, it was she who was inconvenienced rather than Henry. This infuriated Denzil. He had to think of something more irksome. He visited the first floor bathroom early one evening and spent some time looking round. After some technical experiment, he thought he had found a foolproof method of causing Henry Allingham embarrassment. The trick was to apply pressure with a screwdriver or a blunt knife narrow enough for the purpose to the bolt indicator. This he had found to be old and slack in its slot. Once pressed against its housing it could be turned silently so long as the pressure was maintained and the screwdriver didn't slip. This meant that the bathroom was no longer locked. Anyone could intrude and find Henry in his bath.

Of course, Denzil, himself, could not intrude. He had promised Mrs.Ridgeway that he would not. Then Henry's bathtimes were so regular that it was highly unlikely that the others would either. How could he implement his plan? After much thought he decided that he would startle Henry by opening the door but not going in. The occupant of the bath was facing away from the door so if he was quick he would not been be seen. Henry would have to get out of his bath to close the door again. This worked exactly as planned. The door swung open silently. Henry became aware of a draught and was obliged to get out of the bath as modestly as he was able, and make his way dripping to the door before closing it and locking it firmly. Denzil had more than enough time to escape unseen.

He enjoyed Henry's discomfiture but longed to share that enjoyment. He dared not. Whatever he got up to had to remain secret. What next? He decided to bewilder Henry as well as inconvenience him. A few nights later, he opened the door as before, pushed an empty cardboard box towards the bath and closed the door again.

Denzil Elliott did not understand Henry. Henry had little imagination and surprisingly little curiosity. As he got out of the bath, he glanced at the box but paid it little attention. He was preoccupied with his routine. When he had finished drying himself he picked up the box and put it on the windowsill. It vaguely crossed his mind that he had not seen it before and wondered who it might belong to but it was much more important that he should check that the bath was clean, that there were no puddles on the floor, no hairs on the rim and no steam on the mirror. What people left behind in respect of little boxes was not as important as what they left behind in terms of cleanliness and consideration. That is what boarding house life had taught him.

Denzil had no means of knowing what Henry's reaction had been. There had been no vocal outburst. There had been no public announcement. Had Henry noticed the box? Had he been aware that the door had been opened? Was it all worth the bother? What if his luck ran out and he was seen tampering with the bolt? He would have one last try.

Two or three days later, Henry happened to pause in the process of rinsing soap from his hair as he sat comfortably in his bath. Something had distracted him as he had lowered his head but he couldn't think what it could have been. When he had sponged the water from his face he glanced down between the shower curtain and the side of the bath. Why he should do this was surprising in itself. He couldn't remember doing so before. Perhaps his subconscious linked back to the finding of the little box a few days ago. Somehow, the mechanics of his mind had retained the information and had made use of it.

To his astonishment, he could see a shoe. He sat up with a gasp. In a second he had risen Neptune like from the foam ready to deal with any intruder. There were two shoes, side by side. Neither was inhabited. Henry was exceedingly puzzled. His was a logical mind but no logic seemed to account for the appearance of these shoes. In the case of the box, he had assumed that he had overlooked it as he got into the bath. He was certain that he had not overlooked a pair of shoes. He picked them up and examined them. They were not his, they were too small. There were no identifying marks. They were not warm, they had not been worn recently. How had they got there? He examined the door. The discovery that it was unbolted disturbed him. He moved the bolt backwards and forwards and watched the indicating disc revolve. There was no problem as far as he could see yet he was sure that he had bolted the door. Since the door had opened itself some days ago he had been most careful to see that he had bolted it properly.

On the completion of his ablutions, Henry strode towards Mrs.Ridgeway's office, strange shoes in hand. Mrs.Ridgeway did not like Henry's visits, particularly as he always had right on his side. The shoes were evidence and she set about finding whose they were. Denzil Elliott had realised the folly of planting his own but had been unable to obtain a pair of Henry's because Henry always locked his bedroom door behind him. Instead, he obtained a pair from the door next to Henry's. Gerald Frimton, the owner, had gone away for a few days.

The next morning, Mrs.Ridgeway was able to tell Henry that she was fairly certain that the shoes belonged to Mr.Frimton. How they got into the bathroom she could not say but she asked Henry, most particularly, whether or not he could have missed seeing them when he first went in. News of this strange occurrence soon circulated among the others. The possibility that the door was open was never considered. Most thought that Henry must have been absentminded and failed to notice them when he first entered the bathroom. Denzil Elliott was quick to side with this view. At last he could enjoy Henry's discomfort with others. It had been a very good wheeze.

The next day, Mr.Frimton did not return to The Moorcroft as he had planned. Nor did he return on the following day. On the third day, Mrs.Ridgeway began to worry. Mr.Frimton had said that he was going to visit his parents in Huddersfield and that he would be back within two days. He had said that he was claiming two days from work which were owing. If he had changed his mind and decided to stay longer, he should have phoned. He had paid in advance, as had everyone, so she was not out of pocket but she believed in politeness and….she was uneasy. Her business experience had given her a shrewd judgement of character. Mr.Frimton had always been considerate and at the beginning of his stay had not been averse to confiding in her. He had been more distant recently but she still felt that he would have told her if anything had been wrong.

That same evening, there was a problem with the third floor bathroom. Miss Catesby was unable to gain access. Her voice was full and round, it echoed down the staircase and even penetrated the sitting room on the ground floor. Miss Catesby claimed that she had been waiting a very long time, that the light was on inside, that no noise could be heard and that she thought it must be Miss Oxbury. She had encountered her on the stairs an hour or so ago. She must have gone into the bathroom. Perhaps she had been taken ill? Who was going to do anything about it? Were there no men in the house? Where was everybody? Couldn't they hear her?

The other residents were obliged to find out what was the matter. Mrs.Ridgeway soon arrived and gave permission for the door to be forced. Neither Mr.Jackson nor Mr.Elliott, both slightly built, were expected to offer much assistance. It was Mr.Allingham who was asked to apply his height and weight to the side of the door. He was very reluctant to be part of the fuss, but when at the fourth lunge, his shoulder caused the bolt and catch to give way, he was, secretly very proud of his achievement.

The ladies rushed in and screamed in ragged chorus. Miss Oxbury lay forward in her bath, her head beaten savagely. The men were allowed in. One glance was sufficient to send Mr.Jackson reeling to the nearest toilet. Denzil and Henry were made of sterner stuff. Denzil, almost as pale as the thin body in the bath, stretched down and felt the side of Miss Oxbury's neck. He shook his head. Together they ushered the ladies out and drew the door shut behind them. Mrs.Ridgeway hurried away to phone the police but not before she had told them all to go down to the sitting room and stay there until the police arrived.

CHAPTER FOUR

The police arrived in strength headed by D.C.I.Duncombe, the senior detective in the division. Mrs.Ridgeway met him in the porch and showed him into the dining room away from the residents.

Mrs.Ridgeway was a remarkable woman. She was not tall but she was undeniably vigorous and always commanded attention. She had lived in the town all her life. She had married Sam Ridgeway the baker and the two had proved a formidable business team. She persuaded him to expand into a restaurant next to the bakery and she personally ran the restaurant until Sam fell ill and had to retire. When this came about, she sold the bakery and the restaurant without a hint of sentiment and bought The Moorcroft Hotel so that she should be able to look after her husband there. When Sam died, she concentrated her whole interest in the hotel. She had no family, she needed to keep herself occupied and she needed to have human contacts just as she had through all her working life. The hotel supplied these needs.

She was committed and very hard working and the people who worked for her respected her and liked her even if she seemed hard. She was not so much hard as practical and hardworking. She was interested in her guests but thought of them first and foremost as customers. She wasn't the sort of person to take offence or to flare up quickly. She was upset at what had happened but she wasn't deeply shocked. Her thoughts were immediately focused on practical matters such as how to provide best support for the police, how to cope with the meals at this time, what arrangements would be necessary for the body, how to cope with the staff.

"Chief Inspector Duncombe, are you a local man?" Mrs.Ridgeway was used to taking the initiative in conversations. She didn't often pursue her questions but she always remembered the answers. "This is a terrible thing. If there is anything you need, please feel free to ask, I will give you all the help I can." She studied her visitor carefully. Duncombe was not tall but he was well built. He had a calmness and an air of patience about him which inspired confidence and comfort in most people.

"Well now, Mrs.Ridgeway, just let me direct the doctor and his team up to the victim…..the third floor? Right! Is there anyone else up there?"

"No, I asked everyone to stay in the sitting room until you came."

"Splendid! What about the staff?"

"They all finished at 7.30. There is only Jenny the young maid she's still down in the kitchen. I don't think she fully understands what has happened, yet. Shall I fetch her up?"

"Yes, I think you ought. Can she wait in the sitting room for the time being? If you would see to that while I am upstairs?"

Within a very short time the D.C.I and Mrs.Ridgeway were back in the dining room.

"First of all, tell me about that poor woman up there."

"There's not a lot I can tell you, Chief Inspector. She's only been here three weeks. A very pleasant girl, always cheerful, spoke to everyone, got along with everyone. She had a good job, secretarial, with Pinners…."

"Did she have any boyfriends?"

"None that I knew of."

"Where did she come from?"

"She said she came from Catton and this was the first time she had been away from home. Her name was Lucy Oxbury. Her home address was 16 Thorsby Avenue, Catton."

"Thanks, how many other guests have you?"

"There are nine altogether. On the first floor are

Mr.Allingham and Mr.Frimton, on the second are Mrs.Elmwood, Mr.Baxter and Mrs.Jervis, on the third are Miss Catesby, Mr.Elliott and Mr.Jackson. Miss Oxbury had one of the attic bedrooms."

"Was everyone in the hotel at the time of the murder?"

"Everyone except Mr.Baxter. He likes to go out for a drink, I haven't a licence. I don't think he is back yet. Then there's Mr.Frimton who went home on Monday and hasn't returned."

"And where is home for this Mr.Frimton?"

"Huddersfield. I'll look out his address for you."

"Yes, if you don't mind, We'll need to check up on him. When did Miss Oxbury take her bath?"

"I couldn't say exactly. Friday is her Dramatics night. I gather she has something to eat on the way back so she doesn't have dinner here and she has more time to get ready to go out."

"She would go straight from her room to the bathroom while everyone else was having dinner?"

"Everybody doesn't eat at the same time. They can come down any time between 6.30 and 7.30."

"Who discovered the body?"

"I suppose we all did. Miss Catesby shouted down that she couldn't get into the bathroom and that there was a light on but she couldn't get a reply. Mr.Allingham broke the door down and we all went in."

"Did anyone touch anything?"

"Mr.Elliott touched Miss Oxbury's neck, to feel for her pulse, I suppose. Nobody else touched anything. We were only in there for a minute or so then we all came downstairs together."

"Do all of your residents get on well together?"

"Yes they do. Considering their different ages and concerns, it is quite remarkable."

"Has anyone been back upstairs, since?"

"No, I can swear to that. I've been down here ever since and no one has left the sitting room."

They walked out into the corridor. The Chief Inspector swept his glance over the bottom of the stairs, the door to Mrs.Ridgeway's rooms and the door to the kitchen.

"How secure is this building, Mrs.Ridgeway? Could a stranger enter without being seen?"

"The front door is normally kept locked, all the residents have their own key. I've sometimes left it open when we've been cleaning, to air the place. In the summer I leave it open frequently to let the sunshine in but not at this time of year."

"What about the back?"

"That's always locked after cook goes off. It's a yale. I usually put the bolt in before I go to bed."

"What staff do you have?"

"There's Mrs.Hammond, the cook. Been with me from the beginning, a real gem. There's Mary Miles, the part time cook or standby, Sarah Lucas and Jenny Phillips the maids, that's all. Jenny is only sixteen, she lives in, the others all live out. Jenny sleeps upstairs in one of the attic bedrooms."

"Next to Miss Oxbury?"

"Yes, at the other end."

"Have all the staff have a key to the back door?"

"No, only the cook. I usually unlock the door as soon as I get up and it is left on the latch all day."

"So, anyone could come in the back way?"

"They could but hardly without being seen. There's always someone in the kitchen."

"If someone did get in, is there somewhere they could hide?"

Mrs.Ridgeway looked troubled.

"The linen cupboards are all locked. There's nowhere to stand up in them, anyway. They could hide in the toilets or bathrooms but not for long, I suppose."

Are your residents out all day?"

"Usually. Miss Catesby assists part time in a dress shop, she sometimes returns in the afternoons. Mrs.Jervis sometimes leaves later than the others if she hasn't a lecture."

"Were they all out today?"

"Yes, they were all out by ten thirty when Jenny and I made the beds and I didn't hear anyone return until after four."

"Well, Mrs.Ridgeway, a thorough search will have to be made. No weapon was found in the bathroom, it must be somewhere. Every inch will have to be turned over. We'll be very careful but you do realise that we can't put everything back exactly as we find it."

"You must do what you have to do. I'd better warn the residents. They'll grumble, no doubt, but the sooner you get to the bottom of it the better."

CHAPTER FIVE

The second in command of the murder squad was Detective Inspector Johnson. He was tall and lean with black hair and heavy eyebrows. There was a strong sense of urgency about him. His movements were always purposeful. His jaw was long and narrow, his nose very straight. He looked as though he was made of steel yet when he spoke there was a warmth and charm in his voice that came as a great surprise to most people. This was very useful when it came to preliminary interviews.

The interviews were held in the dining room while the rest of the hotel was being searched. Miss Catesby was the first to be interviewed. She was very flustered and gave the impression of being very frail. She wore a dressing gown with Chinese embroidery over what appeared to be a well cut skirt of pale blue green. She was thin and wiry and could have been any age over fifty. Her eyes were red-rimmed from weeping but there was just a hint of eye shadow above them. Her face was lightly freckled and unevenly dusted with powder and Johnson thought that when she was younger, Miss Catesby's face was probably her finest feature. He wondered what colour her hair had been. Now, it was a dull mix of greys.

"I'm Detective Inspector Johnson, Miss Catesby. I hope that you will be able to answer a few questions."

As soon as he spoke, Miss Catesby broke into a sequence of sobs. Johnson turned and called through the door. "Is Policewoman Walls out there? Send her in please!"

A smart and alert young officer presented herself and was promptly despatched to fetch tea. Even with tea and a comforting hand, Miss Catesby proved difficult to calm. Eventually her sobs gave way to whimpers and her whimpers gave way to a curious snuffling. Johnson decided to proceed.

"Miss Catesby, you were the one who couldn't get into the bathroom, weren't you?"

A judicious grasp of the wrist from Policewoman Walls steadied Miss Catesby who was poised for another gasp and sob. A whisper issued forth.

"Yes, Yes, I needed to get ready to go out and it was getting late...."

A further burst of subdued whimpering came too soon for the young policewoman to forestall. Fortunately, the exercise of speech seemed to lend Miss Catesby some heart. She recovered herself without assistance.

"I was going to call on Mrs.Humphrey to discuss the next coffee morning...."

"That's right, Miss Catesby, take your time."

"If only I could have phoned. Whatever will she think of me? Mrs.Humphrey, she's the organiser of our ladies' circle."

"What time was it when you first realised that there was something wrong?"

"Oh it must have been about 8o'clock. I was supposed to be at Mrs.Humphrey's at 8.30 and she lives quite a distance away. I first knocked at the bathroom door at 7.30 then again a quarter of an hour later. It really is too bad that we don't have proper facilities in our rooms." Her voice was becoming stronger.

"You live on the third floor, don't you?"

"Yes, I don't usually have trouble getting into the bathroom."

"Did Miss Oxbury usually have a bath at that time in the evening?"

"I'm sure I couldn't tell you. The young are never considerate these days. I always stop and speak but they seldom have the time or the manners to reply."

"You didn't like Miss Oxbury?"

Miss Catesby shrugged her narrow shoulders impatiently.

"Oh, she was alright but she was always rushing off somewhere, No time to speak."

"Do you think she had any enemies?"

"Miss Oxbury?" the thought seemed to astonish her. "She seemed friendly enough with everyone."

At this, Miss Catesby dissolved into tears again and Johnson thought that that was all he was going to get from her. She was led out and a robust lady was ushered in. The newcomer had an air of superiority about her. She lent forward a little from the waist as though she was giving everybody her best attention. As she walked, it seemed that her knees never quite straightened. In a smaller person this might have looked ridiculous but this lady was of substantial build. She was tall and big boned. Above the waist she was normal for her height, below the waist she was very big. Her face and neck looked almost young but Johnson reckoned that she must be forty. When she spoke, her voice had a controlled boom to it. He noticed that her eyes, a soft brown, were alert and intelligent.

"Mrs.Christine Jervis," she introduced herself, placing a strong brown handbag firmly beside her chair.

"Ah, Mrs.Jervis, how long have you been a resident here?"

"Since the middle of September. I'm deputy Headmistress at Hagworth Junior School and I was seconded to a course here at your Institute of Education. I could have travelled but I wouldn't have had the time to study at home. My husband thought it best for me to stay here during the week and go home at the weekends."

"Was there any particular reason why you chose this hotel?"

"No, the Institute sent me a list of recommended places. I looked at one or two then came across this one. It is very old fashioned but it suited me excellently."

"Why is that, can you say?"

"It is quiet and private. I can get my work done without interruption. Also, I am well fed and looked after.

If it was more up to date, it would be noisier and I wouldn't be able to settle to my work."

"So the other residents don't disturb you?"

"Oh no. Once I'm in my room, I'm entirely undisturbed. Nobody here makes much noise."

"It must come as a shock to you when this happens in such a quiet hotel."

"I simply don't know what to think. Miss Oxbury was a very pleasant young woman."

"Mrs. Jervis, you were one of the first people on the scene, I wonder if you would run through the events of the evening in you own words."

"I'll try."

Mrs.Jervis straightened herself in her chair and leaned her bosom forward.

"I had finished dinner and was watching the tail-end of the news on T.V. when I heard Miss Catesby shouting down the stairs. She sounded quite agitated so I rushed out to see what was wrong…."

"Who was with you in the TV lounge?"

"Mrs.Ridgeway always calls it the sitting room. Let me see, Mr.Jackson , he's always there, and Mr.Baxter."

"Mr.Baxter, I thought that he'd gone out?"

"He must have gone out when I went upstairs. He had his hat and coat with him ready."

"You went upstairs?"

"Yes, I found Miss Catesby standing by the bathroom door. She said that there was someone inside but she couldn't get an answer. The men joined us and we rattled the door but there was no answer. Someone said that we should force the door but I felt that only Mrs.Ridgeway could authorise that so I hurried down to ask her."

"When the door was forced, were you the first one in?"

Mrs.Jervis had to think.

"Everything was so automatic at that point. Miss Catesby was standing next to Mr.Allingham, she must have been the first in. Mr.Allingham held back so I must have been the next, but when I think of us all jammed in there it could have been Mrs.Elmwood or one of the men."

"It was clear to you that Miss Oxbury was dead?"

"Oh, certainly. She was bent forward and there was this awful gash at the back of the head." Mrs.Jervis shuddered at the memory.

"Did anyone touch the body?"

"Yes, it was Mr.Elliott. He felt for the pulse and shook his head."

"Did you notice anything unusual about the bathroom, apart from the body, that is?"

Mrs.Jervis took her time but shook her head.

"No I didn't. There wasn't much chance with us all crowded in. Everything looked tidy."

Mrs. Elmwood? This is a very disturbing business. I'm afraid we must ask a lot of questions."

The Inspector watched the newcomer enter and sit down. Mrs.Elmwood seemed very composed. She carried with her an old-fashioned knitting bag with flat wooden handles which she settled in her lap as though it were part of her person. She was neither so tall nor so well built as Mrs.Jervis but she was above medium height and she kept herself upright. She had a mass of light brown hair, almost blonde, brushed back from her temples and falling lightly at each side of her face, which was broad with high cheekbones. Her nose was generous without being dominant and her mouth was soft and full. Her eyes were a gentle grey-green and lent the face a restful expression, whatever she may be thinking. Could this be another schoolteacher? he wondered

"How long have you been resident here?"

"Quite a long time, Inspector. After Mr.Allingham, I'm probably the longest server."

"So you must have liked it here?"

"I can't remember how I came to find this hotel but

30

once I got here I found it suited me very well."

The voice was stronger and deeper than he had expected but it seemed one with her personality.

"I understand that you are a widow?"

"Yes, my husband died five years ago. I needed to earn a living. I had secretarial skills and I was prepared to go anywhere. A good job cropped up here at Crompton's. It paid well and I didn't really want to set up another home, so here I am, being well looked after."

"You get along with the other residents?"

She smiled. "After so long in the place, I can say that I'm very adaptable. I respect privacy and I expect others to respect mine but I'm interested in people and enjoy their conversation."

"Did you know Miss Oxbury well?"

"She was quite new here but she made a good impression on everyone. She was the kind of person who could talk to everybody. I liked her, she was so lively. What a terrible waste!"

Mrs.Elmwood looked troubled but she recovered herself quickly.

"Did you hear Miss Catesby calling from the top of the stairs?"

"Yes, I was in my room. I had just come up after dinner and was having a short lie down." Here Mrs.Elmwood stared at the Inspector as though testing his reaction to that last statement. Ah, he thought, a little vanity here, a woman in her forties not wishing it to be known that she takes a nap after her meal. She went on.

I heard a vague shouting then footsteps. By the time I got out to see what was happening everyone was gathered outside the upstairs bathroom door."

"You were in time to see the door being broken open?"

"Yes, Mr.Allingham was surprisingly strong. It didn't take him long."

"Did you go into the bathroom?"

"I only got as far as the doorway. That was far enough

as far as I was concerned."

"You did not see the body?"

"I only caught a glimpse."

"You didn't see the rest of the bathroom, you couldn't say if there was anything unusual about it?"

"No. I'm afraid that it isn't the bathroom I use normally. Mine's the first floor bathroom."

Mr.Jackson was next. He was distinctly nervous. He was lightly built with fair hair and blue eyes rather close together. Johnson thought that he was the sort who would be popular with women if it wasn't for his unusually pale face. There wasn't a hint of colour or a single freckle to relieve the whiteness. At this moment his eyes were far from still.

"You don't look very well Mr.Jackson. Is there anything we can get you?"

"No thanks, I'm just recovering from a duodenal ulcer. My digestion is not too good. Something like this doesn't help, does it?"

The thin sharp voice had a whine to it. Johnson sighed inwardly.

"Where were you when Miss Catesby called from upstairs?"

"I was watching TV in the lounge."

"You felt you had to go to MissCatesby's rescue, did you?"

"Well the others rushed out, I thought that I should go along too."

"The others, who were they?"

"Well…there was Mrs.Jervis and… Ernie Baxter…"

"Mr.Baxter went upstairs with you, did he?"

"Yes…er…no! No, now that I come to think of it, he just came to the bottom of the stairs. He must have gone out. He wasn't with us when we broke in."

"How long have you been here, Mr.Jackson?"

"Nearly two months, I think."

"Were you sent here or did you choose to live here?"

"I don't know what you mean."

"Why particularly here?"

"I've got to live somewhere, haven't I?"

"I'm simply asking you how you chose The Moorcroft from all the other boarding houses in the area."

"Why shouldn't I? What's wrong with me living here? If you must know, my firm moved me into the area and they are paying for it. This is one of the places on their list. I liked it. Why shouldn't I stay here? Is there something wrong with me staying here?"

"No reason whatsoever. I just thought that the company might be a bit old for you, that's all."

"I do get out, you know. I go dancing at the Diamond. I happen to get along well with the ladies...."

"Did you get along well with Miss Oxbury?"

Jackson bridled and a hint of colour appeared in his cheeks.

"Here! What are you getting at?"

"You were friendly with Miss Oxbury were you not?"

"So what if I was? That was when she first came. I thought she was very nice and I asked her out. She turned me down flat, that's all."

"Did you quarrel?"

"No, we didn't. She simply said no. I didn't ask her again. You have an instinct for that sort of thing, don't you?"

"When the bathroom door was opened, did you have a good look into the room?"

"Well, I went in but the sight of that bloody head set my stomach off and I had to rush to the toilet to be sick."

"So you didn't have a good look at the room itself?"

Jackson drew an impatient breath.

"No, I'm not a bloody interior decorator you know!"

Johnson's voice turned steely.

"Just what are you then, Mr.Jackson?"

There was something in the Inspector's eye as well as

his voice that quelled Jackson immediately.

"Oh, I'm a sales rep for Ingoldsby's"

"One last thing for the moment, do you always go into the sitting room straight after dinner?"

"Er….yes, always. It's a habit now."

CHAPTER SIX

"Mr.Allingham, you are the gentleman who broke into the bathroom? Do sit down, I'm afraid I must ask you a lot of questions"

Henry was a changed man. He couldn't quite account for it apart from the actual drama of finding the body, but he was excited. Normally, he would have shrunk from all the fuss, he would have hated the tears and the distress, he would have deplored the interruption of his routine. Normally he would have set himself apart but he couldn't set himself apart from this and, to his surprise, he did not wish to. He prided himself on his method and his logic and he believed that here was a situation in which he could be of real assistance.

"Mr.Allingham, where were you when Miss Catesby raised the alarm?"

"I was in my room, reading my newspaper."

"Do you always go to your room straight after dinner?"

"Yes, I'm a creature of habit."

"You heard Miss Catesby cry out and you left your room and went to see what the matter was? Were you first on the scene?"

"No, Mrs.Jervis was there before me."

"But you were already on the first floor. Mrs.Jervis was on the ground floor. How did she get there first?"

"I didn't go straight away. I never like to get involved unless I have to. When I heard voices and footsteps on the stairs I thought I had better go."

"Why don't you like to get involved Mr.Allingham? Don't you get along with the others?"

"Oh, it's not a case of not getting along with them. I've always been a very private person. I let them get on with their own lives and hope that they will let me get on with mine."

"You've been here a long time?"

"Yes, I think I've been here longer than anyone."

"Did you know Miss Oxbury well?"

"Not really. I thought she was a very pleasant person."

"Nobody had quarrelled with her recently?"

"I'm sure that no one had quarrelled with her at all."

Henry was amazed at himself. Never had he been so forthcoming.

"You would therefore say that this hotel has been a happy place?"

"It has been a happy place for me, I can't speak for the others."

"When you forced the bathroom door, did everyone rush in at once?"

"No, the ladies rushed in first. As there was a lady in the bath, naturally the men held back. When the ladies screamed, we pushed in."

"What did you see when you pushed your way in?"

"Miss Oxbury was bent forwards - I can't think why the body was in that position, why didn't it fall sideways? Anyway, the back of her skull had been crushed. Blood had poured out over her neck and shoulders. She was cold. Mr.Elliott felt for her pulse but there was none."

"When you said that she was cold, did you mean dead or did you mean cold in terms of temperature?"

"Dead. I didn't touch the body, but now you mention it there was one very interesting thing. There was very little steam in the bathroom."

Inspector Johnson began to warm to this solid dull looking man.

"Did you notice anything else unusual about this bathroom?"

"Only that everything was tidy. Even the towel on the stool was neatly folded. I appreciate tidiness, myself."

"There were no signs of a struggle?"

"No, none at all. Before I left I had a last look round.

There was no blood anywhere except on the body and in the water."

Henry Allingham was much more alert than the Inspector could have guessed. He hoped that he wouldn't turn out to be a bungling amateur detective.

"Who was last out of the bathroom?"

"I was, I remember closing the door."

"And why do think you particularly remember closing the door?"

"I was thinking of the times I had trouble with the downstairs bathroom,"

"Oh? What trouble was that?"

Henry told the Inspector about the mysterious cardboard box and the pair of shoes and how curious it was that the door had not been bolted. Henry's deliberate manner of speaking would not have endeared him to a reading circle but it was heartily approved by its present listener. What a relief it was to find someone who could make a direct statement without any exaggeration or embroidery.

"I'd like you to show me that bathroom. I'd like to have a clear picture of it."

Henry was happy to go with the Inspector. Together they went down to the first floor bathroom. The cardboard box was still on the windowsill. Johnson called for someone to take it away and a policewoman took it away most carefully.

"Now, about this door...."

Johnson tried the bolt from the inside, watching its movement most carefully then he went outside and studied the indicator as he moved the bolt again.

"Mr. Allingham, you have been most helpful. You say that the shoes belonged to Mr. Frimton? Clearly he could not have put them there himself, do you think that someone was playing a practical joke?"

"I haven't given it much thought until now. I suppose it is possible, but who would want to play such a trick and

37

why?" Henry was genuinely puzzled.

"You haven't quarrelled with any of the other guests?"

"I'm afraid that I haven't paid them much attention."

"You haven't a particular friend among the others?"

Henry coloured. He suddenly found the question embarrassing.

"I suppose I must be antisocial. I hadn't realised but I've never felt comfortable with other people, except at work of course."

Johnson felt sorry for Henry and would have liked to know more about him. For the moment he decided not to pry. He did not want to alienate Henry, he felt he was going to be very useful. He guessed that someone had not liked Henry and had resorted to silly tricks, either that or someone had been practising a dummy run.

"Well, let's leave it for the present. I'm sure I'll have some more questions for you later. Thank you very much for your help."

When Denzil Elliott entered the dining room, his face was the colour of fresh putty and he was perspiring heavily.

"Mr.Eliott isn't it? What can you tell me about this terrible business?"

"Er....well...."

"Let's start at the beginning. How long have you been staying at the hotel?"

"Er.... I came here nearly five weeks ago."

"Oh, you came here about the same time as Miss Oxbury?"

"Oh no, she came more than a week after that."

"Did you come here in connection with your work?"

"My work? Oh....yes. Er I'm not in a regular job at the moment. I haven't told the others but I came into a small legacy recently so I quit my other job and I'm here looking for a better one."

"What did you do before you came here?"

"I was a waiter in a hotel."

38

"Really? Where was that, Mr.Elliott?"

"The Aston in Harrogate."

"I gather that you didn't care for it?"

"No."

"What didn't you like about it?"

Elliott squirmed in his chair.

"I didn't like the hours and I didn't like the people"

"The staff or the customers?"

"Both!"

"What sort of work do you think you'll find here?"

"I ….I want to do some research."

"Research! Do you mean to become a student or are you thinking of consumer research? Wouldn't you have to join a big company for that?"

"I'm not really sure. I'm only getting round to thinking about it."

"How did you get along with the customers here?"

"Pretty well. I think they all like me."

"Including Miss Oxbury?"

"I didn't see much of Miss Oxbury. She was always rushing off somewhere."

"Don't you get out much, Mr.Elliott?"

"Just occasionally. I haven't got used to the area yet."

"You are not married?"

"I haven't had much chance yet. Late hours as a waiter haven't helped me to get out and meet people."

"You are still young, of course. Where were you when Miss Catesby called for help?"

"I was still in the dining room."

"You were still eating?"

"No, I had finished. They had cleared the tables and I was just sitting."

"Just sitting?"

"I sometimes like a cigarette after a meal"

"You didn't think of going into the lounge?"

"Oh, the television's always on there. I can't stand all the news bulletins. That's all people do here, watch news bulletins."

"Was anyone else with you in the dining room?"

"No, they had all left."

"So, you heard Miss Catesby's voice, what did you do?"

"Er....nothing at first, I didn't think that there was anything really wrong. Just another old biddy shouting...."

"Is there a lot of shouting in this hotel?"

"Well, maybe not but I'd had enough of rushing to every old woman's cry. It was only after I'd heard someone talking about forcing the door that I thought I'd better take a look."

"Who did you hear talking about forcing the door?"

"I'm not sure. It might have been Mrs.Ridgeway."

"You heard her from the dining room?"

"Yes, she was on the stairs."

"Who was she talking to?"

"I couldn't tell you."

"Alright, you heard someone talking about forcing the door, what did you do?"

"I followed them up the stairs. They were all congregated round the bathroom door. I gathered that someone was inside but wasn't answering. Allingham put his shoulder to the door and burst in...."

"Who was first in?"

"Allingham, I suppose."

"Didn't you see who it was?"

"Oh yes, I remember, the women all rushed in."

"Did you go in?"

"Yes, the women let out such screams. I pushed through and there she was. Miss Oxbury in the bath with her head all beaten in."

"What did you do next?"

"I thought I ought find out if she was still alive. I've done a bit of first aid so I felt her neck for her pulse but there wasn't any."

"Was the body cold?"

"Lukewarm, I'd say. I don't know how long she'd been dead."

"Then what did you do?"

"There was nothing to do but leave it to the police."

"So you went downstairs with the others?"

"Yes."

"Apart from the ladies, who else was there?"

"There was Jackson....and Allingham, of course."

"Why of course?"

"Oh, Allingham is everywhere."

"You don't like Mr.Allingham, do you?"

"He's a stuffed shirt and a creep, I can't stand him!"

"Is that why you played tricks on him while he was in the bath?"

Denzil was aghast. He had given himself away. He had allowed his spleen free rein. How could he have been so stupid? All he had to do was hold his tongue and no one would have known. He hadn't been tricked. The Inspector had simply waited and his own tongue had trapped him. Under the circumstances, there was only one thing to do.

"Inspector, I think I ought to tell you about that."

"Yes, I think you ought."

CHAPTER SEVEN

Chief Inspector Douglas Duncombe was a restless man.
Several of his officers were inclined to call him
hyperactive. The truth was that he hated the routine
deskwork of his job. Every day the weight of documents
on his desk seemed to increase and the futility of so much
of it was paralysing. He supposed it must be the same for
his Superintendent but wondered if it wasn't simply a
matter of 'handing down'. If only it concerned detective
work he would be happy but much of it concerned
changes in regulations and procedures. It seemed to him
endless trivia better handled by a filing clerk, yet he knew
that he had to digest it all. Secretly, he longed to be out
and about, to be physically active. He was within sight of
fifty and was beginning to worry about stiffening up. He
played a few rounds of golf but was too impatient to
develop his game, besides, he had less and less time for it.
In his imagination, every minute behind his desk
deposited another molecule of fatty substance in his
arteries. He worried about becoming a hypochondriac.

A murder case was just what he needed to get his
blood circulating, to sweep the cobwebs out of his still
plentiful hair and to give him the best excuse for escaping
his office. He was more than happy to leave the
preliminary interviews to his excellent lieutenant, Johnson
and to be able to follow the other members of his team as
they went about their duties. He felt quite rejuvenated as
he studied the wounds at the back of the victim's head
then examined the bathroom for himself. He wasn't in the
least troubled that he got in the way of the doctor, the
photographer and the fingerprint man in the process. He
was happy to stand aside as the body was taken away but
he pressed everyone with questions, many of them
unanswerable at the time. He strode up and down,

popping his head into each bedroom in turn as they were being searched, trying to keep one step ahead of everybody. His presence kept every member of his team on his toes.

When the preliminary interviews were over and the room searches had ended, Duncombe summoned his team for a brief conference. They crowded together in the kitchen away from the residents' ears.

"We have not yet found the murder weapon and we don't yet know what it could be. It will be quite some time before we see the lab report, until then we must use our imaginations. From what I saw of the wounds, it is more likely to be made of metal than anything else, not too heavy and not too long. It must be capable of being concealed even if only for a short time.

"Given the timing of the murder, it suggests an inside job by someone who was familiar with the premises and it is quite likely that the weapon is still on the premises. It would not be too easy to conceal. It is possible that the weapon could have been thrown from one of the windows. Sergeant Green, I want you to get some of your men outside. Search the yard and the lane and the street right round the building. I know that it is dark but it would help enormously if it was found tonight. Have you anything to add, Inspector Johnson?"

Johnson stood up slowly.

"As the chief says, we have little to go on. The weapon with fingerprints on it would be an enormous help. Mrs.Ridgeway will open all the cupboards for you. Don't forget the fire escape. An outsider would almost certainly leave that way and could have dropped the weapon or thrown it from there. Get torches and search every step. If we aren't successful, we must search again in daylight tomorrow. Some of you will be wanted to take the residents' formal statements and their fingerprints. I know that it is late but we must get through all of this before anyone can get to bed tonight."

"Say goodnight to Mrs.Ridgeway for me, will you, Trevor?"

Johnson could never be sure whether his Chief was being ironic or not. He knew that he had a good sense of humour and that, while he was usually blunt, he could be subtle and quick but when his voice became light, he suspected that his tongue was not far from his cheek.

"Certainly, Sir. See you in the morning." He endeavoured to match Duncombe's tone.

They parted on the doorstep. Before he could turn back, one of his men drew him to one side and whispered urgently, pointing up the stairs. He was about to move in that direction when Mrs.Ridgeway appeared at his elbow looking concerned.

"I hope that they can go to their beds soon. Was that the Chief Inspector leaving?"

"Yes, did you want a word?"

"Well, I did hope that he was going to call everything off for the night. Miss Catesby's in a poor way and everyone is getting restless. It's just as well that it's Saturday tomorrow. I don't think any of them needs to go to work."

"I think that we should be finished soon. I was wanting another word with you myself."

They went into the dining room but statements were being taken there so they walked to the bottom of the stairs.

"When did you have your fire escape fitted?"

"It will be all of six years ago. An inspector came and insisted that a new one be fitted if I wanted to have my licence renewed."

"Have you opened it recently?"

"I last opened that door a week yesterday. It was a fine day. We had been cleaning and I wanted some air to take away some of the smell of the polish, it can be a bit strong sometimes."

"You didn't notice any difference about it? No sign of oil?"

"No, Jenny made some comment about it being stiff and noisy as usual at the time. I've dusted along there since and I've never noticed any oil.

"Well, that door opens silently and easily now."

CHAPTER EIGHT

After his interview with the Inspector, Henry Allingham enjoyed a feeling of great wellbeing. His view of the world and his fellow humans had undergone a sea change. He returned to the sitting room and sat in a corner quietly, as usual but without any of his former selfconsciousness and awkwardness. Far from avoiding his fellow guests, he began to take an interest in them and in what they were saying.

Miss Catesby, slumped in one of the larger armchairs, was still whimpering and wiping her eyes. For a while, both Mrs.Jervis and Mrs.Elmwood did their best to comfort her, telling her not to rub her eyes or they would remain swollen for a long time. Miss Catesby was not easily comforted. She seemed to resent what had happened bitterly, but as her conversation increased, it dawned on everybody that she was not concerned for the dreadful fate of Miss Oxbury so much as the damage to her social status by her failure to keep her evening appointment with the ineffable Mrs.Humphrey.

It was a while before Denzil Elliott got back from his interview. He had not looked well before he went out, when he returned he looked dreadful. Mrs.Jervis clucked over him maternally but he ignored her and sat himself down at one end of the hard-looking settee.

There was silence for a while. Walter Jackson was very twitchy. He got up from his chair and strode to the window and back several times. His restless movement gradually impinged on Denzil Elliott's awareness. He had been frozen, staring fixedly at the carpet. Suddenly he shouted.

"For God's sake stop crashing about. What's the matter with you? You are getting on everybody's nerves. Sit down and shut up, for…."

"I'll sit down when I like! Why are you shouting? You are the one who's mad."

"Can't you see you are disturbing everybody? Sit down for God's sake! Sit down!"

The ladies stared at their former idol. Henry was fascinated and amused. Is this what his fellow residents were really like? The sad death was beginning to upset everyone. Henry glanced about him and was aware of a waif-like figure clinging to the other end of the settee. It was Jenny, the young maid. Sometimes she helped to serve the meals and sometimes he had seen her sweeping the corridors.

She was very small and thin with short, slightly spiky fair hair. Her eyes were a light brown and were quite close together. Her nose was narrow and rather pink towards the end. Her mouth was small and firm with a protruding upper lip. There was no trace of lipstick, there was no need, the lips were a bright fresh red. A light sprinkling of freckles and a tiny pointed chin completed the picture of what, to Henry, could have been an innocent twelve year old. He suddenly thought of the child he might have had and the old safety mechanism froze him again and he looked away.

Mrs.Elmwood got up and sat beside Jenny, clearly she felt sorry for the girl who was bewildered by the present company and was puzzled by what was going on. Henry looked back at the girl. She was nervously fiddling with the sleeves and neck of her dress but there was no sign of tears. She didn't appear to be listening to what Mrs.Elmwood was saying yet she smiled ever so briefly and nodded her head as though acknowledging Mrs.Elmwood's kindness.

At that moment, Mr.Baxter entered the room. The Ladies immediately registered delight and relief. As soon as he had opened the front door he had been met by Sergeant Green and made aware of the situation. He was bursting to ask questions but he was beckoned out to be interviewed by Inspector Johnson. Noticing the ladies' response to the foursquare, genial, sympathetic figure, Henry wondered if he would like to be another Mr.Baxter and decided he would not. His attention was then drawn to Mrs.Jervis and Mrs.Elmwood sitting in front of him. They were discussing Mr.Frimton. What had happened to him? Why had he been away so long? Nobody had mentioned him, would he be eliminated from the enquiry? One of them took Henry aback by asking his opinion. The new Henry answered clearly and without hesitation. He did not think that there could be a connection or the police would have asked everyone about Mr.Frimton. Immediately Denzil Elliott was bold enough to sneer at Henry, what could he know about it? This shocked Mrs.Jervis but before she could protest a further wail broke from Miss Catesby. She had sat in silence for some time. Now a monstrous thought had occurred to her. "Who was going to be next?"

There was a great silence. They all looked at each other. It had not occurred to them until now that they might be in the presence of a murderer. They had been in daily contact with each other for quite a time. They knew each other, didn't they? Henry watched their eyes, watched the doubt creeping in and was saddened. It was little Jenny who was most disturbed by Miss Catesby's outburst. She stared at her wide eyed then she turned to Mrs.Elmwood as though to question her. Mrs.Elmwood shook her head gently and patted her hand.

Ernie Baxter returned, bright and breezy as ever, to find his fellow guests very subdued.

"Now what's up?"

Walter Jackson broke his silence with an almost incoherent attack on the hotel.

"I should never have come here. What a stupid mistake that was. I might have known. This sinister old dump and a lot of sinister old people in it. The sooner I'm out of here the better. The old bat is right....who's going to be next? Well, I'll tell you something, it isn't going to be me, that's for sure. I'm not going to be mixed up in all of this. I'm getting out, I'm telling you, first thing tomorrow, just see if I don't!"

Henry had never impressed anyone before because he had always remained in the background. Now he rose to his full height and towered over Jackson. He glared at him until the younger man cowered then he spoke quietly but firmly.

"There is no need for panic, for shouting or for rudeness. There is only one thing to do at this time and that is to sit quietly and wait for the police to finish their work. It is understandable that everyone should be nervous but it is unforgivable that a gentleman should give way to hysterics and frighten the ladies like this."

The ladies turned in admiration. Baxter cried out "Hear, hear!" Jackson subsided into his chair. Denzil Elliott regarded Henry with some dismay. Miss Catesby sobbed to herself, unimpressed by Henry or anyone else about her. There was silence for a while.

Sergeant Green came in to invite them all to make and sign formal statements. They left singly, in alphabetical order and returned in silence to sit in the same places. There was a strange compulsive formality about the proceedings not unlike a stately game of charades. Soon after, Inspector Johnson entered.

"Ladies and gentlemen! This has been a long and difficult evening for you. I appreciate your situation but I have to tell you that our investigation has just begun. You may retire to bed now but you must hold yourselves in readiness to answer more questions tomorrow." He ignored a chorus of moans and snorts of indignation. "I must remind you that this is a murder enquiry. Nothing must get in its way. An officer will be on duty here all night. You should have nothing to fear. Are there any questions?"

"Yes, Will we be able to leave the hotel tomorrow? I have some work to see to before Sunday." Mrs.Jervis sounded very calm.

"Yes. So long as you check with the officer on duty before you go out. I advise you not to leave town or to be away for more than an hour or two at most."

"And how long do you propose to keep us imprisoned here?" To everyone's surprise it was Miss Catesby who spoke. She had risen from her armchair and was standing very straight, her chin out, her eyes quite dry of tears, her body absolutely still.

"With luck, tomorrow will suffice but until this case is solved I may need to see you at any time. By the way, you may not use the third floor bathroom for the present, we may need to re-examine it. One last tedious thing, please go next door and have your fingerprints taken."

"Why? Whyever should we? We are not criminals!" It was Miss Catesby again.

"Miss Catesby, it is necessary to eliminate you from our enquiry. Fingerprints may well prove your innocence...."

"Or guilt!" Jackson could not resist the spiteful comment.

"Precisely, Mr.Jackson. Only the guilty should have anything to worry about."

CHAPTER NINE

D.C.I.Duncombe arrived at the station early the next morning, even so, he met Inspector Johnson on the steps and they went in together.

"Are you going back to interview the domestics this morning?"

"They won't all be there much before eleven. I thought I would get through some of the reports until then."

"What about the search?"

"Nothing last night. Too dark and wet outside. I've got Sergeant Green and his squad searching the outside this morning. One thing, Sir, one of the men found that the door to the fire escape on the third floor had been oiled recently. Mrs.Ridgeway claims that it hadn't been oiled when she opened it a week ago."

"So it could have been an outside job, someone coming and going by the fire escape?"

"That door doesn't open from the outside. It could have been the means of escape or the means of getting rid of the weapon, though."

"Well it opens the possibilities. It could be a combination of inside and outside, someone helping from inside."

"We won't get far without a weapon or a motive. Could there be a financial angle, Sir?"

"We won't know until we have checked with her firm and with her bank. The Estate Agents will be open this morning but we will have to wait until Monday for the bank. I'll get onto Pinners as soon as they are open. Anything else?"

"Nothing. I had to let them get to bed but I got fingerprints from them first…."

"Did any of them kick up a stink?"

"Not really. Interestingly enough, it was Miss Catesby,

old tearful and trembly who objected. Showed a spirit I hadn't expected."

"They're a rum lot. None of them look as though they had enough spine to carry out a killing. At first glance, the ladies look too refined and the men look like wimps. I wonder where the missing lodger Frimton fits in? I've put Hornby onto that, he should come up with something any minute. Well, lets get on with the statements."

Duncombe picked up a handful of papers and handed them to Johnson.

"You take these and I'll get on with the rest."

Johnson retired to his own den, growling to his nearest minion that he was not to be disturbed. Half an hour later he thought he ought to confer again. He found his Chief helping himself to coffee.

"Help yourself, I'm glad you came along. I've put in one or two calls and I'm expecting answers very soon. I've also contacted the parents. They were a bit strange at first. Very distant as though they didn't want to know about their daughter. After I broke the news, they were shocked as far as I could tell on the phone. They are coming over this afternoon. I'll meet them and get them to identify the body then I'll take them to the hotel, I'd like you to be there to interview them."

"Right, I'll wait at The Moorcroft until you turn up."

"The statements I've been reading have been pretty straightforward, no contradictions. The post mortem report hasn't arrived yet, of course, but I can't think that it will have anything extra for us. Now, the blows to the skull, could they have been made equally by a woman as a man?"

"My guess is that they could, given the right speed and swing."

"Two blows almost in the same spot suggests tremendous skill as well as speed. Could a woman do that? Don't forget that our women are past their first youth."

"I think that if the motivation is strong enough, the adrenaline summons up the necessary energy. I don't think that we can rule the women out, not even Miss Catesby. We can't limit the field to tall, short, left handed or right handed. The blows were almost horizontal, they must have been delivered by someone with bent knees."

"Are we looking for a golfer or a tennis player then?"

Johnson smiled grimly. "A tennis player might well fit the bill, Sir, but determination would be a higher factor than skill. There would be only one opportunity. Timing would be critical. There had to be no possibility of failure unless the totally unexpected happened."

" Someone interrupted or the victim looked up or the light went out. O.K. so it could be a woman. Our Miss Catesby had the best opportunity. She could have carried it out, relocked the bathroom door and calmed herself before she raised the alarm, but would she be strong enough?"

"I wouldn't be surprised after her performance last night. All those tears could have been a smoke screen."

"Or even tears of genuine relief and remorse."

"Is there anyone we can rule out?"

The Chief shuffled in his chair and shook his head. "Not yet."

They were interrupted by the telephone.

"Yes, speaking. Oh hello Mr.Gardner, thanks for ringing back Nothing? Well, she didn't have much time, did she? Three weeks! What was your personal opinion of the girl? That seems to be universal. Yes it is very sad. We've no idea as yet. Thanks anyway, you've been very helpful."

"No luck at Pinners I gather?"

"No and I guess it will be the same at her bank. The girl seems to have been honest enough and three weeks is hardly time enough to organise a vast financial swindle, is it? It is just possible that she might have deposited a large sum though. We'll have to check with her previous employers."

"Yes, it could be that it all has to do with the girl's past. The parents should be able to give us a clue."

"Well it won't just be something to do with her past, it will be a matter of how that something coincided with someone or something at the hotel. There's nothing in the statements?"

"Nothing, we don't know enough about our residents. We only know what they got up to in the last 24 hours. I'll circulate names and descriptions and see what records come up with."

"Good, that's a start, meanwhile, the sooner the weapon turns up the better. Did fingerprints in the bathroom tell us anything?"

"No, the interesting thing was that only the front edge of the bath had been cleaned, cleaned of fingerprints and blood. The taps and the rest of the surround had normal prints and smudges on them."

"And the prints on the taps were of the victim?"

"Yes, but why did the murderer need to wipe the front edge at all? Why did he need to touch it?"

"He probably needed to check that the victim was really dead. If he leaned over, he might have needed to steady himself. He was cool enough to see that there was nothing incriminating left."

"What did he wipe the bath with, Sir? We haven't found anything bloodstained and the men examined the toilet bowl carefully…."

"Simple! He would use the sponge and leave it in the water."

Johnson was not happy that the D.C.I. had spotted something so simple and that he had missed it.

"It seems that our murderer had thought the thing out very carefully. The cleaning adds to the problem of timing. How much time could the murderer allow for the entry, the strike, the cleaning up then the exit?"

"We will know that when we have a better picture of

the sequence of dining. You will have a careful check on that, won't you, Trevor?"

CHAPTER TEN

When Henry Allingham awoke he was puzzled by a reluctance on the part of his body to fall into line with his time honoured ritual of stretching and feeling for his slippers and his dressing gown before heading for the door. He had slept so well that his mind was rather slow in functioning. Now he remembered. His life had changed. Poor Miss Oxbury had been brutally murdered. They had all been interviewed by the police. He was now enjoying his existence in a way he had never believed possible. It was as though he had awakened from a long and painful dream.

He lay still. It was Saturday. Normally he treated Saturdays as a form of weekday with a routine to match. He always rose at the same time, took breakfast, walked to the nearest shop, bought a paper, walked to the Central Library, read till lunchtime then lunched at the Civic Restaurant next door. After Lunch he would return to the Library if the weather was bad. If it was good he would take a bus to Fernhead and walk back over the moor. In Summer, he simply varied his walk, often having a pub lunch on the way. He was always glad to get away from people. He returned to the hotel between 5.30 and 5.45 for a hot bath before dinner. After dinner, it was always reading before bed. His reading tended to be of a practical nature, facts being preferred to fiction of any kind. He quite liked history, there was comfort to be found in the logic of the past, the sequence of events.

Today he felt a different responsibility. He did not want to avoid anyone. He wanted to mingle. Again he had a strong feeling that he could help to solve the mystery. He didn't know how, he just felt that if he watched and listened he would find out things. Already he was noting facts in his own mind. It was his capacity for assembling facts in their proper order that was going to be of value. He knew. No jumping to conclusions.

He held to his Saturday morning routine but now he was not simply taking satisfaction from his routine. He was aware of things outside himself and looking forward to the next event. Life was no longer automatic. He smiled to himself as he cleaned the washbasin after him and collected his wash things. As he left the bathroom he met a policeman on the stairs and gave him a bold 'good morning'. Downstairs in the dining room, tables and chairs had not been returned to their normal position. Formerly, this would have disturbed Henry gravely. Today, he volunteered to fetch and carry whatever was needed to prepare the room for breakfast. Mrs.Ridgeway was astonished and relieved. She hadn't slept as well as usual and she was not looking forward to this day. There were going to be many problems to sort out. The first of them had been Jenny. Jenny had not understood much that had happened because, it seemed, no one had bothered to tell her. When, at last, she had been allowed to go to bed she had had bad dreams, so she told Mrs.Ridgeway. She had bolted her door and would not come out until Mrs.Ridgeway had come to fetch her long after the time she should have been downstairs.

Breakfast was late but only Henry was down on time so there were no complaints on that score. There were plenty on others. It was clear from noises inside and outside the hotel that the police were back. How would everyone face up wondered Henry.

Mrs.Elmwood was the next down. She smiled at Henry and sat at the table immediately next to him.

"It has not been an easy night," she said with a solemnity that on another occasion would have been comical. It was as if she needed to say it and would, perhaps have said it if there had been no one there. She was taken aback when Henry promptly replied.

"No, Mrs.Elmwood, I don't think anyone could say

that."

He was mildly troubled by his own hypocrisy. He had slept extraordinarily well. Mrs.Elmwood turned fully towards him..

"I feel particularly sorry for the people on the third floor. I don't think I could set foot in that bathroom ever again. I suppose everyone will have to use ours now?"

"Yes, we will all have to try to be patient with one another, at least until this trouble is over."

"How long will that take, I wonder?"

Mrs.Elmwood had never had a long conversation with Henry during all the time they had inhabited the hotel together. She was amazed and seemed willing to prolong it indefinitely. At this point, Jenny arrived with her tray. Henry studied her. Her eyes were as red as the tip of her nose and she could not restrain a sniff. To Henry there was something appealing about that face, pale and puffy as it was that morning. What a pity it was that she should have been obliged to sit trapped among the adults all last evening, like a tiny bird in a cage with other birds much bigger and stronger. Why hadn't she been allowed to go to bed?

Mrs.Elmwood too, studied Jenny's face as she gave her order. Jenny made a slight bob and left silently.

"That poor innocent girl! Having to listen to all the fuss and noise last night. Whatever will she think of us?"

What a caring woman Mrs.Elmwood is, thought Henry. Instinctively he had thought she had warmth but, as with the others, he had never given her much thought until now.

Mrs.Jervis was the next to enter. She was dressed and made up ready to go out. Her manner was brisk as though all thoughts of the previous evening had been expunged by the business of today. She bade Mrs.Elmwood good morning and nodded in the direction of Henry, as always.

"The weather seems to have improved. I wonder if I will need to take an umbrella?"

"I wonder where our duty policeman keeps himself? I mustn't forget to let him know where I'm going. What's the bacon like this morning?"

The door swung open and Miss Catesby entered. She, too, was dressed ready to go out. This time she wore a deep blue woollen dress buckled at the waist with a cut away coat to match - at least the colours more or less matched, somehow the materials and styles didn't. A blue comb sat in her hair above the right ear.

"Good morning dear, that's a very nice dress...."

Miss Catesby, dry eyed, wiry and erect glared at Mrs.Jervis. Banished was any of the image of frailty and woe remaining from the previous evening. This was the Miss Catesby who had challenged the Inspector only more fierce looking now. They all stared at her, waiting for her to speak. She didn't. She turned and sat at the table furthest away.

Ernie Baxter and Walter Jackson entered together. They merely grunted their good mornings and sat together at the last but one remaining table. Jenny was now fully occupied in taking orders. Mrs.Ridgeway brought in the first hot dishes. Everyone fell silent for a few minutes. Denzil Elliott broke the silence by bursting into the room in a foul mood.

"Someone has been interfering with my property. It's a damned liberty! How dare anyone enter my room?"

Oh, come now, Mr.Elliott! You know as well as we do that the police searched every room last night." Mrs.Jervis sounded just a little on edge herself.

"I know that very well. I'm talking about this morning while I was in the bathroom. Someone has been into my suitcase."

"I suppose it was you in there for so long! I don't suppose you gave any thought to everyone having to use the downstairs bathroom today, selfish young man!" Miss Catesby waxed wrath.

"Look here! Who are you calling selfish? I took no

longer than was necessary."

Henry interrupted, "Is there anything missing?"

"No....er, ...I don't think so, but I'd like to know what someone is playing at."

"Perhaps it was one of the policemen," Henry was doing his best to keep everything calm, "They started very early this morning."

"They should give us warning if they want to search again."

"I hope that they are not going to search everybody's room all day at random," Ernie Baxter put in, "I'd like to think that we are going to have some privacy after last night."

"Fat chance mate! The pigs have their trotters in and that's that."

"Oh Mr. Jackson do be quiet. That's stupid talk and you know it!" Mrs.Jervis couldn't restrain her angry outburst.

"I don't have to be quiet to please you, Mrs.High and Mighty Jervis! I shall say what I like! The sooner I am out of here the better!"

"So you keep saying. I'm sure it will be a relief for all of us!"

Mrs.Ridgeway gave a sharp cough from the doorway.

"Ladies and gentlemen, please! Quarrelling won't help! All this noise is upsetting my staff. If your nerves are on edge, go for a walk or something. Failing that, stick to your rooms! I will not have my staff upset!"

Her presence quietened everyone immediately but the atmosphere remained very strained. Henry reflected on the formal good manners and general consideration that had prevailed less than 24hours before. The present nervous tension and petty squabbling astonished him at first. Later, he acknowledged to himself that under the circumstances it was understandable.

"Will you be going out as usual, Mr.Allingham?"

"I'm not sure, Mrs.Elmwood. Perhaps the police will

want to interview us again."

"I think I'll wait until this afternoon, just in case. I have some shopping to do but it can wait until this afternoon. Our lives have changed in more ways than one, I feel." It seemed to Henry that Mrs.Elmwood had drifted off her usual resolute and forthright course.

"Oh, I don't think that you should let this sad event change your existence, Elizabeth. It is a serious matter, I know, but I'm going to get on with things as before." Mrs.Jervis rose from the table, patted Mrs.Elmwood's shoulder and left the room with a purposeful stride.

"How can she say such a thing? Nothing will ever be the same. How can it be?" Miss Catesby glared at everyone. No one replied.

One by one they left the dining room leaving Henry sitting alone. He had finished his breakfast but he was reluctant to move. He poured himself another cup of coffee and sat thinking. Why did they seem so different to him now? Had they changed or was the change only in him? He considered them one by one, struggling to remember what they had been like prior to the murder. He wished that he had had more contact with them but would that have made his memory more sharp? His memory was sharp enough for having had little to do with them. Miss Oxbury, for instance, she had been a relatively shy girl when she first came but had grown into a confident, smiling young woman within no time at all. He hadn't really spoken to her but he had listened to her talking at meal times. She had a light, clear voice and had always responded brightly when others had spoken to her. He was not surprised that she had joined a choir, almost certainly her singing voice must have been a true soprano. What were the occasions he had met her apart from mealtimes? She was always coming and going. Usually he had encountered her on the stairs as he was going up to his room. When had he last seen her? She had not come down to breakfast while he was in the dining room and she had not taken dinner that evening. He remembered that two evenings before, she had left the dining room early saying that she was going to the Choral Society. She had left at the same time as Henry and when they went into the corridor she had asked, good humouredly, if he was a singer too. He had experienced a little twinge of pleasure at her interest but had withdrawn into his shell immediately. She had not taken offence but had hurried up the stairs ahead of him to get ready.

Her movements had always been quick and light. She couldn't have weighed much. There was a strength of character, an independence he much admired in her. He wondered if she would have remained single for long. She would not have been the sort of girl to marry in haste and repent at leisure. Is that what he, himself, had done? No, that had not been the case with him. Events had taken their course, he never felt that he had had much to do with them. With Miss Oxbury it would have been very different. She had a mind of her own. He remembered only one characteristic movement. She often pushed back her wristwatch with her right thumb and forefinger. It happened just before she stood up or sat down or left the room.

He pondered similar characteristics of the other residents. He had noticed that Mrs.Jervis always slid her hands down behind her legs to straighten her skirt before she sat down. It was a longstanding habit, probably from her schooldays. He thought it must have something to do with her height. Mrs.Elmwood had a habit of raising her left hand, pausing at her brow then sweeping it lightly over her hair, hardly touching it. That too was probably a habit from childhood. Miss Catesby's habit of shaking her head nervously as though to free it from stray hairs must have begun relatively recently.

Mr.Baxter's mannerism was to extend his arms in a little shake of the cuffs. This sort of gesture he had seen in the tailoring department of a big store. He wondered if it had something to do with salesmanship. Jackson had a nervous tic at the corners of his mouth and this was usually accompanied by a reflex glance sideways and down. This wasn't too pronounced unless he was distressed. Last night it had been very pronounced. Elliott, too, had a downward glance, but to each side in turn, in his case it was preceded by a movement of the neck, up and down, not unlike a tortoise. The movement was very limited but, as with Jackson, it was pronounced under stress.

Briefly, Henry tried to contemplate his own unconscious habits and failed. His mannerisms would need to be pointed out to him, he certainly wasn't aware of any. He always thought that everything he did was ordered.

There were raised voices in the hall and a sense of excitement. Henry felt obliged to stir himself and find out what was afoot. He met Sergeant Green outside in the corridor. The Sergeant was examining a metal bar on a cloth.

"Is that the murder weapon, Sergeant?"

"It could be, Sir. It's got blood on it for sure. You don't recognise it, do you, Sir?"

The implication was lost on Henry who stooped to have a closer look. It was a metal bar about 14 or15 inches long, black lacquered for most of its length and with a screw thread at the very end.

"Could be anything, it could be one of those….er….what do you call them?"

The Sergeant looked at him sharply

"Could be from an office stool. We've had a few come apart needing to be replaced."

"Have you, Sir, most interesting!

Sergeant Green went off to find a plastic bag to put the thing in. Henry turned to the constable who had found it.

"Where did you find it, Officer?"

The man hesitated. "In the back garden of a house in Wormald Street, Sir."

"But that's at right angles to this building!"

"Yes, Sir, it could easily have been thrown from here."

Henry was amazed but soon accepted the truth of this. He wondered what sort of strength would be necessary to fling such a bar such a distance. He would look for himself when he went out. He looked about him as he climbed the stairs. The hotel was small, he supposed, as hotels go but it was decorated in an ornate style. The carpets were quite thick and of a dark red colour. The walls were painted pale cream and at changes of direction, such as where the corridors gave way to the stairs, there were elaborate plaster pilasters and arches picked out in white and gold. The stair rails were painted white and the banister rail was of burnished mahogany. At the feet of the pilasters were plants in large pots. How strange it was that he should only have thought of them now.

In his room, Henry stood before his wardrobe mirror and gazed at himself. He had always checked on his appearance in this mirror before going out. Now he lingered, pulling in his stomach and raising his chest. Yes, he would go out, he would 'take the air' - such a silly expression that, where did it come from? It implied exercise without purpose. He had always been purposeful even in small, habitual activities, now he hesitated. An element of enjoyment had crept in, something that had never existed before. He hummed to himself and took time to think about what he should wear. He would wear his raincoat and scarf and he would abandon his usual trilby for his old checked cap. He possessed three scarves and he could see that they were very much alike and decidedly dull. Why hadn't he noticed this before? There was no point in having clothes all the same colour. Perhaps he would buy himself a new one. First he would call a the newsagent's then….he would please himself.

CHAPTER ELEVEN

Henry was not alone in informing the Sergeant that he was going out for some fresh air. Just ahead of him in the porch was the slight figure of Denzil Elliott. Henry had no wish to exchange civilities, genuine or otherwise, with that gentleman this morning so he lingered to allow time for Elliott to disappear. Elliott didn't seem sure where he was going. He stood on the step outside for a while, looking left and right. Eventually he moved off to the right. This suited Henry who intended to cross left towards the newsagent's. He too lingered on the step outside soaking in a little of the sun and breathing deeply. How lucky it was to be alive on such a morning. Then he blushed. How could he have thought that when poor Miss Oxbury….He suddenly thought of his wife. He hadn't thought of her for years. No! It would not do! Best to put all thoughts of her away permanently. He had moved on, not far perhaps, but now he was at an exciting stage in his life, he was going to savour every moment from now on. He strode across the street with almost a swagger.

A little way up Wormald Street was the newsagent and just next to it was the bus stop. Buses were quite frequent and all went into the centre of town. Henry was about to cross towards it when he saw a familiar figure queuing with one or two others. It was Miss Catesby. Henry was a little curious. He had formed the impression that she was ready to go out immediately after breakfast yet here she was still at the bus stop. He did not want to have any conversation with her but he thought he might follow her to see where she was going. His mind spun. That would be most improper, yet he had a strong urge to play the detective.

He did not wish to be noticed so he turned and walked a little in the opposite direction. He remembered that the iron bar the Sergeant thought was the murder weapon had been found in a garden in Wormald Street opposite the hotel. Whether or not he had time to look at it before the next bus came he was not sure. He hurried. Looking up at the hotel from the opposite side of the street, he realised that all the bedroom windows and those of the dining room looked out onto Wormald Street. He had never thought about them before. Occasionally he had looked out at the weather but he had never taken an interest in the street for its own sake. He considered the trajectory of the iron rod. It would hardly have reached the gardens opposite if it had been thrown from the lower windows but any of the bedroom windows would have sufficed. The attic windows were too small and altogether too awkward as they sloped with the roof.

Suddenly he heard a bus turning the corner behind him. He wheeled round and headed as fast as he could towards the bus stop. Conveniently, there was a confusion of people descending and ascending which allowed him to reach the running board before the conductor rang his bell. He thought he would be too visible if he sat downstairs, he decided to sit upstairs on the pavement side. He would watch to see where Miss Catesby got off then he would get of immediately afterwards. It wasn't foolproof by any means. His decision was hastened by pressure from someone who had leapt aboard behind him and was following him up the stairs.

Henry never liked being rushed. As he sat waiting for the conductor, he began to doubt the wisdom of his move. He did not know what ticket to ask for. He would have to go to the end of the route. Then he had not had time to buy his paper, he was so used to scanning the first page as he was sitting that he felt at a loss. He did indeed buy a ticket to the end of the route, which wasn't such a great hurdle. He began to relax and comforted himself that he could concentrate more on Miss Catesby without a paper.

He laughed to himself at the realisation that he could not have seen her if the entrance had been at the back.

Sure enough when the bus reached the first of the broader shopping streets, Miss Catesby descended. Henry marvelled at the lightness of her movement. She may look frail, he thought, but she was full of vigour and there seemed nothing wrong with her joints. She was nimble enough, enough for what? Henry struggled to his feet and battled his way down the stairs as the bus moved off again.

"You've got a long way to go yet, mate!" The conductor was being very friendly.

"Oh! Ah! Yes, I've got er…..I've changed my mind!"

Henry's only escape from embarrassment was to revert to his office manner. The conductor shrugged. He was used to abruptness. His good will was often wasted. Henry stepped off as soon as the bus stopped. Blindly he hurried back towards the previous stop. As it was a Saturday there were many shoppers and Henry found himself buffeted on all sides. It didn't help that he was trying to look at everyone at once. Of course, Miss Catesby could have crossed the street or moved off to a different part of the town. He had no idea which shops, if any, Miss Catesby was likely to have gone into. He sighed inwardly at his own folly. Just at that moment he caught sight of a particular deep blue. There she was inside a dress shop, quite near the window. He turned away immediately, not wishing to be seen. Ahead of him was the undoubted figure of Denzil Elliott in the act of turning away himself.

That was too much of a coincidence for Henry. He strode towards Elliott only to find that that gentleman had stepped quickly to his left and had entered a smart sports shop. This was not the sort of shop Henry was familiar with. He hesitated by the door and tried to peer in. The shop was busy and there was no sign of Elliott. Perhaps he had been mistaken. It had certainly looked as though

Elliott had been following him. He smiled grimly at the thought that the follower might have been followed. Quite ridiculous!

Returning to the dress shop, Henry was dismayed that there was no sign of Miss Catesby. He had bungled it! He had allowed the sight of Elliott, or someone who looked like him, to divert him from his self-appointed task. He must pull up his socks. His first task and he had proved incapable! What next? He needed time to think and to recover his composure. He would buy a newspaper and find a coffee shop in which to sit and refresh himself. He left the main street and headed towards the central library, an area with which he was more familiar. Up a quiet side street was an old fashioned coffee shop he had frequented over a long period. It had originated in the eighteenth century and had many of the original features. He loved the high-backed wooden booths and the narrow marble-topped tables. He did not mind the discomfort of the rigid seats, he revelled in the privacy these booths afforded. The service was always prompt and polite and the coffee was excellent. He would scan his paper then think out some better plans.

He had scarcely spread his paper on the table and stirred his coffee when he was interrupted by a familiar voice.

"Mr.Allingham! Good gracious! Fancy seeing you here! Would you mind if I sat at your table?"

Henry looked up with some misgiving. It was Mrs.Elmwood.

"Oh! Of course not, Mrs.Elmwood"

He suddenly found himself lacking in social graces.

"This is one of my favourite places." Mrs.Elmwood was just a trifle flushed, a little excited as though she was indulging in a small personal treat. Henry thought she sounded rather coy which was altogether at odds with his opinion of her up to that moment.

"Have you been here before, Mr.Allingham? I love the

atmosphere here and the coffee is always good." She took off her gloves and passed her hand lightly over her hair. Henry smiled inwardly at the familiarity of this gesture. "I come here quite often in the cold weather, not so often when the weather is bright…."

Mrs.Elmwood was looking at the other people present. Henry wondered how many she knew from previous visits. He followed her glance but could recognise no one. He had visited this coffee shop many times but had never noticed Mrs.Elmwood among the customers. Of course, he had taken pains to avoid people, busying himself always with his newspaper. He doubted if he could distinguish one person from another. He tried again.

"It is only on Saturdays…."

"Sorry, M.Allingham, what were you saying?"

"Saturdays, only on Saturdays"

"Oh no. Sometimes I come here during the week. The office isn't too far away."

It dawned on Henry that he knew nothing of the work his fellow lodgers did or where they did it. He had never been a party to their conversations. He was almost ashamed of his lack of curiosity, he was determined to make amends. He was about to launch into the necessary questions when the waitress brought Mrs.Elmwood's coffee. Briefly, Henry's eyes followed the waitress as she departed. Before he could return them to Mrs.Elmwood they lighted on a figure peering in at the window opposite them.

"Goodness!" Henry's expletives were always mild.

He looked at Mrs.Elmwood for confirmation of what he had seen but she was busy sugaring and stirring her coffee.

"I am sure that that was young Jenny at the window there."

"Jenny? Our maid? Surely not. She would scarcely have finished her work yet."

They both looked at the window but whoever it was

had gone. They both consulted their watches. It was just a quarter past ten.

"I doubt she would finish before eleven. Anyway, what is she doing in town? She hardly leaves the hotel except to go to the cinema, I'm told."

"She looked so miserable this morning. It can't have been good for her last night."

"No, she looked quite bewildered. I daresay she is frightened too. A murderer in the same house! It 's bad enough for us, it must be much worse for her."

"I'm sure she had been crying when she served us breakfast."

"Perhaps she never slept. I assure you that I made certain that I locked my door last night."

Henry pondered this briefly, it was hard to imagine that the calm and solid lady sitting opposite might be frightened. He himself had not been frightened. He had always locked his door at night out of habit. He had nothing to do with the murder or the murderer, he was sure of that therefore he had nothing to fear. Had Mrs.Elmwood something to fear? Perhaps it was just a woman's reaction.

"I cannot imagine why anyone should want to murder Miss Oxbury, can you, Mrs.Elmwood? It must have been some one from outside the hotel."

"Yes, I'm inclined to agree with you. I thought about it for hours last night. I couldn't think it could be one of us. It must have been someone from outside. It wouldn't be very difficult to enter the hotel, you know, the doors are often open."

"But why should anyone, any outsiders want to kill Miss Oxbury? I thought she was most pleasant."

Mrs.Elmwood smiled at Henry's earnestness and was on the point of teasing him about it when she thought better of it.

"She has hardly been here long enough to know anyone."

"Yes, there hasn't been time for anyone to quarrel with her. Poor Girl!"

"We will have to wait to see what the police turn up. Life is so complicated nowadays. Nothing seems to be simple any more."

"I agree."

Henry drained his cup and stood up. He had talked more that morning than he had talked in a week prior to the drama they were caught up in. He continued to be surprised at himself but he had no wish to turn back. He excused himself to Mrs.Elmwood and said that he must be getting along. She did not detain him.

As he left the coffee shop, Henry felt a cool breeze. The sky indicated that a change was imminent. Such a pity, he thought, it had been so bright when he started out. He stood still for a moment, he had no idea what to do next. He had left Mrs.Elmwood because sufficient time had elapsed and he had finished his coffee. Now he thought of several questions he could have put to her and he was unhappy that he had left without thinking. He turned towards the window and darted a quick glance through it. To his amazement, he saw a figure sitting in the seat he had just vacated, a figure he recognised immediately as Denzil Elliott.

Inspector Johnson arrived at The Moorcroft Hotel well before the day staff. He spent some time talking to Sergeant Green and studying the iron bar with the bloodstains on it.

"Who was it found the thing, Sergeant?"

"P.C.Moscrop Sir. Well, strictly speaking, it was the owner of the garden. He saw Moscrop looking about and asked him if it was what he was looking for."

"The owner found it in his garden earlier this morning?"

"He said that his dog had found it near some bushes."

"So the dog handles it then his master then

71

P.C.Moscrop, then you?"

"That's about it, Sir."

"And had the owner just found it when P.C.Moscrop passed by?"

"Just a few minutes before, Sir."

"Not very muddy, is it?"

"No Sir, and the owner wasn't sure where it had been. The dog had been down to the bottom of the garden twice since the owner had let it out. It was the second visit that produced the bar. The owner, Mr.Garrard, thought it was just something to play with. He took it from the dog to throw it when he saw something sticky near the end. He had just begun to think it was suspicious when he saw Moscrop over the hedge."

"It's all too messy for me. Too much handling, no certain position. Was it wet?

"Yes Sir, Pretty hopeless, I'm afraid. The ground behind those bushes is dreadfully chewed up. It would be impossible to say where the thing had landed. It's a long garden. I reckon it could have been thrown from any of the windows or the fire escape. If it hadn't been for the dog we might have been able to judge."

"Well, it can't be helped. We could still enquire if anyone heard anything last night. Someone walking their dog along Wormald Street might have heard something. Get a door to door organised straight away."

Before he could talk to the cook and the other day staff, Johnson was diverted by the arrival of Mr. and Mrs.Oxbury. Johnson was rather surprised as his Chief had said that they were coming to see him in the afternoon. Mrs.Ridgeway hastened to announce them and to explain that they had decided to visit the hotel first since it was on the way to the Police Station. Johnson thought it a strange logic and smiled to himself as he imagined his Chief's reaction to this change of plan. It was barely mid-morning.

Lucy Oxbury's father was tall and thin with carefully brushed dark hair and a thin moustache. His movements and his manner were stiff and he tended to avoid his listeners' eye when he spoke. Lucy's mother was of medium height and was more heavily built than her husband. She was without makeup of any kind and her eyes, a light brown, were rimmed by dark, round spectacle frames. Her hair was short and just showed beneath the narrow brim of a firmly placed round felt hat. Both were stiffly and soberly dressed in dark colours. Johnson wondered if they always dressed like that or whether they had gone into immediate mourning.

He sat with them in the dining room. After the first polite condolences, Johnson sensed that there might be some difficulty. He asked them about Lucy's background. That was all that was required. Mrs.Oxbury did all the talking. Lucy had been well brought up. She had done well at grammar school and had taken up secretarial work. All had seemed to go well then, all of a sudden, she had applied for a job away from home and had left. They had needed her at home. She had a younger brother coming to a difficult age, he needed her assistance and example. The house was not easy to manage, it took her all her time to cope. There was no reason for Lucy to leave. She had her own room and she had plenty of friends. They had all been shocked when she left. It was particularly embarrassing that she had given no reason. What could she tell people? She had been far too independent, now see where it had got her!

There was a pause in which Mr.Oxbury coughed a mixture of comfort and support for his wife. Johnson waited then asked if Lucy had any boy friends. Oh, she was much too young for boyfriends. She had been well looked after, it was time she took a hand in looking after others. There were plenty of young men about. She could have settled down nearer home in due course, if that had been what she wanted. Johnson asked had she been home to visit her parents. Not once. Yes, she had telephoned. Mrs.Oxbury had been obliged to speak to her sharply. People had been asking why she had left home. What could they say? 'Wanted to be independent' what sort of answer was that?

Johnson pointed out that Lucy had been well liked during her short stay in Maskerley. Mrs.Oxbury dared say. She had always been a popular girl. What sort of things was she interested in? Too many, it seemed. She was always wanting to join things. There was plenty to do at home. Trouble? Of course not. She had been strictly brought up and was an active member of the chapel. Of course, they did not know what she might have got up to here, away from home.

There was a clearing of the throat and Mr.Oxbury interrupted. His voice was light but it carried. He could see no reason why anyone should wish to kill his daughter, away from home or not. Johnson agreed with him saying that everyone was mystified. Both parents said that they could think of no reason for such a dreadful thing. Mrs.Oxbury went on, nothing like this had happened to the Oxbury family before, nor to the Maybricks. What it could do to Aunt Lottie and Uncle Fred! And the Bertrams. The whole congregation would be consumed by curiosity. Tongues would wag. They should never have consented to her coming here, but what could they do? She was over age. There was a lesson for her brother!

Johnson took them upstairs to their daughter's room and went through her things with them. He had hoped for some enlightening comment but Mrs.Oxbury simply muttered about extravagance. He was glad when they went. He had found them exhausting and guessed it was due to trying to be sympathetic against all his instincts. He fully realised why Lucy Oxbury had wanted to leave home and why she had blossomed since she had done so. He marvelled that she had remained so good- natured under all the circumstances.

It didn't take long for Inspector Johnson to interview the cook. Mrs.Hammond; the assistant cook, Mary Miles; and the maid, Sarah Lucas. Sarah had served dinner that night but was hard pressed to remember anything about it, so shocked was she at the news of Lucy Oxbury's death. She did recall that Miss Oxbury had not taken dinner because it was a Friday and she didn't take dinner on Fridays. No she had not noticed anything unusual about last night.

Mary Miles was a little more helpful. She recognised the black rod as one that had come from an old trolley that had been used in the hotel. The trolley had been thrown out long ago but the rod had been useful as a substitute poker for turning up the Aga. It hadn't been used very often and it had lain in a corner on top of the cooker for such a long time that it had been forgotten as far as she was concerned.

Mrs.Hammond agreed. She had sometimes used it to reach the window catch. She was short and inclined to breathlessness. She could not remember when she had last seen it. Johnson pressed her to say whether anyone else in the hotel could have taken it. All three ladies said that they thought it unlikely that any of the residents could have taken it because they never came down to the kitchen. Mrs.Ridgeway did not approve of guests visiting the kitchen at any time.

It was Mrs.Ridgeway herself who claimed to be the last person to use the iron rod. The last time had been in the attics just a week ago. It was difficult to reach their window catches without standing on a chair. It was quite simple to reach up with the rod and give the catches a few taps. She could not remember putting the rod back in the kitchen. Almost certainly Jenny would have done that. That was what she wanted to tell the Inspector. She was worried about Jenny. She had slipped out after washing the breakfast things and had not returned. She had never been out for long. She only went to local shops for sweets or a magazine. She was always allowed a break after breakfast as beds weren't seen to before ten o'clock. When half past ten came, Mrs.Ridgeway began to worry. Now it was lunchtime and there was still no sign of her.

Inspector Johnson shared her worry. He did not like potential witnesses going astray.

Henry was puzzled about Denzil Elliott. Had Elliott followed him? Had he been talking to Mrs.Elmwood about him? That in itself didn't worry him but he did wonder why.

He was near the Central Library, he thought he would fall into his normal Saturday routine. He crossed the road and headed towards it, wondering whether he shouldn't have done so from the outset. It had been rather a wasted morning. Even so, it had been exciting. He picked up his stride and almost collided with a couple as they turned into a shop door to his right. He made to apologise but they had been too absorbed in their conversation to have noticed his clumsiness. They passed on without seeing him. Henry stopped and stared after them. There was no mistaking Mrs. Jervis but the person she was arm and arm with was a stranger. Henry knew that he wasn't Mr.Jervis for he had seen him on one of his visits to the hotel.

He climbed the steps up to the Library entrance and went through into the reference section without being aware of what he was doing. His mind was turning over several unusual matters. Mrs. Elmwood had said that she was going into town in the afternoon but went in the morning instead. Jenny had turned up at the coffee shop when she should have been at the hotel. Denzil Elliott, apparently, had been following him most of the morning. Mrs.Jervis was in town with a stranger when she had stated quite clearly that she was going to do some more research in the library. Miss Catesby had set off later than he had expected. He sat down at a table and thought.

There was no doubt that he ought to keep a record. Things seemed to be happening fast. He felt in his pockets, took out a pen then sighed. He had nothing to write on. There was nothing for it, he had to go out again and purchase a notebook, yes, a pocket notebook. He would keep a careful record of everything he observed.

There was a stationer's further up the same street, Henry hurried, he felt a great urgency. The shop was next door to a bookmaker. Henry may not have noticed had not a familiar figure not emerged as Henry was passing. It was Ernie Baxter. He looked most unhappy at the sight of Henry. He was caught in two minds for a moment then he laid a hand gently on Henry's arm.

"You haven't seen Mr.Jackson have you, Mr.Allingham? I'm worried about him. I thought he might be in here."

Even Henry's simple nature was not deceived. He was no longer the unquestioning fellow he had once been. He shook his head. "Sorry, Mr.Baxter, I'm in a great hurry."

He left Ernie Baxter open mouthed on the pavement. The stationer's had just what he wanted. He took the trouble to try it in his pocket before he bought it. Not surprisingly, there was no sign of Baxter on the way back to the Library. Henry had almost forgotten about him until he came to the end of his list of his morning's encounters. His last encounter had been with Baxter, he decided that he should be added. Quickly, Henry noted down the details of their meeting together with the mention of Jackson's name. Henry was nothing if not thorough, he even made a note of the times - he felt that that was most important.

Times made him think of lunch.

CHAPTER THIRTEEN

D.C.I.Duncombe was not happy that his arrangements had been messed about by the Oxburys, especially as they were neither apologetic nor repentant. He accompanied them to the morgue where they identified their daughter and stood by patiently while they recovered from the shock. They were not very demonstrative and, initially, showed no willingness to speak. Not knowing what they had said to Johnson, Duncombe was uncertain how to proceed. He invited them back to his office and ordered them coffee. They were reluctant to accept but were as unsure as Duncombe as to what was expected of them.

"This is a very troublesome business. There doesn't appear to be any motive behind the death of your daughter. It is just possible that there could be some link with the past. Is there anything at all you can think of....?"

"The past!" Mrs Oxley drew in her breath sharply, "That is absurd! Lucy led a blameless life while she lived at home."

"I'm not suggesting for a moment that she didn't, please believe me, but could she have known anyone, however slightly...."

"Ridiculous! She had a respectable job...."

"Quite! Could anyone at her place of work....?"

Chief Inspector, Lucy worked at Brambles the solicitors. You aren't suggesting that anyone with criminal tendencies could be working for Brambles?"

Duncombe was tempted to reminisce about some errant solicitors of note but he struggled to keep to his line of enquiry.

"No, Mrs.Oxbury, but there might have been some case she was involved with that might have had some significance in her death."

"Well, as to that, you must enquire of Brambles."

Mrs.Oxbury's tone softened a little. Here might be a

possible justification of her daughter's strange conduct. She looked at her husband, he returned her glance briefly and shook his head slightly. Duncombe continued.

"We will certainly do that. We must explore every avenue. Was that your daughter's first job?"

"Yes, she joined them straight from school. She did rather well at school and had no difficulty entering the firm. She got on very well there. We were shocked when she left. I'm sure they were too."

"But she didn't continue to work for solicitors, she joined Pinners the Estate Agents."

"She wasn't articled to the solicitors." It was Mr.Oxbury who broke in, "She was employed as a clerk-typist."

"But I thought you said that she had done well at school?"

"Lucy could have gone to University. She was interested in Law but her mother and I thought that it wasn't a proper sphere for a woman. There are few women well placed in Law."

Duncombe studied the face of the man opposite. Mr.Oxbury did not meet his eyes. He pursued his topic keeping his eyes on Oxbury's face.

"She didn't want to study anything else?"

"She er couldn't make up her mind, she was interested in so many things. We thought it better to settle her in a good job near home."

Oxbury's eyes never left his lap. His wife took over again.

"The question of articles never arose. It would have involved studying and a lot of expense. We couldn't have afforded to send two to university, anyway"

"You have another child?"

"Oh yes. We have a son, just coming up to sixteen with exams next summer...."

A thought suddenly occurred to her. "What effect this will have on him, Heaven only knows!" For the first time,

Mrs.Oxbury gave way to tears, but only a few.

Duncombe asked how Lucy and her brother got along together. Mrs.Oxbury looked sour and assured him that they got on very well in spite of the age difference. After that, Duncombe decided that he would rather conduct his enquiries elsewhere. He stood up and extended his hand to his visitors, thanked them for their help and encouraged them to get in touch if they could think of anything that might shed light on this most unfortunate occurrence. He walked with them to the entrance of the station and was enormously relieved to see Inspector Johnson getting out of his car. He could hardly wait to go back inside.

"What a pair! No wonder the poor girl wanted to leave home. She has all my sympathy."

Johnson grinned. "My sentiments entirely, Sir. They said a lot but told me very little. Was it the same for you?

"Their daughter worked for a firm of solicitors in Catton called Brambles before she came here. Maybe they will be able to tell us something. It seems that the girl was very bright but her parents denied her the chance to go to university. Nowadays, every bright kid goes to university, but not Lucy Oxbury. Oh no! They were going to support their son not their daughter." Duncombe grew pink.

"Well, it didn't seem to make their daughter very unhappy, did it? Everybody says the contrary. It seems she radiated happiness after she got here. By the way, Sir, one serious development, the maid Jenny Phillips has gone missing."

"The maid at The Moorcroft? The young one?"

"Yes. She went out after breakfast without telling anyone. Mrs.Ridgeway says that she sometimes went to the local shops but she should have been back by ten. I think we should put out an alarm straight away. Here's a photograph I took from the hotel, not a very good one I'm afraid. There's another thing, we've got the murder weapon. I've sent it down to the lab. We'll know for sure when the report comes in."

"Good progress at last! What was it?"

"A simple iron rod about a centimetre thick."

"Where was it found?"

"In the back garden of 59 Wormald Street. I've got Green to make a full report. Sadly, because the owner's dog fetched it, we don't know exactly where it was found. Also it was in a messy condition from all the handling by the dog, the owner and our men. There is no hope of fingerprints."

"Any idea where this rod thing came from?"

"It was a support from an old trolley. The trolley was thrown out years ago but this rod was useful for a number of things. As far as anyone can tell it was left lying in one of the attic bedrooms. Usually it was kept by the stove in the kitchen."

"So anyone who knew their way around could have taken it. This means it was almost certainly an inside job."

"Yes Sir, it seems so. It could be the reason for the oiling of the fire-escape door - to be able to get out quietly so as to hurl the thing into that garden without any problem."

"It is obvious that we are not dealing with a simpleton. This was carefully planned. These residents aren't all the genteel oddities they may seem. One of them is cunning and cruel. The sooner we are onto that person the better."

"It would have been just as easy and quicker to throw that thing from a bedroom window, Sir."

"There's always a risk throwing it from your own window, surely?"

"Anyone moving about the fire-escape door would be open to suspicion. It would look more natural to be seen coming and going from one's own room."

"One of the snags in this case is that no one seems to have seen anyone else coming or going from the dining room. As I recall, the three who live on that floor are the Catesby woman, Jackson and Elliott. I suppose that makes Catesby a prime suspect. Who else had time and opportunity?"

"I've made a timetable of the eating times last night. Allingham was first in, promptly at 6.30. He left at about 6.55. Catesby was next, within five minutes of Allingham and left immediately after him. Elliott arrived at 7.05 and Mrs.Jervis and Mrs.Elmwood almost immediately after him. Baxter followed at 7.10. Baxter and Jackson went into the T.V.room about 7.40 Mrs.Jervis followed them at 7.45. Mrs.Elmwood went up to her room at 7.45. Elliott was still in the dining room when the alarm was raised."

Duncombe was impressed.

"Well now, from what you tell me, two of the residents had finished their dinner and left the room in time to carry out the killing….."

"That is assuming that the murder took place at 7 or later. If it took place earlier, any one of them could have done it."

"Let me finish. As you say, assuming that the murder did take place at 7, the Catesby woman had gone upstairs by then. She claims to have seen Lucy Oxbury go into the bathroom. She could have killed her and thrown the weapon out of her own window. An hour later she raises stink about not being able to get into the bathroom. She must have been confident about not having been seen. The others are either half way through their meal or just starting it. Allingham, being a creature of habit had gone into his bedroom on the first floor, who was there to see her?"

"Elliott didn't enter the dining room until after 7. He could have seen her."

"Yes, that is a possibility but he didn't mention seeing her in his statement."

"He didn't mention seeing anyone, yet if Lucy Oxbury went into the bathroom at 7, he should have seen her, shouldn't he."

"Not necessarily, all these times are approximate. We don't even have an accurate time of death. We can't even be sure about Catesby's statement about seeing Lucy Oxbury. It could have been a deliberate red herring."

"Sir, none of them can be above suspicion."

"I'm still waiting for Hornby's report on that man Frimton. It shouldn't have taken long."

Duncombe began to pace up and down. Suddenly he stopped.

"I think I'll have a word with those solicitors. I fancy getting out of this office for a while. Perhaps Hornby will have returned by the time I get back.

CHAPTER FOURTEEN

The new Henry could not follow his former pattern of eating in the civic restaurant. He had no complaint against its food except that it was rather stodgy. It had the merit of being remarkably cheap and he could remain fairly anonymous among the crowd there. Now he fancied a change. He would retrace his steps into town and find a restaurant on the High Street from which he could observe the crowd and see if any of his fellow residents turned up or passed by. He pushed his notebook carefully into a side pocket and left the reference section. At the main entrance he was disturbed to find a crowd sheltering from a shower outside. He hadn't brought an umbrella, it had been such a fine morning when he had started out. He heard someone cheerfully declaring that there was a break in the clouds and that the shower wouldn't last long.

Henry drew back to one side. He would wait rather than get wet. He would give it another ten minutes, if it hadn't stopped by then, he would change his plans and slip next door to eat at the civic. A man just in front of him drew back quickly, catching Henry a blow with his elbow. He turned to apologise but Henry wasn't paying attention. He was staring at the couple who had hurried in causing the man to stagger backwards. It was Mrs.Jervis and the gentleman he had seen earlier. They stood, shaking the rain from their shoulders. They laughed together like a young couple, obviously they had found the rain and their rush to shelter invigorating. Henry strained to hear what they were saying but there was too much noise from the others in the entrance. He had no wish to go closer and reveal his presence. Rather to his surprise, they did not linger in the entrance but moved into the library towards the reference section. Presumably that was where Mrs.Jervis was doing her research. Perhaps that was where she had met her companion? Perhaps....?

There was a sudden thinning out around him. The shower had stopped. It must have been quite a downpour, the gutters were full and the drains had not coped very well. Henry trod warily, others around him were not so careful. He found himself being splashed from all sides. He moved to cross the road to escape this insensitive gaggle when a movement ahead made him pause. Someone had stumbled on the far pavement and someone had gone to assist him. The second figure was familiar, it was Ernie Baxter. At first, Henry couldn't see who the other was. When this person was upright, Henry recognised the fair hair and pale face of Walter Jackson. He had no wish to speak to either of them so he turned away and continued down his side of the street.

It was at least twenty minutes before Henry found a place to eat. He had a natural aversion to chrome and plate glass parlours, which seemed to abound, and he would not queue. Eventually he settled for a small cafe just off the High Street. There were only a dozen small tables and there was little space between them but there weren't many people in it and this appealed to Henry although he vaguely suspected that this might reflect the quality of the menu. He made for a table by the window and tried to arrange that he could see out without being seen. The window panes were small and he was to one side, almost in a corner. He took off his coat, scarf and cap and laid them on the broad window sill, looking out the while to see if he had been observed by anyone he knew, then he carefully adjusted his seat so that he had a clear view without being too close to the window. Hardly looking down, he took up the menu, made his choice and sat back with some satisfaction.

His preoccupation with his role as sleuth isolated him for a while, shutting out the noise of other customers. He peered out into the street without being sure who or what he was looking for. He relished being an observer but, he had, at this stage, no wish to be further involved. Suddenly, he realised that this was going to be a handicap. To find out more, he would have to become more involved. Hadn't he just missed a splendid opportunity? He had seen Baxter and Jackson across the street, floundering in the rain and he had walked away rather than find out what they were up to. His nose wrinkled with disapproval yet his mind told him that he had made a mistake. It was not going to be easy, he would have to change the habit of a lifetime. He drew out his notebook, intending to enter the incident.

It was then that he noticed that his table had not been cleared. The clutter of dishes was intolerable. There were cigarette stubs in one of the saucers and huge red smears on the nearest cup. Pushed towards the centre of the table was a plate bearing the remains of a pie with a crumpled paper serviette thrust into it. Crushed on top of this was another plate with a revolting fish skin smeared with ketchup. Tea had been spilled onto this plate and had followed its slope to create a small brown lake on the tablecloth. Further off were two more plates with half finished meals overlaid with abandoned serviettes and even an empty cigarette carton. Crumbs and splashes of tea and gravy were everywhere. Worse, a bluebottle crawled sluggishly and unabashed over the grubby tablecloth where Henry could just make out finger tracings in spilt sugar and cigarette ash. He glanced at his watch. He had been sitting for a good ten minutes. He turned and raised an arm. He was a big man, hard to miss at the best of times. His raised arm was seen by the only waitress present. She was short and plump and leisurely. It took her a while to push her way between the tables.

"Yerss?" She leaned on one thigh, took a pencil from behind her ear and prepared to give Henry her attention. Henry did not speak, he indicated the uncleared table with a gesture. The waitress chewed and blinked, uncomprehending.

"What would you like then? Fish is nice, I can recommend the pie." She shifted her weight, scratched her waist with her notepad, moved her chewing gum with the tip of her pencil and emitted an undoubted belch. Henry stared at her with growing horror.

"You can't just sit without eating, you know." The waitress smiled patiently through her chewing gum and her lip gloss. "What will it be then?"

She turned and looked at her heel for some unknown reason. Her not inconsiderable weight moved against the table. The angled plate slid inevitably, the glutinous remains of the pie could not hold it. Nor could the edge of the table. It landed with gentle force on Henry's lap then slithered sideways onto the floor. Its path was marked by a trail of mixed ketchup, cold tea and gravy.

"Look now! What a mess!" The waitress glared accusingly at Henry then down at the floor. Henry rose, six feet of mingled wrath, embarrassment and guilt. He was incapable of speech. He snatched at the teatowel at the waitress' waist and rubbed furiously at his leg. The waitress gave a little squeal of outraged modesty and snatched it back. This was too much for Henry, he emitted a low roar, seized his precious notebook, his coat, scarf and cap and charged out, scattering furniture in all directions.

Out on the street, he surveyed the damage. There was nothing for it, his suit had to go to the dry cleaner's. Passers-by began to look at him. They looked at his trousers and shook their heads. He was mortified. Then he had an inspiration. He would buy himself a new pair of trousers and take his present pair straight into the cleaner's while he was in town. He could easily wear dark flannels to his suit jacket. He was delighted with this plan and fell to implementing it immediately. Croxley and Furlong, further up the main street, was a men's outfitters he had long admired. He had always been careful with money and had hesitated to enter such a shop. Now he was different. He entered the shop quite jauntily. He made a very favourable impression on the salesman who thought Henry's scheme admirable, tried to sell him a new suit and settled for an expensive pair of flannels, a new scarf and a set of handkerchiefs. Henry emerged well pleased.

He was also hungry. As soon as he had deposited the stained trousers with the dry cleaner's, he headed back to the coffee shop. He would not get a complete meal but there would be sandwiches, at the very least. Time was getting on, he would be grateful for whatever he could get. At the corner where he had to turn off the High Street he saw the slight figure of Jenny Phillips again. This time, she was boarding a bus. He looked again to make sure. She must be returning to the hotel. It was late but, for all he knew, it might be her day off.

CHAPTER FIFTEEN

It was a frustrating morning for Chief Inspector Duncombe. The unexpected arrival of the Oxburys had interrupted his re-examination of the statements. The lab reports had not arrived and D.C.Hornby had phoned in to say that Frimton had not been home to visit his parents. They had not expected him because he had always let them know when he was coming. They were now worried as to what had happened to him. Hornby couldn't enquire further until Frimton's office opened on Monday. Then Duncombe had difficulty contacting Brambles the solicitors. As it was Saturday, there was no one at the office. There were two Brambles listed in the directory for Catton, neither offered any response to his calls. Just after midday, he tried again. This time he was answered by a lady who said that she was the wife of Victor Brambles, the senior partner. She accepted that Duncombe's call was of a serious nature and suggested that he called to see them after two. Her husband and his brother would have returned from their round of golf by then.

It was twenty four miles to Catton, a large stone built village up a valley away from the noise and smoke of regional industry. D.C.I.Duncombe liked this part of the county. Catton was an accepted starting off point for serious fell walkers even though it could hardly claim to be part of the fells. The roads were still broad enough for two streams of traffic and there were plenty of trees to vary the landscape. There was nothing bleak in the countryside immediately around Catton. The winters could be cold with plenty of snow but there was shelter at this level. Three miles further up the valley with the road climbing all the way, you began to feel the winds. At the top it was wild. Duncombe had enjoyed walking as a youth and he remembered looking down on Catton from the top and thinking that it looked a fine example of a typical Yorkshire village.

As he drove in, he realised that it had grown since his youth. Regulations had obliged builders to use stone in new buildings but that hadn't stopped development. It was almost a town. The church now looked small because it was surrounded by a number of large buildings.

Victor Brambles lived in a detached Victorian house just off the main road on the west side of the village. A smart red sports car stood outside the front door. A short, white haired lady with bright, dark eyes and a wide smile opened the door to him, introduced herself as Mrs.Brambles and invited him in. She led him into a sitting room on the right and left him to seek her husband, who, she explained, had just got back. The room was furnished simply with heavy but comfortable armchairs and a fire was already blazing in a highly ornamental fireplace. Duncombe was just admiring his surroundings when Victor Brambles came in.

The senior partner was a well dressed man in his fifties with flowing grey hair over a suntanned face dominated by a strong, pointed nose. His eyes were blue-grey, clear and steady. He was not tall but he carried himself well, giving an impression of great dignity.

Duncombe explained his mission and Brambles was genuinely shocked. News of the death had not reached the morning papers, Lucy's death came as a complete surprise to him. He spoke very highly of her, saying that she had been very capable and a joy to have about the office. She was so lively and so interested in the work. She had never hesitated to work extra hours or to carry out research for them. They were most upset when she decided to leave. Duncombe asked why she had done so? Brambles couldn't say. The only thing that had occurred to him was that she was not happy at home.

"Why do you think that, sir?"

"I have no factual reason for saying so, Chief

Inspector. It's just that her parents were old-fashioned stick in the muds. I believe that they discouraged her from going to university. She was very bright, she would have done well. She never complained but I'm sure that they held her back. I have friends who knew them well, they told me that they insisted that she should take a job near home so that she could help them and help to look after the younger brother. I applaud her spirit in going for another job, was it with solicitors?"

"No. She was working for an estate agent."

"Oh! She was fascinated by the work here. She would have made a good solicitor. We wanted her to take articles but her parents wouldn't have it."

"She left suddenly, did she, sir?"

"She gave us a month's notice. She asked for a reference, I remember, at the same time. She said she needed to have a change and I could see her point, she had been with us for nearly five years...."

"Was she upset at the time?"

"Oh no. She was never moody. I'm sure I would have noticed."

"Could it have been the result of a row at home?"

"Well, it wasn't that sudden. I rather thought that she had planned the move but that she hadn't a job in mind at the time she gave her notice. That's why she asked for a reference. If there had been a row at home I should have thought that she would want to go quickly. We wouldn't have stood in her way. It was her idea to give a month's notice, it was very considerate of her. A week would have sufficed."

"It seems such a waste. At the moment, there is no apparent motive. She doesn't seem to have had any enemies. Was there anything or anybody connected with your work that could have had some bearing on her death?"

"I can't think that there should have been. Most of our work has been conveyancing. I suppose that could be one reason why she chose to work for an estate agent. From time to time I take on a criminal case - I suppose that is what you are getting at? - but there hasn't been anything sinister for a long time and nothing that might have concerned Lucy at all. There were no complicated settlements or any cases where clients or their disputees have threatened us, if that's what you mean."

"It's asking an awful lot, Mr.Brambles, but could you let me have a list of your recent criminal cases? I won't ask you to go into detail, just a brief note of the people concerned and an outline of the charges. That could help us a great deal."

"I'm afraid that I won't be able to help you before Monday and it will take time to go through all the files. I promise to be as quick as possible but we are very busy just now, there seems to be a peak in house buying at the moment. I'll get my secretary on to it as soon as we get back."

"I'm entirely in your hands, but speed is vital. At the moment we are clutching at straws."

There was a tap at the door and a tall figure entered.

"Ah, there you are, Vincent! Chief Inspector Duncombe, this is my brother and partner, Vincent."

A family likeness was obvious in their faces but Vincent was younger and more glamorous than Victor. He was taller and leaner, with a more stylish grooming to him. His clothes looked more expensive and his suntan was a tone deeper. Here was a ladies man if ever Duncombe had seen one.

"The Chief Inspector has just told me that Lucy Oxbury has been murdered and that he is making enquiries."

"Lucy, our secretary Lucy?" Vincent Brambles was as shocked as his brother had been. "How did it happen? Where was she? When was it?" His questions tumbled out.

Duncombe gave a brief outline of the facts, watching

Vincent's face the while.

"What can you tell me about her, Mr.Brambles?"

"She was a sweet girl, intelligent and natural. She put everyone at ease. She was a marvel with the clients. She came to us straight from school, was with us five years or so. A great appetite for work, we miss her badly. We were never sure why she left."

He spoke easily without affectation of any kind, which surprised Duncombe because he thought that an obvious dandy like Vincent was likely to be affected.

"Do you know if she had any boyfriends while she worked for you?"

"She was a very private person really. Her parents kept her on a rein, I suspect. I don't know of any particular boyfriends. She never talked of one while she was in the office."

"She didn't have much of a social life then, sir?"

"Not that I know of. She belonged to the Methodist Chapel and must have joined in their activities, I suppose. I think that she was very popular. She played tennis for a while last year. I saw her on the courts once or twice and she was surrounded by admirers. Mind you, I doubt whether her parents let her out in the evenings."

"Did you find her attractive, sir?"

"I certainly did. I can't imagine anyone not doing so....Oh, you mean did I play the interested employer?" He gave a little laugh. "No, Chief Inspector, I'm a happily married man. I don't think she thought of me as anything other than an employer, either."

"Thank you for your time and trouble, Mr.Brambles. You appreciate that we have to explore all the possibilities."

The brothers showed him out. Duncombe left with no doubts about their sincerity. He felt that his journey had not been entirely wasted.

CHAPTER SIXTEEN

By the time Duncombe returned to the station it was already dark. He fretted that little could be achieved until after the weekend and he was not in the best of spirits as he   pushed open the swing doors. The desk sergeant greeted him warily.

"Sir, D.C.Hornby is waiting for you"

"Is he bedamned! Send him along to my room."

"Sir....!"

It was too late, the D.C.I. was already half way down the corridor, wrestling out of his overcoat as he went.

When Hornby arrived he was not alone. With him was a thin young man with frizzy hair and a thin, fairish moustache.

"Sir, this is Gerald Frimton."

"Frimton! Frimton!"

Duncombe's cry was so loud that the young man took a hasty step backwards.

"Well now, Mr.Frimton, I think you have a lot of explaining to do, haven't you? Where have you been since last Monday morning?"

Gerald Frimton's chin went up and his eyes met the D.C.I.'s squarely.

"I don't think I need to account for my whereabouts to anyone. I am over twenty one and I am not guilty of anything."

Duncombe held the young man's gaze and signalled for him to take a seat.

"You may or may not be guilty of anything, Mr.Frimton, but you have certainly misled your landlady and your parents. Did you not tell Mrs.Ridgeway at The Moorcroft Hotel that you were going to visit your parents at Huddersfield?"

"Yes, I did, but I changed my mind. Surely that's not a matter for the police?"

"How well did you know Lucy Oxbury?"

"Lucy Oxbury? Quite well, she was new to The Moorcroft. I shared a table with her."

"She confided in you, did she?"

"Well, hardly confided. We enjoyed talking to each other."

"What did you talk about?"

"Oh, the theatre, films, music, anything....but why? What's all this about?"

"I'll tell you in a moment, sir. Where have you been staying while you have been away from The Moorcroft?"

"I've been staying with my girlfriend at 16 Mortimer Crescent."

"Here in Maskerley?"

"Yes, I took two days off. I was going home but something cropped up and I changed my mind. My girl friend and I are planning to get married, I wanted to spend some time with her family...."

"You have been there all week?"

"Yes, but I have been back to work."

"Were you planning to leave the hotel?"

"No, not yet. Our wedding won't be for another month or more. I was going back tomorrow, Sunday. All my clothes are still there."

"Where were you last night, Mr.Frimton?"

"Last night, Friday night? I stayed at Mortimer Crescent."

"You returned there straight from work?"

"Yes."

"And stayed in all evening?"

"Yes."

"Your girl friend's family will vouch for that, will they?"

"Well...they went out about six...."

"So no one can say that you stayed in all evening?"

"I wasn't feeling so good, a touch of flu I thought, so they left me behind. Sally, the girl friend came back about nine. She can testify for me."

"Lucy Oxbury was murdered in the hotel sometime about seven that night."

"Lucy? Murdered?"

There was a long pause. Gerald Frimton stared at the Chief Inspector, his mouth tight, his eyes wide.

Duncombe acknowledged to himself that he knew very little about the residents of The Moorcroft. The young man who had just left his office would need careful checking out but so would all the others. Johnson would be delving further at that very moment.

He could not get out of his mind a connection between Lucy's death and her work at Brambles. It could make sense, a recognition, a need to silence. But that would imply an outside job, someone from outside the hotel and, apart from the oiled fire escape door, the indications were to the contrary. There was a strong possibility that it was a combination of inside and outside. Johnson had checked police records, none of the residents had a record but that only meant that they had not been prosecuted and found guilty. He stirred in his chair, sighed and looked over at his in-tray. On top lay a slim file on recent burglaries. He remembered giving it a cursary glance earlier in the day but he had been distracted by those awful Oxburys. He reached over and picked it up. The list consisted of one in Stafford Walk on the 20th, two in Gabbitas Street on the 23rd. and 25th., reported together on the 25th. and one in Wormald Street reported on the 26th. Duncombe sat up suddenly. Wormald Street seemed too near home to be a coincidence.

All of these burglaries had taken place within a short distance of the hotel. The details revealed a common pattern, rear doors and windows opened without much difficulty, money and jewellery taken. No damage done except where force was necessary at the point of entry. The occupants of the houses were all out on the evenings in question and had returned at times varying between 9.30 and 11.p.m. The neatness of each break-in and the absence of fingerprints suggested a professional burglar or a very careful amateur. The absence of the owners in each case suggested that the thief had thoroughly 'cased the joints'. None of the items stolen were bulky, other valuable items had been left untouched, it seemed that the thief only took what he could carry away in his pockets. A comment in the file discounted the probability of the few local thieves known to the police being involved. Two had been interviewed, they had had alibis and had been unaware of the burglaries. Their grapevine had been ignorant of them.

If there had been a new face, a dedicated amateur, at work in the district, why couldn't it be one of the residents of the hotel? It would have made an excellent base. Duncombe was thinking of the oiled door. The question raised others. Could Lucy Oxbury have been involved? He doubted it but it was something to be considered. That could provide the scenario of inside and outside. A falling out of thieves could be the motive, although the brutality of the killing seemed out of proportion, but then, weren't all killings out of proportion?

CHAPTER SEVENTEEN

Henry Allingham felt better after he had eaten. His favourite Coffee Shop had not disappointed him. A bowl of excellent home-made soup and a generously filled sandwich were all he could have asked for. He shook crumbs from his elegant new flannels and rose to go. His movements were more deliberate than they had been that morning. He was learning. He would not miss anything because of haste. He still regretted his failure to question Mrs.Elmwood, he needed to know so much and their meeting that morning had been an excellent opportunity to find out about his fellow residents.

As soon as he left the doorway, he looked round him carefully. The narrow street was busy but he recognised no one. The light was already beginning to fade yet it wasn't much after three. He was pondering his next move at the end of the street when he thought he could see a familiar figure ahead of him. This, even at a good fifty yards, had to be Denzil Elliott. He was moving away from Henry but there was something characteristic about the slope of the shoulders and the back of the head. The stride, too, was inimitable. There was determination in the stride. This wasn't the Elliott who had been following Henry at leisure, it was an Elliott hurrying with some other purpose. Henry felt a strong urge to follow, he no longer felt any conscience in the matter. If nothing else, it would polish his new found skills as a sleuth.

It didn't help that his quarry returned to the High Street. Henry had great difficulty in keeping an eye on him in the crowd. An awkward encounter with a large lady stooping to pick up a small dog caused Henry to lose sight of his man. At the next corner, some instinct made him look left and there was his quarry disappearing into a railed off area at the top of the rise. Henry thought himself very lucky, he had so nearly missed him. He hurried discreetly.

The railed off area turned out to be a small park, dense with laurels and high privet. Henry had never noticed this park before but that didn't surprise him much. He had never really explored the town. He had been content with his routine, with his familiar places. Here, only a stone's throw from the main street was a park with several tall trees and many bushes. He was filled with curiosity. A very little way in, the path divided, to Henry's great annoyance. A choice had to be made. There was no obvious indication as to what lay down either path though he could hear voices to his right, high pitched voices. He followed the sound and, twenty yards on, turned unexpectedly into an open space. A neatly trimmed area of grass, hemmed in by a high, gloomy hedge, was populated by a host of birds, scuffling after pieces of bread and cake thrown to them by three small children. Henry hesitated, there was no bench or seat of any kind and no adult in sight. To his consternation, the youngest of the children approached him with a big smile, hand outstretched.

"Mister, you throw one!"

The old Henry stiffened and shrank back. The new Henry blushed with pleasure. The hesitation didn't trouble the little girl.

"Go on! It's only bread. See if you can throw it further than our Jack. There's a tiny bird over there, it hasn't got any, see?"

Henry was overwhelmed by the little girl's trust. She was treating him as though he were a family friend, perhaps an uncle. He stooped and took the piece of bread.

"Tilda! How many times have I got to tell you?" A rough hand snatched the little girl's arm and whisked her away.

"Never, never talk to strangers! I've told you time and time again!"

There was a hint of hysteria in the voice. Henry was only dimly aware of a woman and the little girl hurrying away to his left with the two other children scampering after her. He stood frozen for a very long time.

"You all right, mate?"

A small, weatherbeaten man in overalls and a peaked cap stood at his side looking up at him, quite worried.

"What? Oh, ah! Yes, I think so..."

"You look as though you had had a shock or were ill or something."

"Yes, I think I...." Henry was still standing motionless.

"I'm sorry mate, but I've got to lock up. It's nearly dark, I'm late already. I'll have to ask you to go. Perhaps you should see a doctor. Can you manage?"

The park keeper's concern penetrated Henry's daze. He shook himself and looked at the little man.

"Thank you, I'm alright now, I think. I'm sorry to keep you."

The park keeper walked Henry to the entrance, looking at him anxiously from time to time. By the time they had reached the street, Henry had fully recovered. He turned to thank the park keeper once more and saw, almost hidden by branches, a sign pointing up the path to the left. He couldn't read it in the gloom. His memory returned to the figure he had been following and had lost. It was all too late now but he was curious.

"Tell me, is there another way into the park up there?"

"Oh no, them's just the toilets. Are you sure you're going to be alright?"

"Yes thanks, you've been very kind. Thank you."

Henry walked away briskly, leaving the park keeper shaking his head sadly.

CHAPTER EIGHTEEN

About five o'clock, Johnson handed in his reports on the residents.

"These are as far as I've got. Everybody's finished for the weekend."

"Trevor, there's one more for you to add to your list. The missing Mr.Frimton has turned up. D.C.Hornby did a neat piece of work. Having gone to Huddersfield only to discover that Frimton had not been home as Mrs.Ridgeway believed, he returned to Maskerley, went into the Post Office and heard the man in front of him spell out his name to the woman behind the counter. Quick as a flash he stopped him and brought him to see me. The wretched man had been in Maskerley all the time, staying with his girl friend. And guess what? He hasn't an alibi for the time of the murder."

"Has he gone, Sir?"

"Well, you might just catch him. He went to Room 3 to make his statement."

Trevor Johnson's file on the backgrounds of the residents made fascinating reading.

Ernest A Baxter was in the process of retiring from a partnership in a jeweller's shop. He was a widower with a stepson, recently married. His wife had been wealthy and when she died had willed her house to her son. Baxter had been obliged to clear out and allow the newly weds to occupy the house. He was quite happy to do so, his wife had left him a large sum and his share of the business would amount to roughly £50,000. He was in no hurry to find himself another home, he was quite content to live at The Moorcroft while he could afford it. He had no children of his own and his only known relative was a brother in Australia of whom he had not heard in 30 years.

Millicent Catesby had been the daughter of a prominent clergyman. She had been privately educated to no particular purpose. Her parents had not owned a house of their own but had died soon after each other, leaving her what was, thirty years ago, a considerable sum. It had been prudently invested and she was living off the interest. She had never worked or earned any money of her own. When she was younger, she had been well looked after, with a maid in part attendance. She had no wish to take on the responsibilities of a house of her own. She could not have afforded to live in a three or four star hotel and she was horrified at the thought of ordinary lodgings. She had stayed in a number of less glamorous hotels and had found them all trying. Not only that but her expenses were increasing and her source of income was not. Eventually, she had moved to the The Moorcroft and found it sufficiently genteel to serve her well, except that it didn't have private washing facilities. She was a member of a select Ladies' Circle and assisted in a number of charities. She helped in a friend's dress shop on a part time basis and received a small remuneration for this.

Walter Eric Jackson came from the Yorkshire Wolds. His father was a farm worker and a respectable local figure. His mother was a part time housekeeper. He was an only child. There were a number of relations on his mother's side, all living in the same area. He was more ambitious, he left the area as soon as he could. He had worked for the same firm since he had left school. Ingoldsby's was a good firm to work for, they had moved him around a lot but he was used to that. At the moment, he was not 'on the road'. He was helping to set up a branch just out of town, that was why he was staying at The Moorcroft. Normally, he lived in a flat at Wakeham with two friends. He hadn't got a car at the moment but he expected to be provided with one when his present assignment was over.

Gerald Frimton, nothing known yet.

Christine Jervis's parents had been 'Drapers and Outfitters' on Teesside. They had had two daughters late in life. The eldest, Jane, had married a Yorkshire farmer and was living comfortably with a large family about her not far from Thirsk. The two daughters had been well educated and had lacked for little but the parents had not left them as well provided for as they had expected. Christine had decided to go in for teacher training while still living over the shop. When her parents died, she had to find a place to live. She moved to Rendersby to join her first school and met her husband there. He was an accountant ten years her senior. She had ambitions, had become the deputy head of a junior school at Hagworth, not far from where they lived. At present she was on a course at the Maskerley Institute of Education with a view to applying for a headship. She had no family of her own and did not wish for one.

Mary Elizabeth Elmwood was born in Newcastle upon Tyne. She was an only child and, so far as she knew, had no living relatives. She had trained as a shorthand typist and had always done secretarial work. She had worked in a number of towns then had settled in Leeds where she had met her husband. They had been very happy but he had become ill and she had nursed him to the end. That was five years ago. She had needed to escape and to earn a living again. A very good job had cropped up, personal secretary to the director of a large company, Crompton's, with its headquarters in Maskerley. She had applied and got the job. She had no immediate wish to set up another home at the time of her arrival in Maskerley. She had chosen The Moorcroft from a short list supplied by her firm and had liked it so well that she had chosen to stay on a permanent basis. She could afford it, she was well paid and her husband had left her a reasonably good annuity. She lived a quiet life and the hotel suited her.

Denzil Elliott wasn't sure where he was born but his parents had spent most of their lives in Westholm north of

Sheffield. They were not natives of that town, that was all he knew. He had two brothers and an older sister. He did not get along well with any of them. His father was out of work for a long time and there were great difficulties in the family. He escaped as soon as he had finished school. He had worked in a shop, in a cafe then in a bar. He thought he would like to enter the hotel and catering trade. He found a job as a waiter in the Aston Hotel in Harrogate. He believed that he would be able to 'work his way up' through the hotel, learning from every department, but he was told by the manager that he had not been employed as a management trainee but as a waiter. He would not be given the opportunity he had wanted. He had not sat any examinations at school and so could not enrol for a catering course at college so he was stuck. He worked on at the hotel, hating it, then out of the blue, he was left a small legacy by a distant relation. He quit his job immediately and came to Maskerley on a whim. He was looking round for a job but had not found anything as yet.

Henry Allingham had been born in Beverley. His parents had died when he was very young and as there were no known relatives, he had spent seven years in a boys' ophanage. He had learned secretarial skills in his senior school which was a Secondary Commercial School. He had been diligent and had had no trouble in finding employment. While still relatively young and in lodgings he had met a young girl and had married her. They had set up a home and taken out a modest mortgage. Two years later she left him. He had been very thrifty since his institutional days and taking on the property had been a well worthwhile venture. After a decent interval, he sold the property, settled the remaining debt and took to living in lodgings on a permanent basis. Eventually he had ended up at The Moorcroft. He felt that it had been a good move. He had had no children, he was entirely independent, he lived frugally and was able to save something for the future.

Duncombe sat back. They were an amazing crew. He felt sure that only a little further probing would reveal a number of deceptions. For example, why had a travelling rep. no car? Did Elliott really have a legacy to live on, given his background.

At that moment there was a knock and Inspector Johnson entered.

"Just the man! I've been reading your report on the backgrounds...."

"That's what I've come to see you about, Sir. I've done some more checking."

"Right, what've you got?"

"First, Baxter. His stepson didn't really approve of him, he thought that he had married his mother for her money. It was after he married her that he bought his way into the jeweller's business."

"His stepson was probably right, then."

"His partner is glad to be rid of him. He says that he is good with the customers but he has been an increasing liability. He can't keep away from the horses. He suspects that he has been losing heavily and fears that his losses might be subsidised from the till. The settlement has been in the hands of the solicitors for a while and should be completed soon."

"How will the partner be able to buy Baxter out? I gather that it is only the one shop."

"The partner is quite happy about that. He will raise a loan. He says the business is good enough for that. He feels it will be better without Baxter. I asked him if money had actually been taken but he thought not. He was becoming very nervous, though, and that was no basis for a partnership."

"Second, Jackson. He got his job at Ingoldsby's through his father and is only hanging on to it because his immediate boss doesn't want to hurt the family. Apparently he is fond of his drink but his stomach can't take it. He has had a number of spells off work, it's a case of getting plastered then being ill. Just two months ago he lost his licence through drink and was only kept on because they were setting up a new branch near here and he was given the job of helping to organise it. If he doesn't recover his licence, he wont be able to stay on as rep."

"Not a very likeable character but nothing there to link him with a murder."

"Third, Elliott. The Aston say that he was with them for only a few weeks. They suspect that his references were false. While he was there, property went missing from rooms, there was an official investigation and several stolen items were found in the room of someone who worked alongside Elliott. The man swore his innocence but the evidence was overwhelming. They had worked the same shifts, they had had the same opportunities, neither of them had convincing alibis. There was a possibility that they had worked together but both denied it vehemently. They hadn't really had much to do with one another. Elliott was clean. The other man got two years. Elliott left soon after."

"So Elliott is a thief, is he? Well, I have something to tell you now. Four houses have been burgled in the last week, all within a stone's throw of The Moorcroft. I may be jumping to conclusions, but what if one of the residents was responsible? What if the fire escape door was oiled to allow a thief to come and go without being seen or heard? Could not that resident be Elliott? His room is nearest to the fire escape on the third floor. We should check up on that legacy story."

"We can tackle him about the legacy and see if he shifts. When his room was searched there was nothing that might have incriminated him in a burglary."

"Burglars are quick to get rid of the stuff these days. Any news of the young maid?"

"None yet, I'm sorry to say. I just hope she turns up this evening."

"And Frimton?"

"I'm afraid he'd gone long before I got down there. I can wait for him."

Henry Allingham hardly understood the hurt. It had been grievous and overwhelming and he had been stunned by it. He made no effort to comprehend or come to terms with it, he simply sought to escape it. He put it to the back of his mind and hurried on. He had walked almost the length of the High Street before he realised that he could catch a bus. His feet had begun to ache, he must have walked a considerable distance in the course of the day and all on hard pavements. He climbed onto the first bus that came along and sank onto the first vacant seat.

"Twice in one day! Goodness Mr.Allingham, it's almost too much!"

Mrs.Elmwood gave a little laugh and leant her elbow against his. He did not shrink away. There had been a great battle within him but the new Henry had not been totally defeated.

"You are very late, Mrs.Elmwood."

"Yes, I didn't intend to spend all day in town but I met an old friend I hadn't seen for years and we had lunch together. We took our time and had a real old gossip. Then I almost got back to the hotel when I realised that I'd forgotten something so I had to trail all the way back again. I treated myself to a cup of tea at the coffee shop before I could summon up the energy to make the return journey. I didn't see you there this time."

Henry wanted to ask what time she had taken tea but he thought that might be considered rude. Mrs.Elmwood went on.

"You are rather late yourself, Mr.Allingham. What have you been up to?"

Henry contented himself with a brief account of his shopping for clothes and his visit to the library. He was not inclined to gossip and he had no intention of telling anyone about his tailing experiences.

They left the bus and walked the rest of the way together. From some way off they could see and hear a commotion at the front door.

"Oh dear, journalists! I'm afraid the press has caught up with our unfortunate happening. Whatever shall we do, Mr.Allingham?"

"I shall do what I always do, Mrs.Elmwood."

Henry saw no reason to hesitate. He had had no experience of the press. He was tired and in need of a bath, these people would have to make way for him. Accordingly he approached the steps just ahead of Mrs.Elmwood. Immediately, shadowy figures got in his way and gabbled at him at high speed.

"Sir, can you tell us what your connection is......"

"Sir, are you an investigating officer.....?"

"Sir, are you one of the residents here.....?"

"Sir, could you give us an account of this.....?"

"Sir, the Northern Globe would be willing to print....."

Henry moved his bulk forward and sideways. Mrs.Elmwood crept up close behind him. He ignored the reporters and reached forward, his key at the ready. As soon as the door moved, Mrs.Elmwood slipped through it. Henry had more trouble, he had to battle through and also battle the door shut again. He had not said a word nor had he allowed anyone to catch his eye. His size had made the reporters believe that he might be one of the detectives working on the case. He was surprised but calm. He longed for a good soak.

CHAPTER NINETEEN

Mrs Ridgeway was very upset at the onslaught of the press. She told herself that she ought to have expected it but it was much more insistent and troublesome than she could have guessed. The murder was quite enough of a disaster without having to suffer the aggravation of journalists at the door. They would not go away and seemed to think that they had every right to intrude. She had told them that the police would tell them all they needed to know. That was most unsatisfactory to them and they went on clamouring. She stopped answering the door and forbade her staff to do so.

Downstairs, Mrs.Hammond had had a shock. Going out to the bin in the dark, she had been accosted by two young men. It had been totally unexpected and had given her a terrible fright. Her imagination had been heightened by the death of Lucy Oxbury and she had thought she was about to be murdered. Her scream had brought everyone running. The two young men were similarly frightened by the scream and by the flailing attack Mrs.Hammond had made upon them with her dustpan and brush. Mrs.Hammond was not given to fainting even in her terror. Self defence was her instinctive reaction. Later, she regretted that she had not had something more substantial or more messy to hand. The young reporters apologised profusely. They had simply tried their luck at the back door since they were outnumbered at the front. Mrs.Ridgeway saw them off the premises with hard words. They were not rewarded with any story.

It dawned upon Laura Ridgeway that there were more problems ahead. She had found her staff very loyal over the years they had been together. Now they were being tested. They had all been shocked by the death of one of the residents but, of course, they were not very close and the shock would quickly give way to excitement. They would stay with her while the police were carrying out their investigation in order to share in the excitement and learn the outcome. It would be when friends and neighbours began to talk and whisper that they would think about leaving. No doubt they would be pursued by the reporters, they too would have their privacy invaded, their relations would be upset, their friends and neighbours would be drawn in, then they would begin to regret being part of it. She couldn't bear the thought that even Meg Hammond might leave her.

There was one dreadful worry on her mind that exceeded everything. Where was Jenny? Normally, at this time in the evening, her attention should have been on the preparations for dinner. Tonight, her mind was clouded with worry, she couldn't quite focus on questions or answers. Ever present was the hope that the telephone would bring news of Jenny's safety or that Jenny, herself, would slip quietly through the kitchen door. She had agreed to take responsibility for Jenny when she arrived in the summer. Jenny was an orphan, she had been highly recommended by the orphanage and Mrs.Ridgeway had taken to her immediately. She was clean, neat, hardworking and uncomplicated. Her quiet shyness was a bonus. As the weeks had gone by, everyone had come to like her yet she was entirely unspoilt. Laura Ridgeway was not an emotional woman but she had come to think of Jenny as one of her family. Responsibility for her hung heavily at this moment.

A violent hubbub drew her attention to the front door. She was puzzled for a few seconds as she was fairly sure that all the residents had returned. Through the door squeezed the two senior detectives and she greeted them with relief.

"Any news of Jenny?" was her first question.

"We rather hoped that she had returned by now." Duncombe was genuinely sympathetic. "Would it be convenient if we had words with your residents again?"

"Well, dinner's in just ten minutes, could you wait until it's over?"

Duncombe and Johnson exchanged looks and Johnson suggested that it would be alright if, in the meantime, they could speak to Mr.Elliott. Mrs.Ridgeway agreed to this, the meal could proceed. Mr.Elliott could have his later and her staff could get on with everything in reasonable order.

The two detectives climbed to the third floor. Before knocking on Elliott's door they turned their attention to the fire escape door at the end of the corridor. It was dark at that end of the corridor away from the light on the landing. It was quite conceivable that someone could linger there without attracting attention. They opened the door without difficulty. The handle lifted smoothly and the door glided outwards without a sound. Johnson took out a torch and examined the hinges. They had been cleaned before being oiled, someone had been at great pains to ensure silent movement. Inside was a doormat of cocoa fibre. It was typical of Mrs.Ridgeway that every door should have a doormat. Johnson crouched and examined it. It was fairly new and there was little dirt inside its fibres.

They went out onto the metal landing and looked about them. To their right was Wormald Street. Most of the houses were detached and stood in gardens with plenty of trees in them. Duncombe considered them good pickings for an enterprizing burglar. Johnson's attention was on a possible trajectory for the murder weapon.

"Not easy, Sir."

"Too easy, if you ask me. There's plenty of cover, a good distance between them, probably not a burglar alarm in the whole street, poor street lighting, what more do you want?"

"I was meaning the trajectory. It would take a good

aim for that bar to reach the garden of number 59. Look, Sir, there's the hedge between 59 and the next house, in among that shadow there. That only leaves five feet of garden at most before the corner of the hotel gets in the way. Then this door sticking out would be a handicap. Whoever it was would have to squeeze round it before he could throw anything."

"That's not impossible, if someone is determined." He smiled at his Inspector, he was giving him his own back. "It was an iron bar, it wouldn't drift, would it?"

"But that big tree there is just a few feet inside. He'd have to be sure he wouldn't hit it and have the thing bounce back into the road."

"You think it was thrown from one of the bedroom windows, then?"

"It certainly seems more probable now that I've seen this narrow platform."

"Right, let's keep it in mind. Now, where do these steps come out at the bottom?"

"They face into the yard at the bottom. Escape is into the lane from the yard."

"And as it is the last house in the street, it would be very easy to slip into the yard and up these stairs. A burglar could have done the job and skipped up here within half an hour or so. What about the door to the lane, wouldn't it be locked?"

"I don't think Mrs.Ridgeway bothers to lock that door. Anyway it wouldn't take much to climb the wall."

"Now then, this door, I thought it only opened from the inside?"

"Ah, yes....."

Johnson examined the door from the outside. There was only a handle on the inside but the end of its spindle appeared on the outside in the form of a domed rivet. Johnson picked at it with his fingernail until his torch revealed a pair of grooves intersecting at right angles.

"Look, Sir! Here's how he did it. He took the trouble to

cut grooves in the end of this spindle. That must have taken a helluva time, either that or he had some mechanical tool to help him."

"He wouldn't dare use a drill. There's always someone in the hotel to hear him."

"It was either a file or a saw and it would have to be a very hard toothed saw to manage this."

"Why the cross grooves? Wouldn't one do?"

"My guess is that he couldn't afford a slip. He hadn't time and he didn't want to make a noise. He would use something like a cylinder, a box spanner or something like it, with a cross piece built into it. The end of the cylinder would fit over the end of the spindle entirely and prevent it slipping."

"Sounds a bit far fetched to me. Why didn't any of the men see this last night when they did the search?"

"They probably saw the grooves and thought nothing of them. They are neat and trim and harmless looking."

"Pah! We can't be there all the time to tell them what to look for. That should have been discovered when they noticed the oiled hinges. Dammit, it is a murder enquiry!"

A door opened along the corridor. They hurried inside and closed the door behind them. They were just in time to see Denzil Elliott starting downstairs.

"Mr.Elliott, I wonder if we might have a word with you, perhaps in your room away from the others?"

Denzil Elliott was startled. He could not think where the detectives had sprung from.

"I....I was just going down to dinner...."

"We took the liberty of telling Mrs.Ridgeway that we were going to have a word with you and she said she would keep your dinner if necessary."

"Well..."

"In your room, sir?"

Elliott turned back and led the way into his room.

CHAPTER TWENTY

Unlike the previous evening when he had been obliged to admit the tricks he had played on Henry Allingham, Denzil Elliott was very composed. He sat on the edge of the bed and indicated the only chair in the room to Duncombe. Both policemen decided to stand.

"What can I do you for?"

"Mr.Elliott, you say you don't often go out in the evenings. I wonder if you could tell us where you were on the evenings of the 20th., 23rd.,24th., and 26th. of this month.?"

"Eh?" This question took him by surprise. His startled expression changed to a cunning one.

"That would be last Friday, Monday, Tuesday and Thursday?"

"That's right, Mr.Elliott, You have a good memory. Can you remember what you did on those evenings?"

"Easy! I stayed in the hotel. I hardly ever go out."

"Can you go over your evening's routine, we'd like to get it clear?"

"Well, not every evening is the same, Sometimes I stay downstairs and watch the telly, sometimes I come up to my room straight after dinner."

"And what about before dinner?"

"Before dinner?"

"Yes, I believe you often return to the hotel about four in the afternoon. What do you do between then and dinner?"

"Well....I don't do very much. If I've been walking round a lot, I have a quick kip...."

"So you sleep before dinner, what do you do after dinner when you come straight up to your room?"

"What's all this about?"

"Just answer the question, sir."

"Well, I sometimes read..." He watched the detectives' eyes as they looked in vain for any books or magazines in the room. "I....er....listen to my radio a lot," he pointed to a small portable radio by his bed.

"I don't suppose anyone disturbs you once you are up here?"

"No, everybody keeps to themselves here."

"So you would have no witnesses to prove that you did not go out again?"

"Why should I go out again?"

"What do you do in the daytime when you leave the hotel?"

"I've been looking for work."

"You spend every day looking for work?"

"Mr.Elliott, you have been here over a month, do you expect us to believe that you have spent every day, all day, looking for a job?"

"Well, I take my time, there isn't much going"

So far, Johnson had done all the questioning, now Duncombe took over.

"How have you been keeping yourself, Mr.Elliott?"

"How do you mean?"

"What have you been living on?"

"I told you, I was left some money."

"Would you mind giving us some details? Who left you this money?"

"A distant relation."

"Could we have a name and address?"

"I don't really know this woman...."

"Then you should be able to tell us the name of the solicitor who dealt with this legacy. You would get a letter from him."

"No, I didn't keep the letter. Anyway it hasn't anything to do with anybody but myself."

"I put it to you, Mr.Elliott, that this legacy never existed. I believe that you spend your time looking at property and planning break-ins. I believe that you have been living on the proceeds of burglaries you have carried out in this area."

"Rubbish! Where did you get that idea?"

"How long did you work at The Aston Hotel in Harrogate?"

"Just over a year."

"You are lying, Mr.Elliott, we know that you worked there for only a few weeks. We also know that at the time, you were suspected of thefts but, fortunately for you, the missing items were found in the room next to yours occupied by a John William Somers. He denied all knowledge of the thefts but neither of you had an alibi. In the end, he was the one convicted."

"They couldn't pin that on me and you can't pin anything else on me."

"Can't I? Don't be too sure. We are checking on all your previous employers...."

"That won't help you, I'm clean!"

Johnson interrupted.

"How many pairs of shoes have you, Mr.Elliott?"

"What? What is this?"

"A simple question, how many pairs of shoes have you?"

"Two, the ones I've got on and another pair in the wardrobe, why?"

"May I examine them, please?"

Denzil Elliot stared at him for a moment as though he was about to refuse. There was uncertainty in his face. Then he decided to cooperate, albeit with a poor grace.

"Here!"

He undid his laces, slipped out of the shoes he was wearing and passed them over to the Inspector. Johnson turned them over and studied the soles and heals.

"By the way, Mr.Elliott, you haven't used the fire escape at any time have you?"

"Why should I use the fire escape? There hasn't been a fire."

Duncombe tried a hunch.

"We believe that the murder weapon was thrown from the top of the fire escape...."

"I've never been near the fire escape. I don't know anything about it. I thought you were talking about burglaries not the murder."

"We are investigating both."

"I've told you, I have nothing to do with the murder. I didn't know the girl. She was just another resident."

Johnson had been looking in the wardrobe, he drew out a pair of soft soled casual shoes.

"Is this the other pair you mentioned?"

"Yes....those are my casuals...."

There was a silence as Johnson examined the soles and heels of this pair.

"Do you wear these much, sir?"

"No, just for a change, when I'm indoors."

"Indoors, you mean they are only used as slippers?"

"Yes, you could say that."

"There's soil in the pattern of the soles."

"Well, I've used them outdoors in the past."

"But not since you came here?"

"No, it's not the time of year."

Johnson peered at the sole of one of the casuals.

"Chewing gum! I wonder how that got there? I can't imagine that that came from the hotel."

"That must be old as well."

"You say you have never been near the fire escape?"

"Never!"

"Then how do you account for fibres from the fire escape mat sticking to this chewing gum?"

"Where? Where?"

Johnson turned away from Elliott, denying him the opportunity of seeing or interfering with the shoes.

"Evidence, Mr.Elliott. I'm afraid that we will have to take these shoes away for forensic examination. I'm afraid your situation looks rather bad. You admitted that you interfered with the latch of the downstairs bathroom, we found the same kind of scratches on the latch of the bathroom where Miss Oxbury was killed. Next, you say you were never near the fire escape and we find fibres from the fire escape mat on your shoes. Almost certainly, the murder weapon was thrown from the fire escape. What are we to make of all that?"

There was total silence for several minutes. Denzil Elliott sat frozen, the two detectives stood motionless.

"Alright, I'll tell you...."

"Thank you, sir. Perhaps you had better come down to the station and make your statement there."

CHAPTER TWENTY ONE

There was a commotion at the front door as dinner came to an end. Scuffling and excited shouts drifted down the steps then a car drew away. There was a stir of curiosity among the guests waiting for their coffee. When Mrs.Ridgeway entered with the coffee, all she could say was that Mr.Elliott had accompanied the police to the station and she did not know when he would be back. She was tight lipped with worry and in no mood to linger for questions.

Mrs.Jervis was the first to speak.

"Surely, Mr.Elliott can't have been.....?"

"I can scarcely believe......!" Mrs.Elmwood, too, was bewildered.

An abrasive sound came from Miss Catesby.

"I am not in the least surprised!"

She was dressed in a pale green moire silk outfit with a string of large amber beads at her throat.

"There was something down at heel about that young man!"

She was voicing a truth but she was being very unpleasant about it. A small uproar followed.

"Miss Catesby!"

"Oh dear! We know he wasn't well dressed...."

"That's not a very nice...."

"That's right, kick a man when he's down!" Walter Jackson flung down his napkin. "Nobody thought there was anything wrong with him yesterday."

"Nobody knew he was going to be arrested yesterday."

Jackson clasped his stomach and moaned. He had felt unwell all afternoon and had to ask Mrs.Ridgeway for poached fish instead of what was on the menu. Henry the Peacemaker spoke up.

"I'm sorry you've been ill. I saw you stumble this

afternoon, from across the street. It was just as well that Mr.Baxter was there to help you."

Baxter had not been listening. A light film of moisture had gathered on his brow. When Sarah Lucas came into the room with her tray, he quickly asked her if she knew what was the problem with Mr.Elliott. Sarah knew nothing but she was very curious. Everybody 'downstairs' was wondering.

The jeweller stood up, excused himself briefly and hurried out of the room. This in itself was unusual. He was stockliy built and his movements had always been slow and dignified. There was a murmur from the ladies.

"Very unsettling." was all Mrs.Jervis could manage.

"It has been an extraordinary twenty four hours." Mrs.Elmwood sipped her coffee thoughtfully. Miss Catesby sniffed loudly, signifying her general disapproval. Henry Allingham simply sat at the alert. He was longing to ask what had caused him to stumble but Baxter's exit had created a vacuum he could not disturb.

After a pause, Mrs.Elmwood asked if anyone had seen her knitting bag, she hadn't seen it since the previous evening and felt rather lost without it. Henry remembered that, indoors, it was always with her. He struggled to remember last night. When they were waiting in the sitting room, the knitting bag had been alongside the chair where Mrs.Elmwood had been sitting, not far from his feet. He remembered that when they had returned from having their fingerprints taken, he had sat in the same seat but he could not remember seeing the knitting bag again. When they retired to bed, Mrs.Elmwood had been first out of the room and so he could not have seen whether she had the bag with her or not. No one had an opportunity to reply before Inspector Johnson knocked and entered.

"If you've finished your meal, I'd like a word, please."

There was a moan from Jackson and a sharp intake of breath on the part of Millicent Catesby.

"We are still investigating a murder and we will need

to have further words from time to time. I have to tell you that the young maid, Jenny Phillips has gone missing."

There was a chorus of disbelief and dismay.

"You may or may not know that Jenny was an orphan. Obviously, she has not gone to visit relatives and she did not have friends in the neighbourhood as far as we know...."

"But I saw Jenny this morning!"

Henry could not prevent himself from interrupting. Johnson turned his serious gaze on Henry.

"And what time would that be, Mr.Allingham?

"Exactly 10.30. I saw her looking in the window of the Coffee Shop in Bland Street. Mrs.Elmwood was there at the time."

He looked over to Mrs.Elmwood.

"Yes, I remember Mr.Allingham saying that he thought that he had seen Jenny but I didn't see her. We looked at our watches at the time and I said that she couldn't have finished her work by then, it couldn't have been Jenny."

"It could indeed have been Jenny. Mrs.Ridgeway says she went missing soon after breakfast...."

"And I saw her later, in the afternoon, about 2.15. She was getting on a bus."

"Where was this, Mr.Allingham?"

"At the corner of the High Street and...er...Watson Street."

"You didn't see which bus she was getting onto?"

"I'm sorry, I looked twice to make sure it was Jenny this time but I didn't notice the number of the bus. I assumed she was coming back here."

Henry was disappointed with himself. He ought to have noticed the destination of the bus or, at least, its number. Why hadn't he? He was too easily distracted, either that or he had jumped to a conclusion. He was much too inclined to jump to conclusions. He had assumed that Jenny was returning to the hotel after taking a morning off, but then, he had no reason to think otherwise at the time. He heard Inspector Johnson's voice continuing.

"We take a serious view of her disappearance for obvious reasons. She may have been an unwitting witness, not of the murder but to something connected with it. She may simply have been upset, though Mrs.Ridgeway doesn't think it is like her to take off after an upset. She was quite happy here. We have reason to think that she is in danger and we ask you to think of anything that might give us a clue to her whereabouts."

"My dear man, we have no idea where she might be. What do you expect? She was a maid, we hardly saw her, do you expect us....."

"Come along Millicent! You and I have been here a long time. We've known Jenny since she first came." Mrs.Elmwood sounded upset and cross.

"It may be alright for you to befriend all the domestics, Elizabeth, It has certainly not been my habit to do so. I suggest that the Inspector asks the domestics instead of troubling us."

"I am asking everyone in this hotel, Miss Catesby."

"Why not ask the young man you have just taken down to the station? I presume that you suspect him of being the murderer?"

"Mr.Elliott is making a statement, which probably has nothing to do with the murder. He, like you all, is still under suspicion concerning the murder and he too will be asked about Jenny Phillips."

D.C.I.Duncombe took Denzil Elliott to the station, cautioned him and took him through his statement then left D.S.Green to see to the rest. Elliott was not loth to tell of his burglaries and to give details. Duncombe assured him that it was in his interest to do so, however, he was not willing to account for the watches and jewellery he had stolen. He accounted for the money but all he would say was that he had disposed of the other items through a friend. The D.C.I. warned him that his refusal to reveal his accomplice's name would count against him at his trial.

Duncombe had to admit to himself that Elliott had been very professional. There must have been plenty of experience behind his careful planning and execution. To have taken a room at The Moorcroft and to have made a survey of the local properties suggested great coolness and the cutting of the grooves on the fire escape door suggested considerable skill. He suspected that Elliott could have given him a much longer list of burglaries from a number of towns and he promised himself to initiate enquiries into his former employment and whereabouts.

He was turning into the corridor on his way out when he bumped into Trevor Johnson coming in.

"You are back early! I thought you were going to do some more questioning?"

"The man I particularly wanted to see skipped out while I was downstairs. I've told them about Jenny Phillips and I've left Maltby to see if anyone else leaves tonight."

"Who were you gunning for?"

"Baxter. It occurred to me that Baxter was the most likely person to carry Elliott's loot away. He's a jeweller...."

"But he wouldn't be so foolish as to try to dispose of it through his own shop?"

"No, apart from the risk, I think that his partner would soon smell a rat. But Baxter would have contacts and even if he was stopped in the street, it would be most natural for him to be carrying jewellery, wouldn't it, Sir?"

"Good thinking! You'll check on him tomorrow? I've sent the shoes to the lab straight away, they'll be valuable evidence...."

"I don't think they'll be that important, Sir." Johnson had the grace to look sheepish.

"What? Don't tell me....Very neat! Worth a try, especially as it worked. The confession is down in writing. But where does it leave me if he withdraws his confession before the case comes to court? You may try these tricks when you are on your own, just don't try them when you are with me, do you hear!"

Duncombe stared aggressively at his D.I. for a few seconds then smiled, turned up his coat collar and strode out into a very wet night.

Henry Allingham was disturbed by the thought that Jenny Phillips was in danger. The vision of her peering in the window of the coffee shop was firmly in his mind. Why had she been in town? She had been looking for someone. Who could it have been, and why? She had always been shy and, as far as he knew, she had little contact with the residents. He was sorry that Mrs.Elmwood had not seen her. He was certain that he had not been mistaken, that was why he had looked twice when he had seen her getting on the bus.

He was restless and paced about his room, a thing he had not done before. Elliott's leaving with the police officers had perplexed him too. What had Elliott been up to that day? Was there any connection between Elliott and Jenny? He remembered that he had seen Elliott sitting in the coffee shop not long after Jenny had left. Had she been looking for him? Is that why he had been taken away for questioning?

Henry paused by the window, partly drawn by the rattle of the rain against the pane. He peered out, fascinated by the downpour. He watched sheets of rain gusting through the puddles in the gutter opposite. The feeble light from an old-fashioned street lamp seemed to emphasise the rain and its movement. He stood back ready to draw the curtains when he was aware of another movement in the street below. To the right of the lamp was a telephone kiosk and it was the movement of its door that had caught his attention. He looked carefully and saw a figure hesitate then slip out and hurry across the road towards the hotel. He could not be mistaken, it was Ernie Baxter.

Why hadn't he used the telephone in the hotel? He must have made more than one phone call for he had been out for at least half an hour. Henry knew that he had not been anywhere else, he smiled a little triumphant smile to himself. Why had he known this? Because Baxter was not wearing a coat and hat. It was November, Baxter would never have gone any distance without being protected against the cold. It was his habit to wear a coat and hat.

Henry got out his notebook and committed his new observation to writing. He reread what he had already written and pondered the relationship between two such different people as Baxter and Jackson. They had been friendly since Jackson had arrived. He couldn't think what they had in common, considering the difference in age. He considered what he knew about Baxter and the answer came unexpected and clear. Baxter enjoyed a drink, Jackson must do, too. That would account for the stumble in the street. Jackson had been drunk! Henry was astonished at this simple truth. Why hadn't he realised this before? What an innocent he was!

What about Elliott? Why had Baxter rushed out after asking Sarah Lucas about him? Was he trying to get in touch with Elliott? Perhaps he was trying to get a solicitor for him, but why should he do that? He hadn't noticed any closeness between them. Henry sighed, he had hardly noticed anyone, so absorbed had he been in his own routine.

He was tired. He had had an enormously busy day. He would go to bed early. As he was getting ready, he thought about the next day. It was Sunday, he was free to do whatever he liked. He would remain on the alert, he would go on observing and, if necessary, he would go on following. Who would be next? He remembered his

125

failure with Miss Catesby, what a disagreeable woman she was. His last thought, before sleep overtook him, was of Jenny.

CHAPTER TWENTY TWO

Although it was a Sunday, Trevor Johnson was in the station very early. He was eager to know what the lab had to say about the murder weapon and by now there should be reports about the finger prints and various samples taken from the bathroom and the fire escape. There were many routine things to be attended to and he had an irrational urge to see to them all himself. However, there was a team of officers at hand and it was his job to see that tasks were allotted .

He started his own work at the beginning, with the photographs of the body. Lucy Oxbury had been lightly built and it was likely that her bones were not particularly strong. The wounds at the back of the head indicated crushing of the skull. He checked with the pathologist's report, yes, the bones were relatively soft. Examination of the skin suggested that the upper part of the body had not been submerged indicating that either the blows had been struck soon after the victim had got into the bath or that she had been killed and then dumped in the bath. He thought it unlikely that Lucy Oxbury had been killed before she had got into the bath, it would have been very difficult to arrange the body in the position as shown in the photographs. He remembered Henry Allingham's remark - 'why hadn't the body slipped over to one side?' It *was* a little strange but the feet were touching the end of the bath, the knees were drawn up and the arms and hands were limp at her sides, it was consistent with the victim having been struck from behind, possibly just after turning off the taps. The head and upper body had simply fallen forward.

There was no evidence of any cleaning up in the bathroom except on the front edge of the bath. Everything was neat and undisturbed. Lucy Oxbury must have been killed while sitting in her bath. The murderer had turned the bolt and entered the bathroom, struck quickly, wiped the edge of the bath, left the room and turned the bolt back again. Johnson was not happy. There was no shower and no shower curtain in this bathroom. There was no barrier to draught from the door. Surely a naked person sitting in a hot bath would be aware of the draught as soon as the door was opened? If the taps were still flowing, she might not hear the door being opened but she was certain to feel that it had opened, it was November, after all. Could the murderer have struck so quickly that the victim had not even time to turn her head? It would have taken at least three strides to get into position and time to draw back the arm and strike. Yet the head had been facing front or the wounds would have been in a different position. There was no place to hide in the bathroom therefore access had to be via the door, there could be no surprise attack from within.

The lab report indicated no other injury or bruising. There was no sexual motive as far as the lab was concerned, Lucy Oxbury was virgo intacta. Motive, motive, there didn't seem to be any motive. There was no possibilty of mistaken identity, everything was too deliberate. Johnson was certain that all that was needed was the revelation of the motive. His Chief was right, it would depend on what records would come up with and not necessarily police records, he had already explored that avenue. He would have to dig further into the past. He sighed, rose and stretched then went into the operations room. Quickly he allotted tasks to the nearest available personnel.

Soon after that, a telephone call sent everyone scurrying. A body had been seen in the Langton Canal on the other side of town. A team from the fire brigade was endeavouring to recover it.

Johnson decided to investigate, himself, before he

informed the D.C.I. It might turn out to be an old tramp, in which case his Chief would not thank him for such a false alarm. Nevertheless, on the way there, he had a sinking feeling that this would turn out to be Jenny Phillips.

The Langton Canal was almost a sewer. It had not been used as a waterway for many years. Now it was a stagnant menace to health and life. Countless times, local councillors had made it a focus and platform for their oratory. Never had anything been done about it. Ten lives had been lost in it over as many years. The local press would feature it and its victims when they had nothing else exciting to write about. If there had been a private owner, pressure would have forced action. It had been part of a nationalised industry. Promises and plans were discussed, nothing came of them and no one expected anything of them. No one knew what to do with it. Bright new men of business talked of transforming it into a leisure facility. Few of the people who lived anywhere near it thought that a likely prospect. It stank, its water was a dull grey-green, streaked and thickened with oil. The only living thing in it would seem to be a rich fluorescent green slime. Occasionally, the surface would stir as some forgotten debris moved within its depths. Children playing near the bank believed that some monster lurked below the oily surface, hadn't they seen it move?

By the time Johnson reached the firemen, they had succeeded in retrieving the body. Someone was in the process of covering it with a plastic sheet when Johnson stopped him and looked down. It was indeed Jenny Phillips. It was possible to see the light colour of her hair through the dreadful clinging slime and there was no mistaking the pointed nose, chin and thin red lips. There was a glimpse of the same flowered print dress she had worn on the night of the murder under a brown raincoat.

Between the collar and her chin were dull marks. Johnson felt sure that when the pathologist and his helpers had cleaned up the body, these marks would indicate a strangling or attempted strangling. He was used to examining bodies, particularly after accidents, and many had been horrific, but he found this tiny wisp of a body particularly poignant. Trevor Johnson was a professional, a man on his way up, cool and competent. He was troubled that he should be moved by this body but it had reminded him, only too well, of his own daughter Felicity. She was at least two years younger but the same size and weight.

There was no time to waste, he returned to his car and phoned the police doctor then his Chief. It was natural that Duncombe should ask whether the death could have been accidental or not. Johnson said that he thought not but he had called the doctor. Duncombe was on his way, so was a team from the station. An ambulance had already been called.

Johnson looked about him. Where the body had been found, the canal was overlooked on both sides by tall buildings. Opposite was the completely blank wall of a furniture repository, on the same side was a disused warehouse in poor condition. It was a gloomy spot, particularly on a grey November day. It would have been very dark indeed on the previous evening. A hundred yards down the canal was another road bridge with a stone parapet. It was identical with the bridge he had just driven across only it didn't look as though it carried much traffic. The bridge he had crossed had a flight of stone steps from the parapet down to the towpath. There were three bridges within walking range, this one at Broughton Road, one at Gladstone Street, further up, and the one ahead of him at Redworth Road. They all had the same stairways down to the towpath. Jenny and her assailant could have walked down any of these steps.

He examined the edge where the body had been

retrieved. The firemen had nearly packed away their tackle by this time. Sadly they had disturbed the bank with their movements.

"Was there any sign of scuffle or movement on the side of the bank where you found the body?"

The foreman answered. "You mean at this point? No, it's slippery but there wasn't a sign of a struggle. Mind you, that doesn't mean she went in here. There are plenty of other places...."

"But there's no current. The body couldn't drift. I suppose it was floating when you found it?"

"Yeh, but we didn't find it. We got a phone call to say someone had seen it. It was an old bloke walking the dog. He waited and showed us where it was."

"He isn't here now, have you got an address for him?"

"Yes, it'll be with our switchboard. Oh, here are the ambulance men. Well, we wont wait. It's all yours now."

The firemen departed in a cheerful mood. They had performed their task well and they were pleased with themselves. The police task had hardly begun. The doctor was the next to arrive. He was a thin man with a sharp nose and an eagle eye. Johnson had met him on several occasions and had admired his efficiency but he had often wondered if the poor man was overworked, he had a grey look about him. The doctor quickly affirmed Johnson's opinion that the death was suspicious. He wasted no time, he jotted a few notes down ready for the coroner, covered the body, nodded to Johnson and departed briskly. Soon after that D.C.I.Duncombe arrived. He derived great satisfaction from seeing well organised teams of policemen scouring the towpath in both directions.

"What makes you so sure that this girl just didn't fall into the canal?"

"There were marks round her neck which probably mean she was strangled before she met the water."

"Old Simmons didn't linger long?" The D.C.I. was offended that the doctor hadn't waited to speak to him.

"He confirmed that the death was suspicious?"

"Yes Sir. I've sent for the photographer. I hope he hurries up, the ambulance is already here."

"When do you think she was killed?"

"Simmons thought that she had been in the water a long time. We'll have to wait for the pathologist to tell us more."

"Well, it means an appeal for sightings, maximum cover including T.V. I'll see to that if you continue here."

"Right, Sir. It also means another go at the residents of The Moorcroft. Allingham claims to have seen the girl at 2.15 yesterday afternoon in the centre of town, catching a bus. Unfortunately, he cannot say which bus. He assumed she was returning to the hotel."

"A weird sort of bloke, this Allingham. Did anyone back his story?"

"No, Sir."

"So he is the only one to have seen her in town yesterday?"

"Yes, it would seem so."

"There can be no seem about it. I would check on the others if I were you. This Allingham might be leading us astray. How many of them were in town, I wonder? I wouldn't mind betting that there weren't many alibis for yesterday."

"The search of the canal banks revealed nothing that could be connected with the death of Jenny Phillips. Heavy rain had fallen late in the evening but no clear footprints were visible. Door to door enquiries in the nearest streets were set in motion, no one had seen anything suspicious or could remember seeing a young girl answering to Jenny's description.

Johnson made contact with the old man who had alerted the fire service. He told him that the body had been floating just below the surface. He had noticed it as soon as he had come near. There was just light enough at that time in the morning. He had gone to the nearest phone and had dialled 999. The operator had suggested that the fire brigade be called first. He had waited to show them where the body was, then he had gone home to his missus because she would be getting anxious. He had not seen a soul on his walk but he had done the same walk for years now and he could count the people he had met on the towpath at that time in the morning on the fingers of one hand.

The only information concerning Jenny's whereabouts yesterday had come from Henry Allingham. He had said that she had caught a bus at the corner of Watson Street and the High Street. Johnson checked. There were only three possibilities from that particular bus stop. One was a bus going to Langton, a village two miles north west which had given its name to the canal, two was a bus going to the western extremity of the town, passing along Wormald Street, the one Jenny would have caught to return to the hotel, three was a bus to Borfield via Littlebury and Serston, it too would pass near Wormald Street. The first was a number 22 and didn't run very frequently. The second was a number 6 and ran every thirty minutes. The third was a number 17 and ran at approximately ninety minute intervals, it also tended to be a single decker. Johnson felt sure that Henry Allingham would have mentioned it if it had been a single decker. The 6 and the 17 did not run close to the canal but the Langton bus crossed over it at Dewley Road about quarter of a mile to the west. That bridge did not have direct access to the towpath.

Johnson's next move was to contact the bus station. Being a Sunday didn't help, the office wasn't open officially. After a long delay an Inspector answered and from him Johnson established that a bus to Langton was due at that stop at approximately 2.16. There was a number 6 due at that stop at 2.02 and 2.32 and a number

17 at 2.38 but these, Johnson rejected. He enquired about the driver and learned that he would be a Sid Fletcher but he wasn't on shift this Sunday. A long trail to the opposite end of town was nearly a waste of time. Sid Fletcher was in bed suffering from a hangover and his wife wanted Johnson to return later. Mrs.Fletcher was persuaded to rouse her husband as it was a matter of some urgency. It took a while but eventually a dishevelled figure appeared in the doorway, half dressed and unshaven, holding his head with one hand and drinking from a fizzing glass in the other.

"What can I do for you, Inspector?" The voice was remarkably firm. "There's nothing wrong is there?"

"Mr.Fletcher, I'm sorry to get you up like this on your day off but I'm investigating a murder and I think you might be able to help."

Sid Fletcher's eyes gleamed interest beneath lowered lids. He shook his head and winced.

"I'm enquiring about a young girl who was found drowned in the canal this morning. I believe that she caught the bus you were driving yesterday afternoon from the stop just where Watson Street joins the High Street, that would be at 2.15. This is a recent photo of the girl, she was small, lightly built, with fair hair, wore a light coloured raincoat over a patterned dress. Can you remember her getting on your bus?"

Fletcher took the printed hand bill and stared at it. He needed to clear his head and shook it again only to wince more fiercely. He took a longer drink from his glass then asked his wife to bring him a cup of coffee. He looked down at the hand bill again and suddenly gave a little cry.

"Yes, now wait....yes, I remember her and I'll tell you why. She had just got on and sat down when she sees someone through the window and wants to get off again. She wanted to get off at the lights but I wouldn't open the door, I thought she might get hurt. She was almost in a panic. She got off at the very next stop. That's all I can tell you."

"You didn't see who it was? The person she saw?"

"Not a chance, I was moving off in traffic."

"Where was she going, would you know?"

"You mean before she got off? She asked for Langton, I remember because she had no idea of the cost and had to fiddle for change."

Johnson smiled appreciatively.

"You've remembered a lot, how is that?"

"Well, you only remember the unusual ones, the ones who keep you waiting or who want to jump off like this young'un. She didn't seem to know where she wanted to go, I had to tell her where we were going and how much it was. You don't remember the ones who pass through with the right change."

CHAPTER TWENTY THREE

The atmosphere in the hotel at breakfast was depressing. No one felt cheerful enough to speak. It wasn't just the case that they were shocked at the disappearance of Jenny and Denzil Elliott, the residents were becoming wary of each other. Their concensus opinion that the murder of Lucy Oxbury must have been by an outsider had begun to crumble. From the Inspector's remarks, they were not able to assume that the murderer was Denzil Elliott. It seemed it had to be one of them.

Henry had been first down as usual. He greeted Mrs.Elmwood with a smile but she seemed nervous of him and merely nodded. As before, Mrs.Jervis was next down, she smiled and began to speak but the words froze on her lips. She sat down opposite to Mrs.Elmwood who only nodded. Ernie Baxter arrived, dapper as usual but somewhat deflated. He could hardly muster a smile but nodded and murmured, sitting in his usual place. They gave their orders to Mrs.Ridgeway in low murmurs. Mrs.Catesby arrived rather behind her usual time. She was not quite so upright and sharp this morning but she had not lost her voice.

"I wonder if we are going to be free of those news hounds this morning? What do we pay the police for if we cannot stir without being hectored and worried?"

No one felt disposed to answer.

"Why is everyone sulking? I for one am carrying on as usual."

Her last remark rang rather hollow, it was as if she were trying to persuade herself. Mrs.Ridgeway asked Ernie Baxter about Walter Jackson. He suggested that perhaps Jackson was not able to face breakfast on account of his stomach. Everyone looked up at this point. Another missing person? They looked warily at each other.

Mrs.Ridgeway saw them.

"I don't know why you are all so worried. Mr.Jackson is almost certainly still in bed. It is a Sunday, after all. He hasn't always got up for breakfast on a Sunday."

"Would you like me to go up and ask?" Henry was trying to be helpful, he wanted to ease the tension.

"Well, if you would like to go up with me. I don't think Mr.Jackson would like to be disturbed by anyone else."

Henry left the dining room with Mrs.Ridgeway. Suddenly everyone relaxed.

"How considerate of Mr. Allingham." Mrs.Elmwood's soft voice broke the silence.

"Well, I wouldn't like to be involved. One nasty experience is quite enough for me." Miss Catesby shook her head.

"Yes, it's all getting on our nerves. Thank goodness my husband is coming today. I can get away altogether even if it's only for the afternoon."

Ernie Baxter sat crumbling bread. He didn't seem aware of anything around him. His eyes never left his plate.

Soon, Henry returned.

"No need for alarm, Mr.Jackson doesn't want to be disturbed. He said he would get up later if he felt able."

"Did you speak to him personally?" Miss Catesby was as blunt as ever.

"No, we spoke through the door. There was no need to disturb him."

"I have good reason to distrust locked doors."

Henry wondered what had happened to the inconsolable Miss Catesby of two evenings ago. She seemed to have developed an extraordinary toughness. Had she always been like this or had her ordeal touched a hidden spring to release this strength? He tried to remember what she had been like before Lucy's death and found it difficult. Perhaps the weeping and the collapse had all been an act? Henry blushed at the idea of such

137

deception, he had always thought the best of people and it had never occurred to him to doubt them.

They all drifted into the sitting room.

"Ah! The papers have arrived."

Mrs.Jervis heard the noise of Sunday papers being pushed through the letter box in the hall. She waited for the journalists outside to settle then went to the front door. Mrs.Ridgeway was there before her.

"Everyone wants news, this morning," Mrs.Ridgeway tried to sound cheerful, "I think we are going to have a poor time of it."

"Yes, I'm afraid so, Mrs.Ridgeway. It can't be good for your business."

"It can't be good for any of us."

The Moorcroft Hotel was in the headlines. Most of the tabloids had combined the story of the dead woman with the missing girl. There were photographs of the entrance and the front door of the hotel and there were photographs of Jenny Phillips taken from the handbill. The reports were very sketchy because nothing official had been released and no one had spoken to the reporters. The headlines were predictable, "Death Strikes in Maskerley Hotel", "The Moorcroft Hotel Mysteries", "Maid missing from Murder Hotel", "Quiet Hotel Murder Mystery", "Maskerley Maid Missing from Murder Hotel".

This did not comfort the residents. They knew that the press had only begun to focus on them. The pressure would build up. They would have no peace until the investigation was over. They felt more depressed. Mrs.Elmwood wandered over to the sitting room window and looked out. She gasped.

"There are more reporters than ever and still they are coming."

The doorbell began to ring and went on ringing,

"This is dreadful. I wonder if I can phone my husband and tell him to come round to the back. I might just catch him before he leaves home."

Sarah Lucas was clearing away in the dining room and heard Mrs.Jervis through the open door.

"I'm sorry, but there's almost as many out the back. It's going to be terrible getting out and in. These reporters are just like hyenas."

Henry wasn't sure that 'hyenas' was what Sarah meant but the word was somehow appropriate. He wondered what he was going to do. He didn't want to spend all day cooped up in the hotel. He wasn't a church goer, his days in the orphanage had turned him against church-going in all its forms. He had usually waited for the church-goers to depart then he had gone for a long walk, often taking the bus out towards the moors then walking back, enjoying a pub lunch on the way. He had looked out of his window first thing and thought the cloud cover looked as if it might break. This may turn out to be a good day for walking.

There was a distant hubbub from downstairs and D.S.Green came up from the kitchen with another constable. He apologised for all the fuss and warned them of the difficulties they must expect. He instructed the policeman with him to stay on duty at the front door and assured the residents that there was now a constable on duty at both doors, they would try to see that the residents could get through the crowds without injury. Then he told them that Inspector Johnson was on his way and would like them to wait in the hotel until he arrived. He should not be more than a few minutes.

"Really! This is most exasperating! We have planned this...." Mrs.Jervis was vexed.

"I must go to church! This is quite unreasonable!" Miss Catesby drew herself up ready for battle.

"There has been a serious development, Ladies."

"Important! Important! What can be more important than going to church, for heaven's sake?"

Henry was sufficiently alert to guess at the new

development.

"Have they found Jenny the maid?"

"I'm not in a position to say, sir."

Henry was aware of Mrs.Elmwood's eyes upon him but when he turned to her, her face was hidden behind a newspaper. There was a silence for a few minutes then Mrs.Jervis went into the corridor to use the telephone. Miss Catesby turned the pages of her paper with little interest. Ernie Baxter muttered and excused himself. The minutes ticked on.

"I do hope that Jenny is alright." Henry spoke indirectly to Mrs.Elmwood. He had not taken up a newspaper, he was too worried.

"So do I, such a delicate little scrap." Mrs.Elmwood sounded rather emotional. Henry glanced at her, she had not put down her paper. Henry wondered if she was steeling herself for bad news. Mrs.Jervis returned, tutting. She had not been able to get through, her husband must have left home already. She looked at her watch.

"Good gracious, it's ten past ten already!"

"What? This is too bad! I'm getting ready, even if it means taking a taxi. The service is at ten thirty."

Miss Catesby stormed out. Ernie Baxter returned, fiddling with his cuffs and avoiding everyone's eyes. Mrs.Jervis sat on the edge of her seat clasping her handbag. Suddenly she looked at it and said.

"Did you find your knitting bag, Elizabeth?"

Mrs.Elmwood put down her paper and looked at her.

"No, it's most peculiar. I've never been without it. I feel quite lost without it. Wherever could it have got to?"

"Was there anything particular in it?"

"Just some knitting I'd barely started. Oh, and a novel someone lent me. One or two other odds and ends, I dare say. I used to keep all sorts of things in it. It was really a kind of portable dustbin." She laughed lightly. "That's one of the reasons I miss it so much."

"Well it certainly wouldn't be the sort of thing that

anyone would steal, would it?" The two ladies enjoyed a titter.

Henry noticed Ernie Baxter staring at them. Why should he do that? Henry's view of the residents was changing every hour.

A car drew up outside and a hubbub arose. A few seconds later the doorbell rang. Henry thought it odd that the Inspector should ring the bell. Someone rushed by the door to the sitting room and went out. The noise outside grew, there were several shouts then the car door slammed and they could hear it drive away. Sergeant Green looked in then went to the front door. Again the hubbub, it reminded Henry of a child's toy, open the door - hubbub, close the door - silence. There was a brief interval then Sergeant Green came back into the sitting room looking upset.

"It seems Miss Catesby has ignored my instructions and has gone out. I'm afraid the Inspector will not be pleased."

"What will happen to her, Sergeant?"

"That depends entirely upon the Inspector, she has been very silly."

"But she has only gone to church."

Again the hubbub broke out, a little louder this time. A car drew up, the shouts grew louder, one or two flash bulbs popped. Inspector Johnson had arrived.

He was, indeed, angry to learn that Miss Catesby had gone but he made no comment. He gathered everybody together, sending Green to ask Walter Jackson to attend. While they were waiting for Jackson, they were diverted by the arrival of Mr.Jervis. He had great difficulty squeezing past the reporters outside because he wasn't prepared for this experience and perhaps he wouldn't have succeeded if it hadn't been for the constable on duty at the door. Johnson was very civil to the newcomer, he asked him to be patient, saying that it was very important to have further interviews with the residents. Mr.Jervis, a small man in his fifties, bald, with a blue chin and prominent, dark eyes, was happy to stay and listen.

Not unexpectedly, Walter Jackson was furious at being dragged from his bed. He arrived, summarily washed but unshaven, his clothes thrown on carelessly. He was about to create an uproar when Johnson silenced him with a gesture.

"I regret to inform you, ladies and gentlemen, that the body of Jenny Phillips was taken from the Langton Canal earlier this morning."

"Oh no!" Mrs.Jervis gasped out. The others sat frozen.

"It is almost certain that she was the victim of an attack. It is also almost certain that there is some connection between the deaths of Jenny Phillips and Lucy Oxbury. Under the circumstances, I must ask every one of you about your movements yesterday. It is vital that you remember everything. Sergeant Green will deal with the ladies and I will deal with the gentlemen. By now, you must be aware of the procedure. As soon as you have signed your written statements, you may go.

Henry Allingham was in a dilemma. He couldn't admit to following Miss Catesby or Denzil Elliott, he couldn't really explain why he did so. By the time it came for him to speak to the Inspector, he was faltering and embarrassed. This was a different Henry to the one who has spoken so clearly at their last interview. Johnson was very aware of the difference. All Henry could tell him was that he went window shopping in the morning, took coffee at the Coffee Shop where he saw Mrs.Elmwood and Jenny Phillips, visited the Central Library, bought himself some new clothes, went to the dry cleaners, saw Jenny Phillips at the bus stop, had some lunch and took another walk before returning home.

Inspector Johnson was not happy with Henry's recital. He looked at him for a few moments.

"Is that what you would normally do an a Saturday, Mr.Allingham?"

142

"Er...no. I usually buy my paper, read it in the library, have lunch at the Civic Restaurant then go for a long walk."

There was another silence. It was as if the Inspector was giving Henry time to start at the beginning.

"Why did you change your routine, sir?"

"The murder has...changed everything."

"In what way?"

Henry was not a dissembler, nor was he obstinate except in the pursuit of long established habits. He was stuck, he simply did not know how to go on.

"Mr.Allingham, you change your routine, you become the important, the only, witness to the whereabouts of Jenny Phillips, you buy new clothes, take others to the dry cleaners...all on account of the murder of Lucy Oxbury? Please explain."

Henry could only stick to facts.

"I had food spilled on my trousers, I thought I needed a new pair. I changed into the new pair and left the old pair at the cleaners."

"So that hasn't anything to do with the murder?"

"No, I suppose not...."

"Did you normally have coffee at The Coffee Shop?"

"Yes, that is the cafe I normally use."

"Do you suppose Jenny Phillips was looking for someone?"

"Yes, she was peering in the window."

"You wouldn't know if any of the other residents use The Coffee Shop regularly?"

"Mrs.Elmwood said that it was her favourite coffee shop but I don't know how regularly she uses it."

"But Jenny Phillips did not enter the cafe?"

"She was there at the window one minute than gone the next. I don't think she entered. I left soon after that and I would have seen her on the way out, if she had."

"You could have been mistaken."

"No, I would have recognised Jenny anywhere."

"Oh? Why is that?"

"I was sitting opposite her in the sitting room on Friday night, she looked so pathetic, she is still in my mind."

Johnson stared at Henry.

"You were once married, yourself, I believe?"

Henry coloured and drew back.

"You didn't have a family?"

"No, no we didn't."

"Was there any particular reason why you didn't?"

"No, we just didn't."

Henry was offended. He had no wish to recall those unhappy days. There had been so little sharing. He had felt deceived very soon after the wedding. He supposed that he was an unashamed romantic, his wife had been a spoilt child. They had little in common, he couldn't think why they had married. Both of them wanted a home, both wanted to escape their environments. The rush had been hers. He had taken her affection for granted. He realised, all too soon, that she had very little affection for him. She had treated him as a wage earner and little more. Her domestic skills were few and were applied unwillingly. Perhaps she had found him repulsive in some way. Perhaps he had been inadequate as a lover. He had made few demands on her and, as she grew more sluttish, he made fewer. She, herself, seemed unresponsive and when she left him he thought it improbable that she had left him for another lover. She simply sought another home with more money to it. Whether she got it or not never troubled him. He got over the shock quite quickly. His work had occupied him, he enjoyed seeing to himself, keeping everything tidy and in order. The years had gone by pleasantly enough, he had few needs, he had been content. Now, this Detective Inspector had touched a nerve. Deep down he had needed children. He struggled to concentrate on what Johnson was saying.

"We'll get this written down then you can sign it. You

are sure that there is nothing more you want to tell me?"

Henry wanted to tell him the full story of his day. He wanted to help, after all, that what was he had set out to do immediately after the murder. Perhaps at this point he would have done so, but the Inspector had caused the old Henry to re-emerge. He was numb and silent.

Mrs.Elmwood's statement affirmed the meeting in The Coffee Shop and included the encounter on the bus coming back to the hotel. No one else claimed to have seen Henry that day. Mrs.Jervis had done research for her thesis in the Central Library and had returned to the hotel at about four thirty. Mr.Jackson had gone into town and had been taken ill after lunch, he had been brought back to the hotel by Mr.Baxter. Mr.Baxter had gone into town, had eaten an early lunch then had seen Mr.Jackson in near collapse and had brought him home.

No one but Henry Allingham had seen Jenny Phillips. Johnson questioned the hotel staff but they could not help. None of them had been in town that day and none of them save Mrs.Ridgeway had seen Jenny before she went out.

Millicent Catesby's arrival at the police station, escorted by D.S.Green, was noisy but the noise was all bluff. The time she spent in the interview room with an unresponsive policewoman was time enough for her to repent her folly. She was pale and quiet when Johnson came in.

"Miss Catesby, you were present when Detective Sergeant Green asked all the residents to wait in the hotel for me, were you not? Why did you ignore my request?"

"I took it for a request not an instruction! I always go to church on Sunday mornings. There has been disturbance enough, I didn't see why I should not go. The killing has nothing to do with me."

"How can you say that, Miss Catesby? You were the one who shouted for assistance, who asked for the door to be broken in and who found the body...."

"I was not alone in finding the body."

"Nevertheless, you are an important witness and, as one of the residents, you are a potential suspect...."

"I....I....how can you possibly say that....?"

"Miss Catesby, everyone in the hotel is a potential suspect, you must understand that. You must take this seriously. Murder is a very serious matter. You cannot pretend you have nothing to do with it, you are connected with it whether you like it or not. Our investigation must take priority over everything."

Johnson was very fierce. Millicent Catesby's lips began to tremble. He rushed on.

"Now, I need a statement from you as to where you were on Saturday. All day Saturday. The reason for this further statement, as I explained to the others, is that the body of Jenny Phillips was found in the canal this morning. It had been in the canal for some time and it is almost certain that there was foul play."

"You cannot be suggesting...."

"I am not suggesting anything! I need to check on everyone. It is quite straightforward. When you have given your account of your movements on Saturday, I will be in a position to eliminate you, or not, as a suspect. You must realise that your rushing off this morning casts suspicion on you already. It was a very silly thing for you to do and could have led to a charge of obstruction. Now, please! No more shilly shallying! Tell me what you did on Saturday, starting from the beginning."

"Shilly shallying? I have never shilly shallied in my life! Outrageous!"

Johnson glared at her.

"Anyway, I was at the Fashion House all day...."

"Then, can we have the full story without further delay?"

CHAPTER TWENTY FOUR

The D.C.I. was anxious for a conference as soon as Johnson had left the interview room.

"How far have we got, Trevor?"

"Not too far. I've seen the driver of the bus that Jenny Phillips boarded. He was certain it was her. He thinks she saw someone in the street she knew. She got quite panicky when he wouldn't let her off at the lights."

"So your Mr.Allingham was right, she did get on a bus."

"Well, it leaves some time before she was killed, assuming she was killed after dark. It was getting dark about half past three but it wasn't really dark until after four. There can't have been many people on the towpath in the afternoon but I don't think anyone would risk killing someone there before dark."

"Did anyone else see her?"

"According to the statements, all the residents were in town yesterday, only Allingham saw the girl. They were all on their own and only Jackson and Baxter got back before dark and even they could have returned to town, they weren't seen again until dinner. I haven't seen Elliott yet, I'll see him in a minute."

"What about this wretched Catesby woman?"

"She got quite bolshie this morning and went off to church after I had sent a message asking them all to wait...."

"Well, you can't lock her up for that. I suppose she really did go to church?"

"Apart from checking with the taxi driver and the congregation, I have to believe she did. There wasn't time for her to do much else."

"What did she do on Saturday?"

"She claims to have spent all day in the dress shop

where she works part time. It should be easy to check on that."

"It seems that Allingham is the odd man out. What had he to say?"

"He was surprisingly cagey. He claims to have seen Jenny Phillips looking in the window of The Coffee Shop at 10.30. Mrs.Elmwood was there and confirms the time but she didn't see the girl. He didn't do much except wander about but he bought himself a new pair of trousers and left the old pair at the cleaners..."

"Did he? That's very interesting, now why should he do that, I wonder?"

"He claims to have spilt food on them."

"You can guess what I'm thinking. I wonder how many pairs of trousers he has?"

"Later, he saw Jenny Phillips again and the bus driver bears that out. He says he had something to eat at about 2.30 and walked about the town until dark. Mrs.Elmwood was on the same bus he took back to the hotel."

"Walked about town until dark! What sort of cockeyed tale is that?"

"I'm certain he is hiding something. Until today, I would have sworn he was a simple, straightforward sort of chap. He was the one who put me on to the turned bathroom bolt trick."

"Did anyone else see him in the course of the afternoon?"

"No one. But if he was up to no good, why did he say he had seen Jenny Phillips? He didn't have to."

"It all seems to me to be a bit of a con. Perhaps he is playing the innocent just to put everyone off. Perhaps the bathroom bolt story was a deliberate effort to put us onto someone else."

Duncombe scrabbled through a file and took out a sheet of paper.

"Look at your timings. Who finished his meal in plenty of time to carry out the murder and return to his room then come out again when the alarm was raised? You say he was hiding something today? I think we should have him in and question him."

"I don't think we have enough to go on. He could just deny everything. Again, there is no motive."

"He is a very odd bloke, it could be that he doesn't need a motive."

Johnson was shocked by his Chief's casual logic.

"Sir! He may be a loner, that doesn't make him a random killer."

"We've got to bear it in mind. We must look at all the possibilities. Two killings might be just that, random killings linked by proximity and vulnerability. One killing is carried out, Jenny Phillips may or may not have seen or heard something suspicious, the appetite to kill is there, the girl is vulnerable, she is killed."

"That is a very thin thread, Sir. I can hardly believe that it applies in this case."

"Why not? The absence of motive is what makes me think it is a possibility. Think, Trevor, they were both young girls, both very pleasant and unsuspecting, both were ideal prey for an oddball...."

"I cannot believe that Allingham is that much of an oddball! He has been in this town, in the same job, for years without any problem. He has been at the hotel for quite some time too...."

"Who knows when an oddball is going to crack? It may be that the arrival of this new girl, Lucy Oxbury, triggered his desire to kill. He was married once, the marriage broke down, why? Ever since, he could have harboured a grudge against young women...."

Johnson remembered his interview with Henry and his embarrassment when he had asked him about his marriage. He began to think that there might just be something in Duncombe's argument.

"Shouldn't we wait for a few more reports? The pathologist's report on Jenny Phillips for one. The report from the solicitors for another."

"I doubt if either of those reports are likely to turn up anything new. If we are stuck it's over a motive. Without a motive it is means and opportunity. At this moment, the prime suspect, in fact the only one, is your Mr.Allingham."

"I still think we are jumping the gun, Sir. I haven't interviewed Elliott yet, he might have seen Allingham yesterday, he could verify his story. It would be better if we waited one more day."

"I would remind you, Inspector Johnson, that the second killing took place within twenty four hours of the first. What if there is another murder? Is it safe to wait?"

"I don't think we could detain him, Sir. Not enough grounds. We must wait for the pathologist's report to be sure."

"Right," Duncombe sat back, "We'll wait. You interview Elliott and I'll hurry the pathologist. I'll get the team to cross check the statements while you are at it."

Denzil Elliott was not at his best. His forced inactivity had sapped his vitality. He had spent the day thinking over the past twentyfour hours and regretting his confession. He had been caught out over the door. Dammit, why had that wretched girl to go and get herself murdered? He'd been onto a good thing. With proper intervals, he could have gone on for another three months or more. He was just beginning to enjoy himself and build himself a bit of working capital. He knew that there had to be a limit, if you overdid it you got caught. He had observed that rule and had survived until now. There was a limit to how long he could stay at the Moorcroft, he knew that, but he hadn't anticipated how soon it would end. The prospect of a spell inside troubled him more than he was prepared to admit. He was upset that he had been returned to the interview room and dreaded that something had turned up to link him with the murder.

Johnson quickly informed him of Jenny Phillips' death and asked him to say how he had spent Saturday. His spirits sank. He was a suspect again. Not only that, he did not want to admit to following Henry Allingham that morning. There was malice in his action but also a belief that Allingham could be the murderer. He couldn't easily explain that to the Inspector. He was also uneasy about the prospect of betraying his contact. The more he was questioned, the greater the odds that he might let something slip. He took his time, simply saying that he had gone into town on the same bus as Allingham, had been window shopping, had had a pub lunch, had walked about town for most of the afternoon and had returned to the hotel around five.

"That would be after dark, then?"

"Yes, it was dark about four."

"You didn't see anyone from the hotel while you were in town?"

"No."

"So there is no one to back up your story?"

"Well, someone in The Hussar in Watson Street might recognise me, I've been there before."

"Watson Street? I don't suppose you saw Jenny Phillips in that area? What time did you come out?"

"I didn't come out until nearly closing time. I certainly didn't see her then or at any time."

There was something so cagey about Elliott's expression that Johnson was not disposed to accept what he said although, on the surface, it was straightforward enough.

"So what did you do after you left the pub?"

"I just walked around, looked at a few shops, got fed up and returned to the hotel."

"And no one can substantiate that?"

"No....I suppose not."

"You didn't see anyone from the hotel at any time yesterday afternoon?"

Denzil Elliott hesitated. He wanted to say he had tailed Henry Allingham, now was the time to say so if at all, but he could think of nothing to justify it and he was well aware that he had already admitted to 'persecuting' Allingham in the hotel. He realised the awkwardness of his position and remained silent.

"You did see one of them?"

Elliott looked down and said nothing.

"Who was it?"

"What is the problem, Mr.Elliott. What have you got to hide?"

"What do you mean? I've got nothing to hide. I've told you about the robberies, what more do you want?"

"I simply want to know who you saw on Saturday afternoon. I am investigating a murder, I need to know where everyone from the hotel was yesterday afternoon. I'll ask you again, did you see anyone from the hotel after you left The Hussar?"

"No!"

"You know the town quite well?"

"Yes, I know my way around."

"You didn't go near Gladstone Street on your wanderings, did you?"

"Gladstone Street? Why Gladstone Street?"

"Nor Broughton Road?"

"No, I turned the other way and walked as far as Redworth Road."

"You walked up Redworth Road, did you?"

"Yes, as far as the park."

"Only as far as the park?"

"Yes."

"It was dark by then, was it?"

"Well, it was nearly dark. That's when I decided to turn back."

"What time would that be?"

"I don't know what time, do I? It was just getting dark."

"You didn't look at your watch?"

Again Denzil Elliott hesitated. He didn't know what trap was being set for him.

"You came straight back to the hotel after that?"

"I went into Roughley's, had a look round then had a cup of tea on the top floor. After that I caught a number 6 back."

"And you saw no one you knew? Did anyone see you on your return?"

"Er....I don't think so. I have my own key, you know."

"You didn't speak to anyone in the sitting room?"

"No, I went straight up to my room."

"What time do you think that was?"

"It must have been about five, I didn't bother to look."

"That's a pity, Mr.Elliott, when it comes to a murder investigation it is important to be certain about times."

"I tell you, I know nothing about the murder!"

"Let me go over Saturday with you. You went into town in the morning on the same bus as Mr.Allingham but Mr.Allingham didn't see you. You walked about window shopping for nearly three hours but no one you knew saw you. You went for a drink in The Hussar and came out about three and wandered about the main street until dark but no one you knew saw you. You came back to the hotel at about five o'clock but no one saw you come in. In short, no one saw you the whole day until D.C.I.Duncombe and I interviewed you in your room at 7 p.m."

"Someone in The Hussar is bound to have seen me!"

"We will check on that, you may be sure. You know that the park in Redworth Road is less than a hundred yards from the canal, do you?"

"The canal, what canal?"

"The Langton Canal, I thought you said you knew the town quite well, Mr.Elliott?"

"I've never been near the canal. Why should I go near it?"

"Redworth Road crosses the canal, it wouldn't take you

long to get from the park to the canal."

"Why should I want to get to the canal?"

"You could have walked to the canal and back, caught your bus and been back to the hotel in plenty of time for dinner."

"What are you talking about?"

"Didn't I tell you? That's where the body of Jenny Phillips was found. In the canal."

CHAPTER TWENTY FIVE

The residents of The Moorcroft were in some disarray. They were acccustomed to pleasing themselves what they did on a Sunday. Some went out for the whole day, others made arrangements with Mrs.Ridgeway to have a cold lunch then went out for the afternoon. This Sunday was different. They had been put off their stride by three things. One was the news of Jenny's death, two was the taking of Miss Catesby to the police station and three was the horrid clamouring of the reporters.

Mrs.Jervis had been the first to pull herself together. The making and gathering in of statements had taken up too much of the morning for her liking. She was not going to wait any longer. She beckoned her husband and headed for the door. Her husband had been fascinated by the whole business. He had sat by the sitting room door watching and listening to everything. He longed to know more but his wife was in no mood for lingering or for answering any more questions. Together they fought their way through the front door onto the steps. The duty policeman made a path for them and they put down their heads, ignored the howled questions and financial offers, squeezed themselves into their car and drove off.

They didn't see Miss Catesby return from church, nor did they see her being driven away in a police car soon afterwards. The pressmen and photographers had roared at this sight and cameras flashed all over the pavement. Miss Catesby had little chance to adjust to her situation. Her expression, as captured on film, was an extraordinary mixture of bewilderment and defiance.

Mrs.Elmwood confided to Henry that she was very sorry for Millicent Catesby even though she was rather difficult at times. She did not think that she deserved to be driven off like that, after all, it must have seemed to the reporters that she was under arrest. Henry replied that, as the Inspector had returned to the station, it was logical that she should report there.

"But why shouldn't she have been allowed to make a statement to the policemen left behind here?"

"Perhaps it was because she went out before the Inspector arrived."

"A way of punishing her, you mean?"

"No, not exactly, but murder is a very serious business, you know. I'm surprised we are free to do as we please after what has happened to poor Jenny."

"But they couldn't detain us unless they charged us and we cannot all be guilty."

Henry thought that Mrs.Elmwood was being rather ingenuous, he changed the subject.

"Are you going out to lunch, Mrs.Elmwood? The weather is rather encouraging."

Mrs.Elmwood looked out of the window and gave herself a little shake.

"No, I'm not sure that I'm up to facing all these reporters...

I don't really like to ask, but.....I wonder if we couldn't have lunch together somewhere? I think that it might be safer, somehow, if we were together, don't you think?"

Henry was surprised to find Mrs.Elmwood so nervous but he agreed that there was safety in the idea. At least, if they had to make any more statements, they could confirm each other's whereabouts. He hastened to reassure her but warned her that he had little idea about good eating places, he had always eaten sandwiches on his walks. They made plans and left by the back door. Luckily for them, the hubbub at Miss Catesby's departure had drawn the newshounds from the back lane round to the front. Only one was in evidence and he was at the Wormald Street corner, looking the wrong way. They turned and hurried in the opposite direction as quietly as possible. They were not pursued.

They had to walk a long way before they could turn towards the bus route. Mrs.Elmwood had suggested that they tried a hotel on the western edge of Maskerley. Henry was more at ease with the suggestion than he could have anticipated. He found Mrs.Elmwood's company pleasant and comfortable. They travelled in relaxed silence until they reached the hotel. Unfortunately, the hotel was very popular and all the tables had been reserved. They asked the barman if he could recommend anywhere else and he directed them to a smaller establishment called The Granby in Beresford Road. He went one better and telephoned to reserve them a table.

"You're lucky, they've just had a cancellation. Who shall I say wants the table?"

Neither of them had any idea where Beresford Road was so they took a taxi. They smiled at the idea of retracing most of their steps but they were delighted when the driver stopped in a little driveway dominated by a huge monkey puzzle tree and they saw that The Granby was a neat and quiet licensed restaurant. The barman was most welcoming and they treated themselves to generous schooners of sherry.

Sitting at the bar, Henry suddenly felt awkward. He had enjoyed their excursion so long as they had been mobile and they had joint decisions to make and new surroundings to observe. They had shared delight at finding The Granby welcoming and convivial and they had giggled together when ordering their drinks but, once the drinks had arrived and they had murmured their appreciation of their first sips, they fell silent. It seemed that, simultaneously, they felt a lack of ease, not knowing what to say to each other. Henry was at much more of a disadvantage in that respect than his companion.

Mrs.Elmwood was about to break the silence when the barman broke it for her. He declared that their table was ready and that they could go into the dining room as soon as they wished. They finished their sherries quickly and moved into the dining room. Mrs.Elmwood was very relaxed, taking the lead quite unselfconsciously. Henry found this a great help. The dining room was not large but it was full. On his own, Henry would have been very embarassed, entering late and imagining that he was the object of every eye. As it was, he was happily pre-occupied with seating Mrs.Elmwood, with sharing a study of the menu and with discussing the wine list.

When the waiter had been dispatched, Henry began to feel a little uneasy about the wine. He had enjoyed his sherry, it had left him with a cosy glow deep inside him, but he was not used to drinking more than an occasional beer with a sandwich while he was out walking. Mrs.Elmwood noticed his expression.

"You aren't worrying about the wine, are you? I think we need something to take our minds off this terrible weekend. I am sure you deserve it, Mr.Allingham....oh, I can't go on being formal on an occasion like this, tell me, what is your name, mine's Elizabeth."

"Mine's Henry, pleased to meet you Elizabeth."

They shook hands across the table and laughed. Henry was amazed. He had never made a joke, consciously, that he could remember.

"I don't often...."

"It's been a...."

They paused to give each other the chance to begin. Henry was happy to give way.

"It is good to get away, isn't it? I was so content at The Moorcroft then this has to happen. It's quite unbelievable!"

Henry was aware that they should be thinking of other things, that they should be taking the opportunity to forget what had happened, at least for a while, but he was also aware that he had nothing to talk about. He wanted to know more about his companion but he didn't want her to know more about him. Life for him seemed to have begun at The Moorcroft, he had no wish to talk about what had happened before. He was very aware of his limitations. Mrs.Elmwood continued.

"I never thought I would have to leave it, everything was so ordered and calm. The food was good, too, and Mrs.Ridgeway was so obliging. I enjoyed the company and I liked the independence. Nobody troubled anyone until now. Everything has changed...."

The soup arrived and they drank it eagerly, not pausing to speak. The silence stretched beyond the laying down of their spoons. Henry ventured to break it.

"That was very good. We must have been ready for it."

"Yes, I think we were. Tell me, Henry, what are your plans?"

Henry felt that Mrs.Elmwood had been studying him. Before he could reply, the waiter brought the wine and waited for Henry to taste it. He did what he thought was right, sniffing, sipping then nodding approval. Briefly, he reflected that he would not have been able to distinguish one wine from another, good from bad.

"I mean, will you stay on after the investigation is over?"

"Oh, I haven't given it a thought. Like you, I rather liked it, I had got used to it."

He pondered what these questions were leading up to. He had no wish to change his circumstances. He raised his glass and drank. Mrs.Elmwood watched him and went on.

"When I first came here, I chose The Moorcroft because it was solid and had some atmosphere. It was clean and comfortable, not too far from the centre of town yet not too near either..."

The waiter brought their main course. They had both chosen ragout of lamb for no other reason than that it was unusual. It is not possible to give this dish a bright appearance, to dress it up in any way, but when the cover came off, the spicy aroma was truly mouthwatering. They ate with gusto. The spices gave edge to Henry's thirst and, while Mrs.Elmwood sipped gently at her wine, Henry took his in generous gulps.

"These vegetables are delightfully crisp. I think that we could not have chosen better."

"I agree entirely. This is an excellent meal. Considering the circumstances," Henry glanced round the dining room, "It isn't so very expensive. I'm not surprised that it is full. How lucky we were to get a table. More wine, Elizabeth?"

"No, Henry, not just yet, but don't wait for me, help yourself, by all means."

"You are not from this area, Elizabeth?"

Henry could think of nothing better to say. His companion continued to watch him.

"No, my husband and I lived in Leeds. When he died, I came here to work...."

"Oh, I'm sorry..."

"No need to apologise, it was a long time ago. I've got used to living on my own, we didn't have any children, I didn't have any ties in Leeds. I'm happy in my work here. I just don't know whether I can go on living at The Moorcroft when it is all over."

"Work! This weekend seems so long that I've almost forgotten about work."

Indeed, Henry was quite disappointed to have his thoughts directed towards work again. A mere two days ago he had been conditioned to think of his job as the most important element in his life.

"I just want to forget about these awful deaths and all the tension and suspicion. I'm not nomally given to nerves but I don't know how long it is going to take to clear up and I don't know how long I can stand it."

Henry couldn't imagine this calm and comfortable woman opposite him having a breakdown. He put his glass to his lips as though to mask what he was thinking. The wine was good.

"There have been signs of strain in most of our fellow

residents, poor Miss Catesby and Mr.Jackson in particular."

"And what did you think of Mr.Baxter last night?"

"Ah, Mr.Baxter! Now his is an interesting case...."

"Why, Henry, you sound just like a detective. I thought you were observing everyone, right from the time we were all together in the sitting room. I suspected that you had some ideas."

"Ideas?"

"Ideas about the murder. You don't say much but you notice things, am I right?"

Henry was not vain but he was susceptible to flattery, if it was not too obvious. He smiled conspiratorially and drained his glass. He decided to confide in Elizabeth.

"I have a systematic kind of mind, Elizabeth. An orderly, logical mind. Something to do with my work, I suppose. It occurred to me that I might put it to some use in connection with these terrible events. Having been rather distant from everyone in the past, I'm afraid, could be an advantage. No preconceptions, no flights of fancy to get in the way...."

"Marvellous! I can see we shall have to be very wary...."

"Oh, no one but ourselves must know. It would never do. No one should even guess. Everyone should speak and act as normal, only then could I make a useful contribution to the investigation."

"Yes, I see. But what progress have you made? What have you seen? Have you had time to come to any conclusions?"

"It is much too soon. All I have done, so far, is to make a few observations. I've been jotting them down in a notebook."

"How exciting! I'd love to see it."

"I will show you when I have sufficient entries," Henry had a momentary thought that Elizabeth might have been teasing him but there was nothing in her face to confirm it. "Of course, it isn't easy, everyone is under suspicion and I only see everyone at mealtimes."

"But you notice things when you are out and about too, don't you? When you got on the bus, last night, you looked as though you had seen or heard something very important. You were very preoccupied. Had it anything to do with Jenny?"

Henry was taken aback. Why should Elizabeth have thought that? He had seen Jenny earlier in the afternoon but by the time he had got onto the bus he had had other things on his mind. His hand moved instinctively towards his pocket as though he had unwittingly wanted to record her question but he relaxed. Jenny was on everyone's mind and Elizabeth had been very kind to Jenny, it was only natural that she should ask if he had been thinking of her too.

"Well, you remember that I told the Inspector that I had seen Jenny twice on Saturday, it was certainly true, I'm just sorry that I didn't notice the bus's destination. It's silly isn't it...?"

"Not really. Why should you? You saw her get on a bus, why should you trouble about which bus?"

"It might have been very important."

"If she was found in the canal, she couldn't have gone far on the bus."

"That would depend on where she fell into the canal. If she had visited someone first...."

"But she didn't know anyone in or around Maskerley. She was a very shy girl. Mrs.Ridgeway said she was an orphan and hardly ever left the hotel except to go to the pictures once in a while."

Mrs.Elmwood stared hard at Henry.

"Are you sure it was Jenny you saw?"

"Oh, I'm certain of that. I looked again to be sure, that's why I didn't see where the bus was going."

"And you didn't see anyone else?"

"Well, no one I knew."

There was a silence. They had ordered coffee and they sat back to enjoy it. It seemed that they had nothing more to say to each other. Henry was the first to break the silence.

"I'm sorry, Elizabeth, it looks as though I've drunk most of the wine. Is there anything else I can get you?"

She gave a little shudder as though she felt a cold draught.

"Do you know, I would rather like a brandy. Would you care for one? That would fortify us against whatever lies ahead."

"I rather hope that there will be no more dramatic happenings."

She laid her hand lightly on his.

"At the very least, there are bound to be more questions. I'm afraid our lives are not going to be the same."

CHAPTER TWENTY SIX

Henry was not accustomed to paying big restaurant bills. The old Henry jibbed but the new Henry prevailed. It had been a delightful afternoon and he had found Mrs.Elmwood excellent company. They stood at the entrance to the Granby and wondered what to do next. It was only 2.30 and the sun was quite strong for a November day.

"It is so pleasant, let us walk back, it can't be far."

Henry was grateful for this suggestion, he had eaten well and the brandy, on top of quite a large quantity of wine, was making him feel drowsy. They headed off in what they thought was the right direction. They walked for some distance in silence. Henry had no small talk and he dreaded stumbling into something personal as he had done earlier. He waited for Elizabeth to open a conversation but she was too deep in thought. He thought that a comment on the lack of traffic was too trivial, everything he thought of seemed trivial. Eventually, they reached a familiar street.

"It seems we are heading in the wrong direction, Elizabeth. This street joins the main road at the bottom there, we are going towards the town centre."

"I don't think it matters, Henry. Let us go on by all means."

There was nothing visual to stimulate their conversation. The last two streets they had passed along were of brick built terrace houses with small gardens at the front, all very like each other. It was not a rundown area even if the houses were old. There was something sedate about this part of town. Being a Sunday, all was quiet, nothing moved except for an occasional freewheeling cat. Suddenly, round the corner at the far end of the street, two young girls appeared, the first people they had met since leaving the restaurant. They were walking rapidly, locked in animated conversation. They passed without so much as a sideways glance at the middle aged couple on the same pavement. Elizabeth took Henry's arm in a firm grip.

"Did you notice, Henry? The girl on the inside, don't you think she looked like Jenny?"

"I'm sorry, I didn't notice...."

"Very like her face, not quite the same hair."

Henry was on the point of saying he wasn't too alert as yet when he realised that this would not help the image that he had been projecting of himself as a keen observer and amateur sleuth. He had no time to speak.

"I liked that girl. It is a dreadful thing that has happened to her. Could we...it's an awful thing to ask, I know, you'll think me strange... could we go and look at the canal?"

Henry stared at her in astonishment.

"It must seem gruesome to you but I have a strong urge to see where the poor girl met her death."

"Elizabeth! It will only distress you."

"I'm stronger than you think. Please Henry. We don't need to linger. It can't be far from here. I'm not the fainting kind, you know. If you are keen to help the investigation, it might help you to view the scene of the crime."

This last argument was a powerful one as far as Henry was concerned. It overcame his scruples. In any case, his scruples had been on behalf of his companion not himself.

"If you are really sure you want to go, Elizabeth."

They continued their walk

"Do you really think that looking at the canal will help your memory of Jenny?"

"I don't know, I just have this powerful urge to see it."

"You don't suffer from nightmares then?"

"I dream, or I believe I do, but I rarely remember what I have dreamed when I awake. So far, I haven't had any bad dreams but I can't be sure that I won't have any before this is all over."

"Then why take chances?"

"I can't explain it, I just have to go. You can leave me if you like. Nothing will happen to me in broad daylight, if that is what's troubling you."

"No, I wouldn't think of it. I'll come along."

They proceded the length of the High Street then crossed at Broughton Road. Only a hundred yards at most and they were looking over the bridge into the green-brown murkiness of the canal. The shadow of the bridge stretched in front of them, beyond it, the sun had turned the colour of the canal's surface into a strident yellow-green, brassy and impenetrable. Henry peered into the shadowed surface directly below them.

"It is almost impossible to see into this water, it is thick with slime."

He turned to Elizabeth at his side. She was not listening. Her eyes were fixed in the distance, her face twisted as though she were about to weep. Henry had no experience of comforting anyone, his first thought was to rush on with some distraction or other.

"It could almost be oil, it is so thick. I'm surprised even the weed can grow in it."

He glanced back at her, guilty because he could offer her no consolation. He wanted to speak of Jenny but felt inadequate in the face of another person's grief. He stumbled on.

"Do you want to go down to the towpath?"

"No,no, I don't think so. Where do you think they found her body?"

Her voice was rather distant as though it was someone else speaking. Henry watched her as he spoke.

"I have no idea, no doubt the newspapers will tell us tomorrow. I think you should come away, Elizabeth. You are only upsetting yourself. Nothing can bring the poor girl back. This is a terrible place."

He had eventually found the words, he was emboldened to take her arm and turn her towards the way they had come. She resisted for a few moments then seemed to pull herself together and fell into step beside him. He glanced again at her face and saw that she had entirely recovered.

"Do you feel better now?"

"Yes thank you, Henry. Let us find a bus, it's beginning to get cold."

On the bus home, Henry and Elizabeth discussed the deaths of both Lucy Oxbury and Jenny Phillips. They discussed the abrupt removal of Denzil Elliott and the words of Inspector Johnson. They thought it strange that he should be detained unless he was to be charged. They thought that the Inspector must have been bluffing but they wondered why. They rather hoped that Denzil Elliott was guilty then, since he was locked away, there would be no more trouble.

"That reminds me, Elizabeth, just after I left the coffee shop yesterday morning, I looked back and saw he had taken my place at your table."

"Why, so he did! I'd quite forgotten. He didn't stay long."

She omitted to tell Henry of the disparaging remarks Elliott had made about him. Henry paused, thinking that Elizabeth would offer an explanation or comment, but she added nothing.

"He was in town yesterday, I suppose it is possible that he killed Jenny, too...."

He broke off in horror as he became aware of strangers in the seat in front, tilting their heads in order to hear what they were saying. They remained silent until it was their turn to get off the bus. After the bus had gone on, Henry held back.

"Before we go to face the reporters and everyone else, do you think it is worth me carrying on?"

"Investigating, you mean? Oh certainly, Henry. It isn't all over yet. Perhaps Mr.Elliott is not guilty. I tell you what, let us both keep our eyes and ears open and pool our observations. It can't do any harm. Two heads are better than one, after all."

Henry agreed, but reluctantly. He suddenly felt that he was about to lose the independence he so valued. The secrecy he enjoyed would be lost. He believed that he could trust Elizabeth but it would be difficult communicating in a close knit community like the hotel without giving the game away. He felt compromised. Nevertheless there was a relief in someone else knowing. He felt a strengthening of resolve. As they pushed their way through the reporters, Henry decided that his first priority would be to record all the comings and goings of everybody in the hotel. This was essential. He should have thought of it before.

When Henry had completed his ablutions and had entered the dining room he found that there were only three residents present. Neither Mrs.Jervis nor Mr.Baxter had returned from their afternoon out. Although the meal was well up to Mrs.Ridgeway's standard, Henry had lost most of his appetite. He was unaccustomed to eating well in the afternoon and he was still rather giddy from the wine and brandy.

Walter Jackson sat on his own, scowling, his head bowed over a folded newspaper. Miss Catesby and Elizabeth sat together, chattering in low voices. Henry was obliged to sit in his usual place and be silent. After the intimacy of the afternoon, he suddenly felt at a loss. It wasn't possible to join in the conversation of the ladies, partly because their voices were too low and partly because he had become aware that the conversation seemed only to be about clothes. Neither of them looked up and he was unable to catch Elizabeth's eye. He swallowed his disappointment, ate quickly and was the first to leave.

Upstairs, he took out his notebook and pondered his day. He had an urge to use his notebook as a diary and to fill it with the details of his wonderful afternoon but he held back. His orderly mind jibbed at such muddling of procedures. The notebook had a prescribed function. In it were to be recorded only such observations that pertained to the murders. He laid back on the bed and thought. The canal, why had Elizabeth wanted to see the canal? What was it.... he found himself beginning to doze off. This would never do! He shook himself and sat up. What was he trying to remember? Oh yes, he remembered being taken by surprise when Elizabeth had asked him whether he had been thinking of Jenny when he had sat on the bus beside her last night. Why had it seemed a strange thing to ask? Surely she didn't think that he had anything to do with Jenny's death? No, none of the rest of her conversation had reflected this, he must be mistaken. Nevertheless, he entered the question in his notebook together with the visit to the canal. He added the names of those at dinner and wondered if the absence of Mrs. Jervis and Baxter had any significance.

Baxter's behaviour had been very suspicious. Why had he been so concerned about Denzil Elliott? Baxter had been the only resident not on the premises at the time Lucy Oxbury's body had been found. That didn't mean that he could not have killed her. She had been dead before they broke into the bathroom. Baxter had also been in town yesterday, who was to say that he hadn't met Jenny and disposed of her before returning to the hotel.

Henry felt dispirited. He knew so little. He had no idea why anyone should want to kill Lucy Oxbury or Jenny Phillips. There had to be a reason yet how could there be one. Nobody knew Lucy well, as far as he was aware. Suddenly, he guessed that, in the general pattern of formality in the hotel, nobody really knew their fellow residents. He wasn't unique in that respect. The ladies were closer to each other than the men but did they really know each other? Baxter and Jackson were reasonably close acquaintances but did they really know each other? Nobody had really known Denzil Elliott, unless it was Ernie Baxter, why else had he panicked so visibly?

Had anyone exchanged confidences? Had anyone revealed their inner selves? In the course of the afternoon, in all the time they had spent together, neither Elizabeth nor himself had volunteered much about themselves. They had been nervous, certainly he had, but they had only talked about the meal, their surroundings and Jenny. How strange! He felt closer to Elizabeth Elmwood than anyone else yet he knew nothing about her except that she and her husband had lived in Leeds before he died.

To be fair, he had had no wish to speak of his past, it would have been too painful. He was glad that Elizabeth had asked no personal questions. Was it the same for all of them? If they were all similarly distant, there could be no motive. There had been no connected robbery, no hatred or malice, no jealousy, no lover's quarrel. Denzil Elliott had not been charged with the murder, what motive could he have had? He had turned out to be a practical joker, that could hardly have provided a motive for the murder.

He yawned. The food, the wine and the sunshine had all conspired to make him sleepy. He would not fight it, he would have an early night. It was work tomorrow. Perhaps the routine of work would help him figure things out rather better.

CHAPTER TWENTY SEVEN

The next morning's newspapers were full of the recovery of Jenny Phillips body but with no details of how and exactly when she died. Much was made of the fact that she was the second person from The Moorcroft Hotel to die in two days. Mrs. Ridgeway was most upset at the headlines and the speculation. She resolutely refused to talk to the press, continuing to refer all questions to the police. However, she could not place an embargo on either her residents or her staff, try as she may. She was particularly incensed by a paragraph of nonsense purporting to come from her assistant cook and part time help, Mary Miles. Mary's photograph appeared in two of the papers delivered to the hotel, alongside it were paragraphs referring to "a happy family atmosphere, but who could you trust nowadays?" There were different interpretations of remarks about Mrs.Ridgeway herself. "Fair but strict", "Guardian Dragon gives nothing away - what has she got to hide?" had been two of the sub-headings.

"Now then, Mary, look what this has brought you?"

Mrs.Ridgeway found Mary almost in tears. Not only were the photographs far from flattering, she found her words twisted beyond recognition.

"Mrs.Ridgeway, I didn't say all those things. All I said was that we were a happy family working here but we couldn't speak for the residents. I promise, that is all I said."

"I told you not to speak to reporters, you can never trust them, never! They promise you everything and give you nothing, then they trick you and twist your words. Did they give you any money?"

"No, Mrs.Ridgeway, they didn't."

"No, and I suppose they took your photo without

asking?"

"They take photographs all the time...."

"Mary, it'll get worse. You'll have to be ready for them. Until it's over, then they'll disappear, interest, promises, the lot. Don't let them flatter you, just look how that photo turned out, and do they care? They only care about their money and their jobs. You refer them to me. I don't care what they print about me, I'll be the dragon they want! They'll get nothing out of me."

Mary was impressed by Mrs.Ridgeway's rage. As she said to Mrs.Hammond later, she knew Laura Ridgeway was tough but she didn't know how fierce she could be. Sarah Lucas, the only maid now, had trouble getting in the back door even with a constable to help her and when two reporters squeezed through into the back yard after her, Mrs.Hammond felt obliged to rush out to defend her. Meg Hammond was light on her feet in spite of her bulk, the reporters didn't know until she was among them, elbows flailing, teatowel flicking and her tongue at its most violent.

The domestic staff had a solemn meeting later that morning. They shared their anxieties and their woe. They even managed to share a laugh or two, but the upshot of their deliberations was that they would all arrive together and depart together as far as possible. Mrs.Ridgeway would simplify their working hours and provide them with a taxi so that no individual would be pestered. It wasn't a foolproof arrangement but it was reassuring.

Breakfast was brisk and silent. The pattern of the previous week was repeated almost exactly. Henry was first down followed by Elizabeth then Mrs.Jervis, Walter Jackson, Miss Catesby and Ernie Baxter. Henry was first out as usual. He had not had an opportunity of speaking to Elizabeth as Mrs.Jervis was hard on her heels. He was thinking of his plan to record the comings and goings of the residents as he climbed the stairs. How could he do this when he was always first in and first out? As he turned towards his door, he had a startling thought. They had all forgotten about Mr.Frimton. So much had happened that he hadn't given that quiet young man a thought. At that very moment, Gerald Frimton came out of the next bedroom.

Henry stood stock still and gawped. Gerald Frimton nodded, smiled, and went on down the corridor, as he had always done at this time in the morning. Henry went on to the bathroom and washed his hands and brushed his teeth automatically. He put on his scarf, coat and hat without thinking. His mind was whirring, trying to work out Mr.Frimton's absence and reappearance in the scheme of things.

Once out of the hotel and through the reporters, Henry pulled himself together. By the time he arrived at his office, he was his old self again. The daily routine quite absorbed him and for the next hour or two he forgot about the previous weekend. It was at the official mid-morning break that it all came back to him.

One of the typists had the temerity to follow him into his private sanctum. The old Henry bristled.

"Excuse me, Mrs.Sibley...."

"Oh, Mr.Allingham, sorry I'm sure, but I was wondering...."

"I was about to...."

"Did you see the news on T.V. last night? Was'nt that...."

"Mrs.Sibley!" Henry interrupted her furiously.

"Well, I'm sorry, I'm sure but I thought that was where you lived...."

"Out! Out! Mrs.Sibley! I will not be disturbed while I am having my tea!"

Mrs.Sibley was unabashed by Henry's wrath, indeed it had confirmed what she wanted to know. She turned slowly towards the door, an unmistakeable look of triumph on her face.

173

Henry was horrified. There had always been a distance between the people under him and himself. Now he was aware that they knew more about his circumstances than he could ever have believed. He could ignore the behaviour of one individual but the word would pass round the typing pool within seconds and the whole typing and accounts section would present a much bigger problem. Mrs.Sibley had meant mischief.

In fact, Henry's years of remoteness stood him in good stead. The old Henry prevented the new Henry from being stung. He was able to ignore the stares and glances, the nudges and attempts at conversation. He had the good sense to leave the company premises to have his lunch and was able to return in the afternoon well able to resist any tormentors. Unfortunately, yet naturally enough, there were many awaiting their opportunity.

D.C.I.Duncombe and his second in command could hardly wait for Monday morning. Now they could really get on with their enquiries.

The first thing to concern Inspector Johnson was Gerald Frimton's background. He set his team to work and very soon built up a substantial dossier.

Gerald Frimton was a management trainee at Tremlow's, a large chemical plant on the South side of Maskerley. He came from Huddersfield where his family still lived. His father was a factory storekeeper, his mother did not go out to work. He had a younger sister who worked as a sales assistant in a large store in Huddersfield. He had joined Tremlow Chemicals at Huddersfield straight from school. His industry was commended and he had attended day-release courses and evening classes to assist in his work. Eventually, Tremlow's had transferred him to their Maskerley plant as a management trainee. The Maskerley manager claimed that he was a very reliable and promising young man.

Frimton's girl friend was Sally Ferguson, she worked

in the office of Pinner's the estate agents. Her father was a surveyor who doted on his only daughter. There was an older brother, Thomas, still living at home, who worked for a building society. The mother shared ownership of and worked in a beauty salon in the town. The combined income of all four earners was considerable and they lived in some comfort in Mortimer Crescent.

Johnson could think of no reason why Frimton should have been concerned in Lucy Oxbury's death, yet there was a link with Lucy via the estate agent. There was also a very tenuous link between surveying, building societies and estate agents. He was tempted to visit Pinner's himself but he decided to send D.C.Green.

D.C.I.Duncombe was busy confirming Lucy Oxbury's activities as a member of Maskerkey Choral Society and the Maskerley Players when the pathologist's report on Jenny Phillips came in. It was as Johnson had suspected. Jenny had been strangled before her body had reached the water. The killer had little difficulty, the neck was thin and the girl was not strong. There was little bruising, indicating little or no struggle. Most probably, the girl had been taken by surprise and shock would have played a big part in her death. The position of the bruising suggested that she had been attacked from behind.

For a brief moment, the D.C.I. contemplated a random killing. A young girl on the towpath in the dark, alone, and vulnerable. A homicidal stranger lurking nearby. It was not impossible but it simply came from the idea that she had been strangled from behind. He put it firmly aside, the coincidence with the death of Lucy Oxbury was too glaring.

He reached for the residents' statements concerning Saturday and re-read them. He was not happy and when he was not happy he was restless. He put on his overcoat and called on Johnson on his way out.

"The pathologist's report is in. You were right, Jenny

Phillips was strangled, very little force used. Killer could have been male or female. I'm going back to the hotel. I'm not happy about Jenny Phillips. I want to do my thinking where she lived."

Later in the afternoon, there was a call from Victor Brambles. So far, his secretary had not turned up anything of significance. None of the criminal cases he had taken on during Lucy's time in their office was in the least sinister. One or two of the characters involved had gone to gaol but he could recall no expressed grudges and these would not have been extended to Lucy, she was only their office assistant. It was rather a hopeless task. If he was to be of any help, he would need to have some names to go on. Johnson gave him the names of all the residents and those of Mrs.Ridgeway's staff. The senior partner said he would scc what he could do but he thought it would turn out to be a wild goose chase. Johnson was inclined to agree.

By the end of the day, he had learned that Lucy Oxbury and Sally Ferguson had been good friends and that they were both members of the Maskerley Players as was Gerald Frimton. Sally Ferguson had attended the Friday evening rehearsal in the Co-operative Hall. Gerald Frimton had not been up to it and had stayed at home. She had been surprised and disappointed that Lucy had missed the rehearsal too. She could think of no reason why anyone should kill poor Lucy, she was so nice and straightforward, she wouldn't have hurt a fly.

Inspector Johnson sighed. The mixture as before - nice girl, hard working, happy, well liked, no reason why anyone should kill her. In his experience, people were murdered out of jealousy, or for revenge, or in the course of robberies, or because they stood in the way of someone who wanted to inherit or to marry, or because they posed a threat of some kind. Lucy Oxbury stood in no one's way, she was not murdered for her wealth, nor out of jealousy, as far as he could tell. Was she a threat to anyone? How could she be? So far, Brambles hadn't turned up anything and there was nothing in her lifestyle in Catton or in Maskerley that might give a clue. He would just have to go on digging.

He was on his way out when he met his Chief returning.

"Did you find anything, Sir?"

"Not in Jenny Phillips' room. I've never seen a room so bare. An old Teddy Bear was the only personal possession, poor kid! There weren't many clothes, either. There was an old toffee tin at the bottom of the wardrobe with five pounds in it, that was all," he paused, "Why can't people tell you things straight away? Now Mrs.Ridgeway tells me that Jenny Phillips locked herself away in her room until she had to knock for her at breakfast time. I wonder if there was something in particular that frightened her?"

"Her nearest bathroom is on the third floor, the same as Catesby and Elliott. Did she see any of them moving in the night?"

"I would remind you that we had two men inside all night and two outside. If there was anybody moving about we would have been told."

They had been standing in the foyer, suddenly they were aware that there was a local reporter taking a keen interest in what they were saying.

"See you in the morning, Inspector."

"You are making a statement to the press tomorrow, aren't you, Sir?"

CHAPTER TWENTY EIGHT

Mrs. Ridgeway was not too happy at the reappearance of Gerald Frimton. She had felt let down by his failure to keep her informed. In view of everything that had happened, it had been most inconsiderate of him. She trusted him no longer and even harboured a vague suspicion that his absence may have been connected with the murder. What made her day more difficult than ever was the arrival of a television crew at her door. She had taken the telephone from its rest soon after breakfast and so had had no warning. She was appalled that this crew expected that she would give them an interview as a matter of course. She told them roundly that they could go away. She did not care who they were or who they represented, she was not interested in the prospect of fame, she did not want their money, nor did she care what expense they had incurred in coming to the hotel. Finally, she asked the policeman at the door to see them off. This was an extra burden she could well have done without.

The residents were all filmed as they returned to the hotel that evening. Only Walter Jackson had shown any willingness to listen to the cameramen but he had second thoughts and pushed his way in like the others. They were very subdued when they met again in the dining room later. The only cheerful member present was Frimton and he was not prepared to be communicative because he didn't want to expand on the reasons for his absence. Miss Catesby was very snappy and the others left her alone. Elizabeth Elmwood was very thoughtful. Henry was meditating upon how much his office staff knew about him. Mrs.Jervis was most unusually jumpy. Neither Baxter nor Jackson wanted to talk to anyone.

Mrs.Jervis was called away to the telephone. It was unusual for anyone to be called out in the middle of a meal. When she came back she looked very disturbed. She sat down and tinkered with her food.

"Is everything alright, Christine?" Mrs.Elmwood couldn't help asking.

"Everything is going from bad to worse!"

It was strange hearing this coming from Mrs.Jervis. She had been the least troubled of them all. Henry awoke from his introspection and took notice. Mrs.Jervis's face looked puffy under a heavy layer of powder. Had she been weeping? He could hardly imagine this robust, no-nonsense person weeping. She had been all for carrying on undisturbed by the fuss, the police and the press. What could have happened? Instinctively he reached for his notebook. Elizabeth saw him out of the corner of her eye and smiled. Gerald Frimton addressed then all.

"I've been told about the murders. It must have been a bad time for you."

"You can be certain of that…."

It was Jackson who leapt in but they were all interrupted by Mrs.Jervis who staggered to her feet, pushing the table away roughly.

"Dreadful! Absolutely dreadful!" She rushed up to her room.

"Dear oh dear, I'd better see what's wrong with her."

Elizabeth Elmwood looked down then, slightly bewildered, shook her skirt and followed Mrs.Jervis out. Henry had been watching and guessed why she had hesitated. She had been looking for her knitting bag. It had been her constant companion until the night of the murder. Seeking to help her, he tried hard to remember that evening. He recalled seeing the bag at the side of the armchair where she had been sitting when she went to make her statement. He remembered that when it was his turn, Elizabeth had moved it to allow him to pass. She had taken it onto her lap but he couldn't remember if she had left it behind when she went to have her fingerprints taken. He was sure that it wasn't in the room when he left

179

to go upstairs. She herself must have taken it upstairs. Had she left it downstairs, Mrs.Ridgeway would have found it. He remembered that Elliott had claimed that someone had interfered with his suitcase - was there a thief in the hotel as well as a murderer?

Up in his room he committed his thoughts to his notebook and added the simple fact of Frimton's return. He had put his notebook away and was gazing vacantly out of the window when there was a discreet knock at his door. Henry was astonished to find that it was Elizabeth.

"Can I come in for a moment, Henry?"

"Er….well…." Henry had a well-developed sense of propriety.

"Just a private word."

"Well….er….come in Elizabeth. Is it urgent?"

"Not really, but I thought it wouldn't do to be seen discussing together."

Henry was not sure that Elizabeth should be seen entering his room either. He hurried to draw the curtains and was embarrassed when one of them stuck and he was obliged to stand on a chair to free it. His visitor stood on the other side of the bed waiting patiently.

"I can't help Mrs.Jervis, she's deeply upset about something but I can't get her to tell me what it is. But I wanted to talk to you about Mr.Frimton. Don't you think it a bit odd that he should return immediately after the murders?"

"Elizabeth, he left the hotel last Monday and I think I heard someone say he was going to see his parents."

"That's what he told us at breakfast but I saw him on the Thursday and again on the Saturday. On the Thursday, I thought he had returned but when I got back, I realised he hadn't so I thought I must be mistaken. When I saw him on the Saturday, I was sure it was him but he didn't return to the hotel then, either."

"Did you tell the police?"

"I didn't think to. It didn't seem important then."

"You didn't speak to him?"

"No, both times he was on the other side of the street. Henry, you do know what this means? He was staying in Maskerley. He has been within reach of the hotel. That means we can't rule him out, can we?"

"Elizabeth, we mustn't jump to conclusions."

"Remember, Mr.Frimton sat at the same table as Lucy and talked to her every day."

"That doesn't give him a motive, Elizabeth. Why should he want to kill her after such a short acquaintance.

"We don't know why anyone might want to kill her, do we? We only know that Mr.Frimton had more to do with her than anyone else and that he wasn't telling the truth when he said he was going to visit his parents."

"Well, that is…."

They heard the door of the next room shut and realised that he might have heard them. Mrs.Elmwood turned to go.

"Get that written down, Henry, and we will talk again soon. Goodnight!"

CHAPTER TWENTY NINE

About ten o'clock the next morning, a telephone call came in from a jeweller from Broughton. He was very suspicious of someone who had left some bracelets and a watch for appraisal with the intention of selling them. They were very expensive items and the would-be vendor didn't seem to belong to them. His story had not been convincing. Johnson immediately sent two of his men to check.

Another call came in from Victor Brambles, his secretary had drawn a blank, none of the names she had been given appeared to have any connection with any of his cases. This troubled Johnson who, more than his Chief, had hoped that this was where the solution lay. He relayed the message to his Chief. D.C.I.Duncombe was not too surprised. He had taken up the file on the Ferguson family and was digging into the connection between Sally Ferguson and Lucy Oxbury. He was not a happy man. Earlier he had granted an interview with the press and had had a rough time. They thought he had kept them waiting an unnecessarily long time. One or two intrepid souls ventured to suggest that there was some kind of cover-up going on. Duncombe handled them coolly, pointing out that he had simply waited to see if there would be more he could tell them. What irked him most was that he had to admit there had been little progress so far. Impatient as ever to be out of the office, he left soon after his coffee break to interview Sally Ferguson personally.

Soon after that, the officers who had gone to speak to the jeweller in Broughton phoned in. All the pieces offered to the jeweller matched items listed as stolen by Denzil Elliott. Johnson told them to stay there and apprehend the man when he returned to the jeweller's.

Accordingly, the rest of the Inspector's afternoon was occupied in interviewing one Terence Wilby, a petty thief with a long record of offences and convictions. Wilby obstinately claimed that he was trying to dispose of the jewellery for a friend and that he couldn't divulge the name of this friend. It took a long time to squeeze the name of this friend out of him and it was only the suggestion that the jewellery was connected to the murder at the hotel that undermined Wilby's stubbornness. The friend he was helping was Albert Ernest Baxter. He admitted doing similar services for Baxter from time to time. He had never used the Broughton jeweller before, he had always gone further afield and he cursed himself for his lack of caution.

It was only when Baxter returned to the hotel that evening that he was arrested. His departure in the custody of two detectives caused great excitement among the reporters. Meanwhile, D.C.I.Duncombe had returned from his contact with the Ferguson family. He greeted the news with genuine delight.

"So right again, Inspector Johnson! I hope your cap still fits! Well now, we'll have to work on Baxter and try to recover the loot.

Ernie Baxter's departure had gone unnoticed by the other residents. They were only aware that he had gone when they were sitting at dinner. All that Mrs.Ridgeway could tell them was that Mr.Baxter had been taken away for questioning. The news was greeted with incomprehension.

"Two detained? Whatever are the police playing at?"

As ever, it was Miss Catesby who was the first to comment.

"Perhaps they were working together."

Elizabeth Elmwood looked sharply at Mr.Frimton. He had made this remark with an air of innocence and continued to eat methodically. Walter Jackson was in a quarrelsome mood.

"Working together in a murder? Rubbish!"

"Why not? It's been done many times. I've read lots of stories...."

The sight of Frimton eating away nonchalantly while he talked without apparent concern was too much for Jackson.

"Stories! Stories! This isn't a story! This is for real, don't you understand that? Good God, are you thick or something?" His voice rose almost to a scream.

"There is no need for that, young man!"

"I agree with Miss Catesby, shouting at each other will not help. We are all suffering from nerves."

Henry maintained his peace-keeping role though he had had another trying day and was less tranquil than he had been. He and Mrs.Elmwood exchanged glances. She entered the conversation.

"We must be on our guard. There will be more questioning."

"Mr.Baxter has always been well dressed. I cannot believe that he could have had anything to do with the murder...."

Mrs.Jervis had been deeply preoccupied but this remark seemed to touch a nerve. Henry saw her face crumple. Miss Catesby continued.

"....in any case, he had nothing to do with Miss Oxbury, why should he, she was just a strip of a girl...." There was a startling noise from the corner. Henry could hardly believe his eyes. Mrs.Jervis was clutching her napkin to her mouth, desperately trying to restrain herself. A moment ago he had thought she was on the verge of tears, now it was clear that she was laughing hysterically.

"Well! Upon my....is she ill?"

Miss Catesby rose, her face quite pink. Mrs.Jervis was unable to meet her eye, she simply waved her away with a dismissive gesture of one hand. Miss Catesby left the dining room in a fearful rage. Elizabeth Elmwood turned to Mrs.Jervis.

"You shouldn't have done that dear, you know what Millicent is like."

"Oh...." Mrs.Jervis was making a heroic effort to pull herself together. "Oh, excuse me....that woman, she really....she really is the end...."

She wiped her eyes and mouth, mopped her face and patted her hair.

"I don't know what came over me but I couldn't help myself. With all the things we have had to worry about, she comes out with platitudes about people being well dressed...."

"Nevertheless, dear, I think you have behaved rather badly."

"Do you know, Elizabeth, I think I have behaved naturally for the first time in years. I'm sorry I've hurt Millicent, of course, and I shall have to apologise but I do feel a lot better for it."

Mrs.Ridgeway entered with the coffee tray.

"Is everything all right?"

She had heard Miss Catesby rushing upstairs.

"Miss Catesby's a bit upset."

"Upset? We're all upset. This place is a madhouse. The sooner we get out of it the better!"

"There is no need to be rude, Mr.Jackson. We are doing our best. No doubt we will all be relieved when it is all over. Meanwhile, we must all endure the strain as calmly as possible."

They drank their coffee in silence.

Almost an hour later there was a knock on Henry's door. Thinking it was Elizabeth, he opened it without hesitation. It was Mrs.Jervis looking chastened and a little pale. Henry backed away and Mrs.Jervis followed him thinking that it was an unspoken invitation to enter.

"I won't disturb you for more than a minute, Mr.Allingham. I just wanted to apologise to everyone for my conduct just now. I've had a great personal disappointment and it has affected me more than I could have wished. I am also feeling a little unwell. Fortunately, Miss Catesby has accepted my apology on that account, but I have to say that I did find her rather funny, didn't you?"

At that point, Mrs.Jervis remembered that Henry had never demonstrated a sense of humour. Her smile faded, she seemed to become dizzy and suddenly slumped onto the chair by the bed.

"Mrs.Jervis, are you alright? Can I fetch you something? A drink of water, perhaps?"

Henry became agitated as Mrs.Jervis's eyes fluttered and moisture gathered on her upper lip. He would bring her a glass of water from the bathroom. Having patted her hand for at least a minute while he thought, he let the hand drop and ran out to fetch the water. When he got back, he found Gerald Frimton holding the same hand and fanning its owner with a newspaper.

"Can we lift her onto the bed, old man?"

Henry was incensed. He was not an old man and did not care for the familiarity of being so called. Also, Mrs Jervis was not only an embarrassment, she was a very well-built embarrassment. It would take them all their strength to lift her and, in any case, he could not do with a strange woman on his bed.

"Certainly not!" He whispered hoarsely. "What we must do is get her back to her room as quickly as possible."

They both looked down at Mrs.Jervis, wondering how they were to proceed. Just as Frimton was opening his arms by way of calculating their path about her chest, Mrs.Jervis opened her eyes and stared about in amazement.

"What happened?"

"I think you must have fainted, Mrs.Jervis."

"Did I really?" she looked at Henry most suspiciously, "I am not normally given to fainting."

She looked about her and struggled awkwardly to her feet. She was far from steady.

"I think I'd better go and lie down."

"Will you be able to manage?"

She gave Frimton a withering look.

"Certainly…."

She moved rather uncertainly towards the door. Frimton made to take her elbow but she shook him off indignantly. She straightened her back, rose to her full height and strode off down the corridor.

Frimton turned to Henry and grinned.

"You'll have to be more careful who you let into your room, Mr.Allingham!"

Henry glared ferociously and sucked in his breath.

CHAPTER THIRTY

D.C.I.Duncombe called Inspector Johnson into his room as soon as he arrived at the station the next morning

"I spent a long time yesterday talking to the Fergusons. The girl, Sally, was open enough. She had a high opinion of Lucy Oxbury and was fond of her even though she only knew her for a few weeks. She told me that she and Frimton are to be married after Christmas. That was the reason he stayed with them last week, they wanted to sort out their wedding arrangements."

"Why didn't he tell his parents that, Sir? Wouldn't they be involved in the wedding?"

She wasn't quite so straight about that, mumbled something about seeing them later."

"Could it be that the Frimton parents didn't approve?"

"I asked Frimton himself about that. He said that he didn't want them thinking that he was marrying for money."

"That sounds as though he was."

"I'm not sure but there is no doubt that the Fergusons are well heeled and the Frimtons live much more modestly."

"Are the girl's parents happy about the marriage?"

"Yes, Father Ferguson dotes on his daughter and she is head over heels about Frimton. So long as his daughter is happy, he couldn't care if Frimton had webbed feet. Mother is happy with him, too. She thinks he is a splendid young man with his foot on the ladder of success. She thinks that he will be managing director of Tremlow's in no time at all. The only thing is that she hopes that they will stay in the area after they are married and that, to me, spells trouble. Tremlow's is a big company and he is almost certain to be moved."

"What about the son, Sir?"

"Oh yes, Thomas Ferguson. He's a different kettle of fish. Now there could be something wrong there. He was extremely nervous. I couldn't make out what was troubling him. He has a steady job, one that would bore most people but he is content in it, seems he takes it in his stride yet he started to sweat when I began to ask questions. I checked with the manager of the building society and he was very satisfied with him. He said he was most conscientious in his work but he was a very private person and never said much about himself. His prospects were good but he didn't seem to want promotion. He seemed content with his present position and keen to stay in the area. My guess is that he doesn't like Frimton very much...."

"A touch of jealousy, Sir? An upward mover showing up the man who wants to stay put?"

"Could be. Well, they could almost be opposites. Thomas Ferguson is nothing like his sister, she's open and cheerful, he's secretive and slightly dodgy. I think that she will want to get away from home sooner or later while he is the complete home bird, probably a bit of a mammy's boy. The only thing they have in common is sport. They both play badminton and go skiing in the winter. The whole family goes skiing, they can easily afford it."

"Nothing as far as the murder is concerned then, Sir?"

"No, but I'm going to follow this young man up. The branch manager is going to do some checking for me, just in case. I'll know fairly soon. The rest of the family seems clear."

"There aren't many leads, are there? I was rather hoping that the Brambles would turn up something."

"Yes, that was disappointing, but we had to try them. By the way, have you got someone tracing Baxter and Elliott's loot?"

"Yes Sir, I've put Green and Hornby onto that. It may take some time.

That day, Henry was fully occupied with his routine but he couldn't help noticing that his immediate manager, Mr.Turnbull, came into the workroom twice in the course of the morning. He simply looked round and departed. It was most unusual. For several years, Mr.Turnbull had left everything to Henry, contenting himself with an occasional question when they met in each other's offices, which they had to do from time to time. The typing pool was most curious and Henry had to be extra frosty with them.

During his lunch break, Henry reflected on Baxter's arrest. He had been right, Ernie Baxter had been up to something when he was making those phone calls from that box. He still found it difficult to believe that he had any part in the killing of Lucy Oxbury, he hadn't been there at the time. It dawned on Henry that the most important thing to know was the exact time that Lucy had been killed. He had noticed no steam in the bathroom nor moisture on any of the surfaces he had glimpsed, even allowing for the extractor fan - but the extractor fan could not have been switched on. He would have heard it. Henry recorded his latest thoughts in his notebook

After dinner, Henry sought out Elizabeth. He had not been able to speak to during dinner and there was no privacy in the sitting room. He was obliged to find her room. This was more trouble to him than he had anticipated. He was not absolutely clear which was her room and he had no wish to stumble in on Mrs.Jervis. Fortunately, his first guess proved correct, Elizabeth opened the door and invited him in.

His first impression was of a lighter and more airy room than his own. There were all manner of glass jars and bottles crowding the dressing table, there were several prints and pictures covering the walls and there were books and magazines everywhere. Henry was almost overwhelmed by the friendly brightness he encountered.

Nothing could be farther from the Spartan simplicity and gloom of his own bedroom.

"Er….I hope that I'm not disturbing you, Elizabeth, but there was no opportunity for speaking to you downstairs."

Elizabeth smiled and passed her hand over her hair in that typical gesture.

"That's all right, Henry, I was only reading. Do sit down."

"Well, I won't keep you long. It's just that I've been thinking about Baxter and his arrest. You know that he went out immediately after dinner, before we broke into the bathroom. Everyone thought that he couldn't be the murderer. But what if he had killed her before dinner?"

"Before dinner? I don't see how he could, Henry."

"Everything depends upon the exact time that she was killed and we don't know that."

"I thought Milicent Catesby said she had seen her going towards the bathroom at 7 o'clock."

"I've thought about that. Mrs.Catesby didn't leave the dining room until nearly 7 but it was 8 o'clock before she said that she had seen Miss Oxbury 'about an hour ago'. Those were her very words, weren't they?"

"Yes, I think you are right."

"Supposing she was mistaken? Supposing she had seen Miss Oxbury going to the bathroom earlier, say on her way down to dinner, not on her way back as everyone assumes. Ernie Baxter could have been the killer…."

"So could you, so could any of us."

"Miss Catesby was very vague…."

"The police seemed very happy about it, Henry."

"Baxter had every opportunity to dispose of the weapon when he went out."

"The police were satisfied about the time…."

"We don't know that. They didn't tell us. The papers said that the victim died between 7 and 8 but I have my doubts."

Elizabeth stared at him. "Doubts? What doubts?"

"Would you say that the bathrooms are large here?"

"No, they aren't. What are you driving at?"

"It was the steam, you see. There was no steam."

"Of course not. The extractor fan would have taken it all away."

"That's just it, Elizabeth. When we broke in, the extractor fan wasn't working."

The following day began with frustration for Duncombe and Johnson. Their lines of enquiry were tediously slow and unrewarding. The Chief Superintendent had called for Duncombe's appraisal and had tormented him with questions about motive. Duncombe had to confess that he had none and could only hope that further digging would unearth one. The Chief Superintendent had given Duncombe a long look and had said that he hoped so too.

They were, therefore, excited and reinvigorated by news from The Moorcroft that Mrs.Ridgeway had found a curious metal tube in one of the bedrooms while she was making the beds.

"That must be what Elliott used to get through the fire escape door."

"I wondered what happened to it. It didn't turn up in the search, did it?"

"No, that's very odd! Now it turns up under the edge of someone's mattress. Guess whose? Your Mr.Allingham's"

"What would he want with Elliott's spanner and how did he come by it?"

"More mysteries concerning Mr.Allingham! Perhaps he needed it to get rid of the murder weapon."

"He wouldn't need to, Sir. The door opens and shuts from the inside."

Duncombe glared at his Inspector. He could do without nitpicking, especially after his meeting with the Chief Superintendent.

"If your mysterious Mr.Allingham wanted to leave the hotel secretly and return later, he would need to shut the fire door then open it with this tool when he wanted to return, wouldn't he? I wouldn't be at all surprised if he couldn't throw the damned thing and had to deliver it by hand to the garden where it was found!"

"But why should he hang on to the spanner, Sir? Why not get rid of it at the same time as the rod, the murder weapon?"

"That's what I intend to find out. He's an odd bird and I'm not happy about those trousers."

"But we checked with the dry cleaners. The woman there was sure that the stains were not blood."

"Would the average woman know what bloodstains look like? I think we should bring him in for questioning. Now!"

CHAPTER THIRTY ONE

To the delight of a number of the workers in the office, Henry was obliged to leave his work and accompany two officers to the police station. There he was confronted by a very unsympathetic D.C.I. Duncombe. For nearly two hours he was questioned about the box spanner, his activities on Friday and Saturday, his attitudes, his present life and his past. He had to tell the story of his marriage and its failure. It was all a very harrowing experience. He had no idea what a box spanner was until the actual object was brought in, even then he was mystified as to what exactly it was and how it came to be in his room. His air of baffled innocence seemed to goad Duncombe. Step by step he took him through his statements, disputing every point, worrying him like a dog a rabbit. Henry could do nothing save answer patiently and thoughtfully. Early in the interview he was tempted to admit that he had followed Miss Catesby and Elliott and that he was playing sleuth but Duncombe's pace and aggression didn't allow for it.

At first, Henry couldn't understand the significance the D.C.I. put on the stained trousers he had taken to the cleaners. In his innocence, he could only repeat what he had said in his statement. Baffled by Henry's simplicity, Duncombe invited him to admit that everything was a pack of lies. Henry had carried out the murder of Lucy Oxbury and had told the story of the bolts to cast doubts on someone else. His trousers were bloodstained and needed to go the cleaners. Henry was stunned and horrified but the sure knowledge of his innocence was a second skin. He was deeply hurt but not angered by Duncombe's brutality. He did not panic but answered every question and suggestion as logically and clearly as he could.

Having failed to shake Henry's accounts, Duncombe left him and sought out his Inspector.

"I can't shake him. He's as stubborn as a cartload of mules!"

"Perhaps he is innocent, Sir. I thought he was hiding something about Saturday but I can't believe him guilty of murder."

Duncombe glowered but he felt a sneaking respect for the way Henry had stuck to his line.

"He is definitely odd. You have a go at him, Trevor, see if you can get somewhere."

Johnson was more than happy to do so. He knew Duncombe well enough to understand that his ideas often became fixed. Once he had an idea, he would chew over it until he was sure there was nothing left. If he abandoned it, it would be for good reason and it was usually without hesitation or regret. While he had the bone, it was almost impossible to take it from him. Here was a chance.

Johnson tried different questions.

"Mr. Allingham, you remember that a pair of shoes was placed in your bathroom one evening? They belonged to Mr.Frimton you said."

"Mrs.Ridgeway said they belonged to him."

"So, Elliott took them from Frimton's room while he was out. How did he do that?"

"I believe that Mr.Frimton left his door unlocked while he was away. He often left it unlocked."

"So everyone trusted each other. Did you leave your door unlocked?"

"Oh no. I always lock my door behind me. It's a habit from years ago."

"Even when you go to the bathroom?"

"Yes, invariably."

"Does Mrs.Ridgeway make the beds every morning?"

"Yes, every morning except Sunday."

"How long could such a thing as this spanner remain

under a mattress without being discovered by someone making the bed?"

"I'm sure I don't know. It would depend on the state of the bed and how much making up there was to do."

"Do you leave an untidy bed, Mr.Allingham?"

"I don't disturb it much."

"So, assuming that you didn't put it there yourself, someone could have put it there between Friday night and this morning?"

"But that person would have to have a key."

""Yes, that is so. Could Jenny Phillips have gone into your room without you knowing?"

"Jenny Phillips? I cannot imagine. She would never dream of going into a room without permission. She was a very timid little thing. Anyway, I've just remembered, the linen is changed every Monday. They would have discovered that thing on Monday. Jenny went missing on Saturday, didn't she?"

Johnson acknowledged to himself that that was a long speech from Henry and that all the questioning seemed to have loosened his tongue.

"Let us go over Saturday, Mr.Allingham. I thought you were hiding something. Is there anything more you wish to tell us about Saturday?"

Henry remained silent, unsure what to do.

"Mr.Allingham, you are in a difficult position. You can't afford to keep anything from us."

There was another long pause, then, fortified by a feeling of sympathy in Johnson's voice, Henry told him about his trailing of Miss Catesby and Elliott.

"So you were playing the amateur detective? And it led you nowhere?"

"Yes….but…."

"It never pays and it often obstructs! If we had known about it, it might have saved you from having to come in today."

The Inspector couldn't say more than this, he wasn't at

all sure that the revelation would be sufficient to reassure his Chief. He himself had a great belief in Henry. He had a sharp eye for character and his earliest meeting with Henry had convinced him that there was an extraordinarily uncomplicated individual beneath a stiff and sadly diffident exterior. He may seem to be a very distant and complicated person but there was an admirable simplicity in the man. He felt sure that Henry could never hurt anyone, not knowingly anyway. However, he was vulnerable and it seemed that someone was out to do him harm.

Henry took out his notebook, rather reluctantly.

"I have made a note of everything I have observed. I had only limited access…."

Johnson pushed it back gently.

"Mr.Allingham, I'm inclined to believe everything you have told us. I'm not sure that I can persuade the Chief Inspector to see it my way. My advice to you is to leave everything to us. Now, can we get back to the business of the spanner? It seems to me that it was planted in your room and we need to know by whom and why. This time it could not have been Mr.Elliott up to his tricks. Is there one of the others you may have offended or may have a grudge against you?"

Henry had been battered all morning, he could hardly think. He shook his head miserably. A knock on the door drew Inspector Johnson away and he was left sitting exhausted.

"Something interesting has cropped up, Trevor." Duncombe had lost all his aggressive manner. "The Building Society manager has been checking the Ferguson boy's accounts and has found one or two irregularities. He thinks I should look into them." Johnson whistled softly. "I'll go down there myself and see what threads I can pick up. You finish with Allingham and let him go, will you?"

Trevor Johnson was flabbergasted. His Chief had bombarded Henry Allingham all morning in the sure conviction that Henry was the murderer, now he was coolly departing on another trail leaving him to clear up what was left behind. Well it wasn't the first time it had happened and it was partly what he was paid for, he had better get on with it. He put on a cheerful countenance, at least the heat was off Henry, for a while.

It was a very relieved Henry who was escorted back to his office in another police car. The typing pool was all abuzz. Henry had only time to smooth himself down before he was summoned to Mr.Turnbull's office. Mr.Turnbull did not speak but escorted Henry to the Senior Manager.

The Senior Manager, Mr.Ormesby-Phelps, made it clear to Henry that he did not like employees missing time for whatever reason. He commented favourably on Henry's loyalty over the years but pointed out that the whole firm was anticipating a programme of modernisation. Modern machines would soon be installed and the clerical staff would, inevitably, be reduced, possibly drastically. He couldn't say when it was all to begin. Perhaps later this year, maybe sooner. He felt that this was an opportunity to inform Henry. Dreadful though it may seem, at a time when the firm was, apparently, prospering, not even his own job, he coughed self-deprecatingly, was safe. That was all.

The implied threat was not lost on Henry. It was almost the last straw. He got through the rest of the day on autopilot. He hardly knew what he was doing, only routine sustained him. When it was time to go, he put on his coat and hat and walked out slowly, oblivious of the open sneers about him.

Inspector Johnson was thinking hard. The discovery of the box spanner meant that the murderer was still at The

Moorcroft or had an accomplice there. Someone had tried to implicate Henry Allingham. Why? Why bother? Why not let things take their course. What had the murderer to fear? Was the murderer aware that Henry had done some sleuthing? Did he or she think that had discovered something without realising its significance? He was sure that if Henry had discovered something really important he would have told him while he was in the interview room.

He went down to speak to Denzil Elliott. Elliott was remarkably cheerful. He had been told that someone had agreed to stand bail and he expected to be released at any minute. Johnson asked him directly about the turning device. As soon as he introduced the topic, Elliott cried out that he had wondered what had happened to it. On the morning of the murder, while he was in the bathroom, someone had taken it out of his suitcase. He had been upset because it was tucked inside the lining at the corner alongside one of the strengtheners where it should have been safe. The policeman who had searched his room the previous night had rummaged through all his clothes but had missed the extra hard piece in the corner of the suitcase. He hadn't been able to guess who had taken it.

Johnson asked Elliott where the suitcase had been while he was in the bathroom. Elliott assured him that it was on his bed because he had looked in it for a new packet of razor blades and had left it open. Johnson was surprised that Elliott should have kept his suitcase 'in use' when there were drawers and cupboards available. Elliott smiled and declared that he had always been ready for a 'quick flit', after all, in his profession, he never knew when he would need to make a run for it.

"So, the suitcase was open on your bed. Did you lock your room door before you went down to the bathroom?"

"Nah. There was a run on the bathroom that morning. We all had to use the one, if you remember. I'd already been down once. I heard somebody coming back up the

199

stairs and thought they must have finished so I just ran. Anyway, no one goes into anybody's room in The Moorcroft."

He met the Inspector's eye and had the grace to blush.

"How did anyone else know what to look for? You saw the thing had gone immediately?"

"Yes, the lining had been torn, enough to catch my eye straight away."

"It couldn't have been Baxter?"

"Nah, he's never been in my room."

"Maybe whoever it was went instinctively for the corners. No one saw you coming through the fire door?"

"No, I was careful to look and listen before I came in."

"What about seeing you from the outside?"

"It's possible but it was always dark and I was always careful."

Johnson fell silent. The corridor to the fire door was very dark. So too was the other end of that floor where the stairs went up to the attic. If the stairs to the attic were not lit, it would be almost impossible to see anyone standing there. Elliott's room was the nearest to the fire escape, if he came in quickly and rushed into his room, he might not see anyone watching him. He made a mental note to check this for himself.

"This box spanner, you had it specially made?"

"Yeh. I couldn't make it myself, could I? I have a mate who's a blacksmith, he made it for me."

"How did you cut the slots in the bolt head?"

"Er...I filed first then I used a hacksaw. Took a few spells, I can tell you!"

"You must have started soon after you came here?"

"Yeh, as soon as I found my way around....I've been helping you, haven't I? You'll mention that, won't you. When I'm in front of the beak?"

D.C.Duncombe did not take long over his visit to the Maskerley and District Building Society. A nervously fussy manager, Mr.Thompson, met him at the entrance and ushered him secretively into his office. On his desk, carefully arranged, were two heavy ledgers and some passbooks. The manager indicated a chair next to his and proceeded to open the first ledger at a previously marked page.

"I wouldn't have noticed anything wrong if a customer hadn't questioned his interest this morning. His passbook entries were in order but the entries in the ledger did not correspond for two months."

"So your customer got no interest on the sum he had paid in for two months. I presume that Ferguson himself made good these sums?"

"Yes, the writing is his and it has happened at least twice, as you can see."

"Has it happened to anyone else?"

"I won't know until I've checked every passbook. That will be an enormous task."

"Was it an elderly customer?"

"Yes he was. Do you think....?"

"Well, often an elderly person doesn't think of checking his interest. He trusts his Building Society."

"Quite!"

"I'd better see your Mr.Ferguson. Is he at work?"

"Yes, I haven't had time to see him about this. Since you enquired about him only yesterday, I thought I would get in touch with you straight away."

Thomas Ferguson was shocked to learn that his foolproof system of borrowing had been discovered. He had carefully chosen the investors he had borrowed from. They had to be elderly investors who made the occasional large deposit in cash and who seldom made a withdrawal. He took a chance that no change of pattern would occur to disturb his plan. Under pressure, he admitted to using the borrowed money to gamble with. He lived carefully enough to be able to repay the sums borrowed in a relatively short time. He had not gone mad at his gambling, he had not lost heavily, in fact he had had some modest wins and thought that given time he could become very successful at it.

It didn't take Duncombe long to discover that Ferguson was not as happy at home as he at first believed. He was the quiet, less able member of an extravert and successful family. He felt his position keenly but kept his resentment to himself. He had plans to become independent in a big way. He didn't want to escape so much as to be high in the esteem of the other members of the family. He didn't want to advance in the Building Society. For his scheme to work he needed to be 'on the counter'. Duncombe asked him about Lucy Oxbury and Ferguson was quick to say that he found her attractive. Pressed further, he said that he would have liked to know her better. He had only met her once, when his sister had brought her back after a rehearsal. He hadn't asked her out but he intended to do so when his sister next brought her round.

"I must ask you, Mr.Ferguson, where were you last Friday evening?"

Ferguson looked at him sharply and sat thinking.

"Last Friday…. I was at home, I think. My parents went out to dinner and my sister, Sally, went to her play rehearsal. I was alone in the house."

"You did not go out again?"

"Oh…I went down to the corner shop on Waverley Road for some envelopes. I'd written a letter and couldn't find an envelope to put it in. It must have been about nine o'clock because my sister came in soon after I got back. She usually gets back about 9.15.

"So there is no one to corroborate your story?"

"Corroborate?

"Yes sir. And while I am about it, where were you on Saturday afternoon?"

"Oh, I went to the football match at Castor Park."

202

"You went alone?"

"Yes, I often go alone. Sometimes I go with my father."

"What time did you return Sir?"

"I stayed in town and went to the pictures. I didn't get back until after eleven."

"Did you see anyone you knew there?"

"How do you mean?"

"Could any one say that they had seen you either at the match or at the pictures?"

"No, I don't think that there was anyone, I didn't see anyone."

"Mr.Ferguson, I would like you to come down to the station and make a sworn statement."

"You mean that Mr.Thompson is charging me?"

"He may do so in due course, sir, but I am more concerned at the moment with a murder case. I want to be sure that you are telling me the truth about Friday and Saturday."

"But...."

"Collect your coat and hat, Mr.Ferguson, we shouldn't be long. I'm sure that Mr.Thompson will want to see you when you get back."

CHAPTER THIRTY TWO

Henry lingered long in the bathroom for the very first time. He found the hot bath relaxing and he certainly needed to relax. He also needed to think. He had worried all the way back to the hotel and his mind was not yet clear. He found the Senior Manager's news most disturbing. He had been badly shaken, particularly by the thought of being made redundant, but as he lay, the threat of redundancy receded. In its place came something more disturbing. Inspector Johnson's voice took over from that of Mr.Ormesby-Phelps. Someone had tried to implicate him in the murders by planting that metal object in his room. Why? Who could it have been? His orderly mind struggled to assert itself. As it did so, the shock and pain of the afternoon left him. He became the new Henry again. His notebook would help him to organise his thoughts. He hurriedly dried himself and rushed to his room. He did not hear a quiet voice trying to attract his attention.

He was methodical, he never left his door unlocked. Could it have been someone on Mrs.Ridgeway's staff, even Mrs.Ridgeway herself? Henry couldn't bring himself to believe this. It made no sense unless it was meant as a joke. It would have been a very sinister joke! Elliott might have tried it but he had not been released, as far as he was aware. Neither had Baxter. The bad-tempered Jackson might try a trick of that kind but why should he and how could he have got into the room? Henry consulted his notebook and saw at once that there had been three residents in his room the previous evening.

Elizabeth had called to see him but Mrs.Jervis and Frimton had both been in the room while he was fetching the glass of water. Either of them could have pushed the wretched thing under his mattress. He sat and thought it all over. Frimton had known Lucy Oxbury better than anyone in the hotel. According to Elizabeth, he was in town on the Thursday and the Saturday and was therefore within reach of the hotel. He could have carried out the murders of both Lucy and Jenny. He had no idea why he should do so. Could it be that Lucy had rejected him? Henry sighed, it was difficult when he knew so little.

He knew Mrs.Jervis a little better, or thought he did. She seemed predictable enough until Saturday when he had seen her with that stranger. Then she had been upset and had laughed at Miss Catesby. Had she knocked at his door just so that she could plant the metal tube? But why should she want to kill Lucy Oxbury and why should she seek to implicate him? Perhaps she had simply taken an opportunity to get rid of the tube that presented itself by chance. Henry could not believe that someone he had known for some time would choose to be wilfully malicious towards him. A Mrs.Sibley, yes, a Mrs.Jervis, no!

There was a light tap on his door. Henry rose cautiously and went over to it. The tap was repeated. He opened the door a fraction. It was Elizabeth.

"You didn't hear me when you were on the stairs. Something is bothering you, Henry. What is it? Have you discovered something else?"

Henry was reluctant to speak. He wanted to confide in Elizabeth but he knew that if he began he would find himself telling her everything that had happened that day. It would have been too much.

"Nothing for you to worry about…Elizabeth."

He was astonished at himself. He had almost called her 'dear'. Had their relationship advanced so far? They sat in silence. Suddenly Henry remembered the glimpse he had had of her room with its warm femininity. The bottles and jars on her dressing table, the pictures on her walls. He looked about his room and saw it for what it was, bare, Spartan, cold.

"Tell me, Henry. A worry shared, you know."

Henry hesitated.

"I was asked to go down to the police station today."

"You, Henry, whatever for?"

"They found a piece of metal under my mattress. It was used to open the firedoor."

"The firedoor?"

"They assumed that as it was found in my room, I had opened the firedoor and I was the murderer."

"Oh no, surely not!"

"Yes, I'm afraid so, that is the Chief Inspector thought so. Inspector Johnson thought someone had put it there deliberately to incriminate me."

Elizabeth was shocked.

"Why should anyone wish to do that, Henry?"

"What is more to the point, Elizabeth, who was it? I have noted that, apart from yourself, two other people were in my room yesterday, Mr.Frimton and Mrs.Jervis. Not long after you had gone, Mrs.Jervis came to apologise for the fuss she had caused for laughing at Miss Catesby. She suddenly felt faint so I went to the bathroom to fetch a glass of water. When I got back, Mr.Frimton was in here seeing to her. Either of them could have pushed the thing under the mattress while I was out."

Elizabeth was staring at him.

"I can hardly believe it! You are implying that one of them is Lucy's murderer?"

"And of Jenny Phillips."

"But I have known Christine Jervis for…." She broke off.

"That's just it!" Henry grew animated. "Do any of us really know each other? Look how Mrs.Jervis broke down the other evening, that was quite unexpected. Laughing at Miss Catesby was not in character either. I can't think why Mrs.Jervis should want to murder them, but she is certainly strong enough. Perhaps there is something wrong with her?"

"But what about Mr.Frimton? He talked to Lucy more than anyone else. Perhaps he had a reason to kill her, he was in town..?"

"Yes, I remember you said so. I think I should tell the Inspector, even if it is only a suspicion."

"Oh, I don't think that would be wise, Henry do you? Not yet. There is simply nothing to go on. He might think that you were over-reacting....in self defence."

"Yes, I see. You mean it is too soon after my interrogation? He asked me at the time if I knew of anyone who might have done it and I couldn't think. He might think it strange if I went back now."

"Yes, Henry, I think you should wait another twenty four hours."

"I'm not happy about it Elizabeth. What if he tries something else?"

"We must keep our eyes and ears open. We should be particularly careful that we are not overheard. We should only meet in my room. If I wanted to see you urgently I could knock on your door, say four times, and you could follow me up."

Henry smiled briefly. There was something disarmingly childlike about this proposal that took away some of the tension in his situation, but after Elizabeth left he thought of his future again and he became very depressed. He had never doubted the permanence of his occupation. He had saved a modest sum and had invested in a reliable insurance policy. He would not starve but he could hardly contemplate life without the inevitable routine. There was something almost shameful about being made redundant. He had believed himself invaluable, what was he to think now?

Inspector Johnson was busy tidying up loose ends concerning the robberies when D.C.I.Duncombe brought Ferguson to the station. Sergeant Green was assigned to take down Ferguson's statement while the Chief spoke to his Inspector.

"We have another suspect, Trevor. The Ferguson boy was on the fiddle at the Building Society but it turns out that he was interested in Lucy Oxbury and he has lied about where he was on Friday night. It may not be significant, of course, but the coincidences are interesting. Could the murder have been an outside job after all?"

"I've just been thinking about that, Sir. That top corridor where the stairs go up to the attic can be very dark. Someone could have hidden there then left by the fire escape, but he would have had to know the place and have to get in without being seen...."

"There are two outsider possibilities, this Mr.Ferguson and our Mr.Frimton. Now, here's the interesting thing - Ferguson claims that he was home alone on Friday night, so does Frimton. Both of them couldn't be alone because Frimton was staying at the Ferguson house at the time."

"Well, they couldn't have been working together or they would have given each other alibis."

"All very interesting! I'm going to put some pressure on this young man, he doesn't know he's made a mistake yet."

"Sir, Elliott and Baxter are both out on bail. Baxter has arranged it for both of them."

"Fine! Fine!" The D.C.I. was eager to get down to the interview room.

Johnson shook his head. If it was Ferguson who committed the murder, he couldn't have planted the box-spanner. However, Frimton could and it could be that it was Frimton who wasn't home that night. But what was the point of planting that wretched spanner - a temporary diversion? It would have been temporary unless Henry Allingham had confessed. Had the person who planted it expected Henry to confess? Why? Perhaps that person thought Henry could be pushed into a confession. That had proved to be a mistake. Henry Allingham may look as though he was 'on the brink', in fact he was eminently sane. Johnson was absolutely certain of that.

Unless Ferguson could come up with one, Johnson could think of no motive for Lucy Oxbury's death. The more he thought, the more he was convinced that the secret of it all lay with Lucy herself. They simply didn't know enough about her. She had not been in Maskerley long enough for there to be a motive as far as the locals were concerned. Even if Frimton or Ferguson were passionately in love with her, there had not been time for them to develop sufficient jealousy, rage or frustration to provoke them to such a deed. She had not been wayward or provocative, she had been friendly and pleasant to everyone.

Johnson had been at his desk too long. It was his turn to feel the need to stretch his legs. It was time to find out more about Lucy and that meant a visit to her home.

CHAPTER THIRTY THREE

It was dark by the time Inspector Johnson arrived in Catton. It took a while for him to find the right street and the Oxbury house was at the far end. All the houses were impressive stone-built semis having large front gardens with ample room for trees and bushes. The hedges on each side of the Oxbury house were tall and forbidding. Johnson was glad that there was a moon, even so, the path was often in total shadow. He had to peer at the doorframe to find the bell. First, a powerful outside light above his head took him by surprise and dazzled him, then, when the door opened, the light inside the porch was so poor that he couldn't tell whether it was Mr.or Mrs.Oxley who had opened the door. He hastened to show his warrant card.

It was clear that he was most unwelcome but Johnson had not anticipated anything else. Mr.Oxbury led him into the sitting room, switched on a light and left him standing there. He had hardly spoken. A moment or two later, Mrs.Oxbury entered looking extremely angry.

"I don't know how we can help you, Inspector, I thought we had said everything there was to be said when we were down at Maskerley."

"Well, Mrs.Oxbury, we need to know as much as possible about Lucy. We are most baffled…."

"That may well be, Inspector, but is that any reason why you should be troubling us at this time in the evening?"

"Mrs.Oxbury, we are engaged in a murder enquiry. There is no rest for anyone until the murder is solved. I should have thought that you, the parents, would be most anxious to help, whatever the time of day." Johnson's voice was steely.

"Yes dear," Mr.Oxbury was standing behind him, "it's

not very late. I'm sure the Inspector is right. We must help him as much as possible."

Mrs.Oxbury snorted, turned and sat herself down in an armchair. It was her husband who invited Johnson to sit, he chose to sit on the settee opposite the fireplace. There was an electric fire in the grate but no one moved to switch it on. The room was cold and uncomfortable. Mr.Oxbury crossed to sit in the armchair on the other side of the fireplace and stooped to switch on a small table lamp at its side. Now there was a hint of warmth, but how dark the rest of the room still was! The only other light was the very low-powered standard lamp in the corner near the door which had been switched on when Johnson entered. Johnson adjusted his coat and pulled fussily at his trouser creases to give him time to look round. Though it lacked light and heat, the room was well furnished, almost cluttered, he thought. There were sideboards, two or three side tables and several pictures in broad frames. The mantelpiece was crowded with vases and ornaments.

"To help us picture Lucy, we wanted to know about her school and her friends"

"You could have asked…?" "Well, now," Mr.Oxbury was determined to forestall if not to contain his wife's ill humour, "Lucy went to Catton Primary and Junior School then won a place at Broughton High. She did very well there."

"Broughton is quite a distance away. What is it, sixteen miles?"

"Not too far by bus. It only took 40 minutes. Lucy never lingered unless there was a hockey match."

"Lucy was a good athlete?"

"We understand she was."

"Did Lucy have many friends?"

"Of course she had friends…!"

"Lucy was friendly with everyone."

"Who were her particular friends?"

"Well now…."

"Once she started work she forgot her school friends. She had to look to her new life."

"Were these particular friends local?"

"Oh no! There weren't many…."

"Don't forget Marjorie Forster and Dorothy Herbert, dear! They were girls who lived nearby, one of them lived at the bottom of our street."

"As I was saying, none of them came near once Lucy went out to work."

"Was Lucy close to them when she was at school?"

There was a snort from Mrs.Oxbury expressing astonishment at the Inspector's obtuseness. Her husband continued patiently.

"They sometimes came here to discuss homework…."

"They came here far too often. They simply used Lucy. I warned them off."

"What about in the Sixth Form? Isn't that the time when most friendships become set?"

"We don't know about her friends in the Sixth Form. She didn't bring any of them here. Of course, she had a lot of studying to do for her 'A' levels."

"But what about the holidays, Mr.Oxbury? Did she not have friends for the holidays or go on holidays with friends?"

"Oh!" It was Mrs.Oxbury again. "There was no money for holidays or for entertaining visitors. We lived very quietly and the children did too."

"After she started work, did she have friends or visitors?"

Mr.Oxbury hurried in. "She was friendly with a number of people in the Tennis Club and in our Chapel. I don't think there was anyone in particular."

"I simply wanted to talk to someone who knew Lucy at school or at work who might shed light on what happened to her. Can you give me the addresses of those girls you first mentioned?"

"Well now, for a start, Marjorie Forster's people

moved away from Catton last year. I'm not sure what became of Dorothy Herbert. We don't see many people…."

There was a call from the corridor outside. The door opened and Johnson was aware of a tall, thin figure standing hesitating, not quite inside.

"Certainly, darling! Come along, there's no need to concern yourself with us."

Mrs.Oxbury rose quickly and ushered her son out before her. Her voice was all concern. Whatever her son wanted, she was going to see to without hesitation. The change in her was amazing.

Johnson rose. He thought he was wasting his time. He made for the door and was just in time to see Mrs.Oxbury escorting her son into what must have been the kitchen, her arm around him, her voice a soft murmur.

"Is it possible I might see Lucy's room?"

Lucy's father looked at Johnson sharply.

"What would be the point of that, Inspector?"

"It might just help me to understand your daughter, Mr.Oxbury."

"Very well, follow me."

Johnson was led into a small bedroom at the back of the house. There was a single bed, a wardrobe and a dressing table, all bare. He ignored his host and unceremoniously opened the wardrobe, it was empty. So were the drawers. He turned fiercely.

"I don't understand, Mr.Oxbury. Is this not your daughter's bedroom?"

"It used to be our son's but when Lucy left home we let him have the bigger bedroom."

"But where are all her things? Surely she must have left some clothes and other things behind?"

"My wife had them removed."

"Removed?" Johnson couldn't prevent his voice rising. "You mean destroyed?"

"You must understand, my wife has been very upset."

Johnson bit his lip.

"I think I must point out to you, Mr.Oxbury, that if your wife destroyed your daughter's possessions after she was killed, she has placed herself in a very difficult position."

"And what do you think you are doing, Inspector? This is a monstrous intrusion!" Mrs.Oxbury had followed them upstairs.

"Mrs.Oxbury! Do you not understand? I am conducting an enquiry into a murder, the murder of your daughter! There are many things I need to know. You may have destroyed valuable evidence when you threw your daughter's things away. In view of your attitude, I could bring a charge of obstruction against you." He turned sharply to the husband. "Mr.Oxbury, I would be grateful if you would see to it that your wife fully understands her position. Nothing, nothing at all that has anything to do with your daughter must be touched, moved or tampered with in any way until the investigation is over. If necessary, I will post a constable here to see that nothing more goes amiss."

Johnson was furious, he could hardly contain himself.

"Now, I'll thank you to let me see anything that may have any connection with your daughter. If you object in any way, I will get a search warrant and, tomorrow, I will turn this house upside down. No stone will go unturned until your daughter's killer is found. A very obvious conclusion will be drawn from any further obstruction!"

"Mother!" A further cry from below had Mrs.Oxbury racing away downstairs. Her husband stood stock still, unable to speak.

"Is this the other bedroom?"

Oxbury could only nod. Johnson found it the very antithesis of the small one. It was tidy but it bore all the evidence of being lived in. The bed had a cosy covering. A table near the window had a smart desk lamp shedding warm light on open books. There was a small, well-filled bookcase. Old toys were piled high on the wardrobe. A smart portable radio stood on a corner table. Near it were two photos in frames. Johnson looked carefully at them. One was the son with his parents when the boy was about eight years old, the other was of a group of the boy's school friends.

"Are there no letters or photographs belonging to your daughter?"

Oxbury shook his head and avoided Johnson's eye. Johnson snorted and made his way downstairs. He had had enough! As he moved towards the front door he brushed against one of the side tables in the hall and something fell. Instinctively, he stooped and picked up the object. Boldly he turned it over, his normal studious politeness had evaporated. Even in the poor light he recognised a small white cardboard box as the sort in which pieces of wedding cake are sent through the post. He deliberately read the address. In spite of the scrawled writing, the name Lucy Oxbury was clear enough.

"When did this arrive?"

"Only this morning."

"And what were you going to do with it?"

"Well….we couldn't give it to Lucy, could we?"

"It didn't occur to you that we might be interested in it? Have any other letters or parcels come for Lucy?"

"Not since…." The thin voice died away.

"Could you tell me who might have sent this?"

"It could have come from…Dorothy Herbert…."

"I thought you said…how could you know that?"

"Well…a wedding invitation came two or three weeks ago."

"So Lucy and Dorothy *were* close?"

"Well…."

"Did Lucy attend the wedding?"

"Er…no… we didn't send the invitation on…."

There was a long pause.

"Where does Dorothy Herbert live?"

"Her parents live in Ventnor Gardens just down the road. I wouldn't know the number."

"Goodbye, Mr.Oxbury. I shall be calling on you again, you may be sure. Once again let me warn you about obstructing the police. It is a very serious matter!"

Trevor Johnson had always believed himself to be a tolerant and amiable person. When, eventually, he knocked on the door of the Herbert household, he was not in a humour to be denied anything. As it was, he found Dorothy Herbert herself, visiting her parents that very evening. This was a piece of luck that instantly restored his good humour.

He asked about Lucy and was greeted with noises of disgust from all present.

"She didn't even answer our Dot's invitation."

"They were friendly for years, weren't you Dot?"

"Stuck up, she was!"

"I blame her parents, they didn't want their Lucy having anything to do with our Dot!"

"Oh Lucy was alright. We got on well. She would always help me with my homework. She was always kind. We had lots of laughs. She was very funny was Lucy. Mind you, I was very disappointed when I didn't hear from her. When we were at school, we swore to come to each other's weddings, we had a right giggle about it. I hadn't seen her for ever so long. I left Broughton High after 'O' levels. Then I saw her once in the High Street and she told me she was working at the solicitors. I wasn't surprised. I told her about John. 'Mind you send me an invite', she said and I told her we weren't even engaged yet. That's why I was so sure she would come to the wedding."

"You read about her murder, did you?"

"Murder?"

"Yes, Dot, I'm sorry we didn't tell you but you were still on your honeymoon. When you got back, you went straight into your new flat and we haven't seen you till now."

"Murder? Lucy? Not Lucy? Why would anyone want to murder Lucy?"

"That is why I am here. We have no idea what the motive could have been. We are wondering if there was anything to do with the past, something you might remember."

"Lucy lived a very quiet life. Her Dad and Mam hardly let her out. She was fun at school, you'd never believe it when you think of her stuffy folks. She was a bit of a madcap but she never got into real trouble, she always knew when to stop. She was quite tough really."

"You said that you weren't surprised that she went to work with the solicitors."

"No, well she was very bright was Lucy and she was always interested in that sort of thing."

"What do you mean?"

"The law, things to do with the law. We once went on a visit to the County Court. I thought it was boring but Lucy lapped it up. She went back the very next day and sat in the press box. She got permission from Miss Stanley on account of her doing a project or something about it."

"Did Lucy have any other close friends?"

"Eeeh, I don't think she had. Not from school anyway, that I know of. Not close. I don't think her Mam and Dad let her have friends. They never invited anybody for tea or anything like that. I was hardly let into the house. Once or twice Madge Forster and me went to do some homework together. We sat in the back kitchen. Madge got the giggles and Mrs.Oxbury sent us off and that was the end of that."

"Lucy didn't have a boyfriend?"

"I don't think so. There were a lot who fancied her. She was a good looking girl but she didn't fancy anybody in particular. She liked a laugh with the lads and that was about it. Anyway, she wouldn't have been allowed out and I can't imagine any of the lads standing up to her Mam. She was a proper tartar.

"What about Lucy's brother, were they close?"

"David? Completely spoilt! He was only little when we were there. His mother doted on him. Wrapped him up in cotton wool, she did. Wouldn't let anyone touch him, not even Lucy."

CHAPTER THIRTY FOUR

It was almost a week since that dreadful evening. Millicent Catesby pondered as she took up her washbag in its crocheted linen cover. She dusted it lightly with the fingers of one hand, sadly it had seen better days. Her Aunt Lottie had made it for her when she was a very young woman. Those had been golden days. All three of her aunts had been kind to her. They had helped her to be well dressed and had seen to it that she received many invitations. Her Mummy and Daddy had been too preoccupied with their church work but they had encouraged her to visit, to attend parties and social functions of all kinds. They had been generous, too. It had all come to this.

She regarded herself in the long mirror of her wardrobe, bracing herself and stretching her neck. She turned her head slowly from side to side, opening her eyes wide and touching her skin with the slender fingers of one hand. She thought she still had style. She was sound in wind and limb and there were only a few wrinkles round her eyes and mouth. She dressed well and held herself as well as any woman half her age. There was no reason why she should not grace the top table at any worthwhile function. She was about to give herself a self-congratulatory twirl when she sensed the incongruity of the washbag still in one hand.

Sighing, she picked up her favourite towel, the one with the pale pink embroidery - they didn't make them like that any more, no one would bother to spend time embroidering the dreadfully thin towels one saw in the shops nowadays - and went towards the bathroom. Again she was seized with anxiety. She believed that the feeling of anxiety would always plague her every time she approached the bathroom. Perhaps she would have to leave The Moorcroft. The thought of having to establish a new retreat brought a tear to her eye. She brushed it away angrily, she was made of sterner stuff! Come Christmas, it would all be forgotten.

She stretched a hand to turn the doorknob and found that it was turning itself. She stepped back to allow whoever it was to emerge and was so shocked at the sight of Denzil Elliott that she gave a little scream and promptly fainted.

"Whatever is it now?" Mrs.Ridgeway had been fetched from the kitchen again. It seemed as though this was a rerun of the previous Friday evening's events. Miss Catesby was sitting on the top stair, shivering and whimpering. Beside her stood Mrs.Jervis and Denzil Elliott, the latter in a welter of embarrassment and rage.

"It must have been the shock." Mrs.Jervis was saying.

"I am not responsible for the old bat's hysterics. I'd just come out of the bathroom, perfectly natural. She let out a scream and fell in a faint. It gave me a right old turn, I can tell you! What is wrong with her?"

"She hasn't got over the night of the murder. You can't blame her, can you?" Mrs.Elmwood had joined them.

"It was the shock of seeing you, we all thought that you had been taken away." Mrs.Jervis was blunt.

"Well, I'm back, why should that cause a fuss?"

"Yes, ladies, both Mr.Elliott and Mr.Baxter are back so we must get used to seeing them again. Mrs.Jervis, would you mind helping Miss Catesby back to her room? She can have a nap before dinner…"

"I don't want a nap, thank you. I'll use the bathroom now." Miss Catesby quickly pulled herself together. Although there were tears still on her cheeks, she elbowed the others aside and quickly bolted the bathroom door behind her.

"Well!" Mrs.Jervis was astonished.

"Millicent always makes a special effort on her Ladies' Circle nights." Mrs.Elmwood smiled and made her way downstairs.

There was much awkwardness at dinner. Miss Catesby sat in silence, totally unwilling to look in the direction of the table where Elliott and Baxter sat together putting up as normal a performance as possible under the circumstances. Mrs.Jervis sat stiffly, hardly able to stifle her curiosity. Sarah the maid was obviously nervous and didn't like to linger at their table and, soon, Mrs.Ridgeway took her place. Walter Jackson was discountenanced by finding his usual place next to Ernie Baxter taken by Denzil Elliott. He was unable to satisfy his immediate curiosity without raising his voice and risking a snub. He possessed just enough sensitivity to feel he must wait. Henry was too involved with his new self-imposed task of listening and observing to converse with anyone. Only Mrs.Elmwood was relaxed enough to ask about their experience without giving offence.

Henry marvelled at the way Elizabeth was able to soothe everyone she spoke to. She was genuinely interested in everyone. She had such a gentle manner, she never seemed to intrude and always showed concern. He smiled in her direction.

The two men on bail responded remarkably light-heartedly. They had said that they had been 'helping with enquiries' and had been held over because there were several matters the police had asked them to assist them in. They ignored a snort from Miss Catesby and assured Mrs.Elmwood that they had been told not to talk about it while the investigation was proceeding. Most of their audience were convinced that it was the murders they had been questioned about.

Mrs.Jervis couldn't restrain herself any longer. She asked them what progress had been made then hastened to hope that the two men would soon get over their ordeal. She blushed at what was a possible faux pas and chose to concentrate on her coffee. Henry fished out his notebook again.

"Would it interest you to know that an obsession can develop in a very short time?"

"What sort of time do you mean, Sir?"

"A matter of a few days, certainly a couple of weeks."

D.C.I.Duncombe was expanding on his latest idea. Inspector Johnson was hankering after a well-earned sleep but he wanted to have a word with his Chief and he had to indulge him first.

"This Ferguson boy developed an obsession about Lucy Oxbury almost from first meeting her. He admits that she was never out of his thoughts, says it was love at first sight. He thinks that Lucy Oxbury hardly noticed him and that made it much worse. He was determined to see her and to invite her out and couldn't wait for the next time his sister invited her home. He went to The Moorcroft but was too nervous to go in and ask for her."

"Did he know what time she usually left for her rehearsal?"

"Well, he claims he went to meet her coming out on her way to the rehearsal. Obviously, she never came out. He thought she had probably gone early but he still hung about, in case. He was there quite a long time but he sticks to his story that he was too nervous to go in. I've had his father on the phone, he's bringing a solicitor with him. When they come, I'll have one more round of questions then I'll let him go. We'll have him back first thing tomorrow morning."

"Sir, I wanted a word. I've been out at Catton, visiting the Oxburys...."

"Oh, that's where you've been? I was looking for you earlier. I wanted you to have a go at Ferguson to see if you could get anything different out of him."

"I'd like to follow a line on Lucy through her school tomorrow."

"What? Where do you think that will lead? I'll bet you

got nothing out of the Oxburys…."

There was a commotion out at the front desk.

"That will be old Ferguson. I'd better go. I'll need you here tomorrow, mind. After that you can go where you like." Trevor Johnson was not troubled, he knew that he could make further enquiries by phone.

CHAPTER THIRTY FIVE

Henry Allingham woke the next morning in a more determined mood than ever before. He was acutely aware that his life was at a crisis point but he was also aware of a new sense of purpose. It was a different feeling to that exhilaration he had felt on the morning of the murder. He felt a new need to fend for himself. After a good night's sleep, his mind had cleared. He had been menaced on all sides. Now he felt strong and capable of standing up to everyone and everything. He must anticipate change and welcome it. He must be prepared.

As he walked to the bathroom, he re-appraised his surroundings. The parlour palm in the pot at the corner just before the stairs was vigorous and upright. Its pot was a generous ceramic container, something to be admired. Today, Henry saw it as something quite different. It was tall enough and broad enough to offer a screen to anyone who cared to linger either side of it. There was a similar plant at each corner to the stairs. If one of the corridors was unlit, the subdued lighting on the stairs would make it quite easy for someone to stand behind such a plant unseen. The corridor lights were on time switches to save electricity, there were plenty of opportunities for concealment. Henry began to understand how anyone might make their way about without being seen, just a pause to see that the coast was clear then a rush to the shelter of the next plant.

He tried it for himself when he came out of the bathroom. He reached the third floor astonishingly quickly and was wondering what to do next when he heard someone unlocking their bedroom door. He glanced back from the shelter of the palm fronds and was able to see Miss Catesby entering the third floor bathroom. He did not linger but returned to the safety of his own room and completed his dressing.

It was easier to move around the hotel than he had guessed. Before this he had believed it difficult to move at all without someone or other noticing. Apparently the secret lay in a combination of speed and silence. He had always been slow and deliberate in his movements, now he was thrilled to think how quickly and easily he had moved. There were two other requirements, an anticipation of others' movements and the capacity to reconnoitre.

As he breakfasted, he thought of the ceramic plant pots. They were large enough to hide behind, perhaps they were large enough to hide something in. The murder weapon had been found the next day, could it have been hidden overnight then thrown away the next morning? If the weapon had not been thrown away as the police had suggested, it must have been carried from the bathroom and hidden until an opportunity occurred to get rid of it later. But the police had been very thorough, surely they would not have ignored the ceramic pots?

His thoughts were disturbed by the others arriving one by one. No one was very communicative. Henry could understand why. Even Elizabeth gave him a sharp look as she came in. He had no time to tell her of his new thoughts. He left for work soon afterwards.

Inspector Johnson knew it was to be a crowded day so he made it his business to look up the number of Broughton High School as soon as he got to his office. After a number of attempts, he managed to speak to the Headmistress before she needed to go to morning assembly. He thought it easy to picture Miss Stanley from her voice. It was light and firm and encouraging with a strong hint of sharpness behind it.

"Lucy Oxbury? We were all shocked to read about her murder. Such a pleasant girl, very able too ….how can I help you? Oh, I remember, it was rather unusual, a party went to the County Court, part of a Civics lesson. Yes, Lucy went back the next day, she had permission because she was doing a small project on….'Criminals and the Law' I think it was. It was an original idea though most of it was culled from newspapers. She wanted to put something up-to-date in it, something she could write herself. She was awarded a prize for it. No I can't remember any of the cases in it, I just glanced through it before the adjudication. After all, it is eight or nine years since she wrote it. Ah, it would be Miss Webster, she left us four years ago, she married and went abroad somewhere. Sorry about that, is it important? I see. I think I understand. It must be very frustrating. Look, Inspector, I must go now. I'll make an enquiry or two but I can't offer much hope. Goodbye!"

Further investigation of Tom Ferguson proved difficult and tedious. His solicitor was keen and efficient. Ferguson didn't seem troubled by being caught out in a lie. His solicitor claimed that it was the action of a young man who was infatuated and, being shy, felt guilty about his wish to see the object of his devotion and was very confused. Ferguson had not known what time Lucy Oxbury would normally leave the hotel. He insisted that he had gone there as soon as he could that evening. D.C.I.Duncombe was relentless in his questions about times. Why had Ferguson been in such a hurry to leave the house when he didn't know when Lucy left the hotel? Why had he spent so much time hanging about? If he had not known the hotel, how had he found his way there so quickly? Ferguson stumbled and hesitated again and again, provoking further probing. He showed no understanding of the awkwardness of his position. After further attempts to establish accurate timings and to shake the fragile testimony, the D.C.I. asked Johnson to take over.

As ever, Johnson's approach was less abrasive but no

less penetrating. Step by step he went over the evening. Again, Tom Ferguson stumbled over the same ground, hesitating, repeating himself, slipping but always sticking to the same story. The Inspector started at the beginning again, patiently and gently. It made no difference. Again, slips and hesitations but the same story. Ferguson had left the house at about 6.15, had taken a bus to the top end of Wormald Street. He had not known exactly where the hotel was, he had simply guessed. He had walked to the front of the hotel, had approached the front steps but had had cold feet. He had crossed to the other side of the street and had gazed at the door, hoping that Lucy would appear. After what seemed a very long time he had strolled round into Wormald Street, staring up at the windows and wondering which was Lucy's. Eventually he had gone into the back lane, wondering if Lucy might leave by the back door. After a while a woman came out and walked in the opposite direction. He had hoped that it might be Lucy but it was an older, well-built woman. After another long wait in which he thought he had missed Lucy, he decided to take a bus home. As the bus was driving off he heard a police siren but had no idea that it was heading for the hotel.

It was a poor tale and exceedingly badly told. Trevor Johnson knew that his Chief could not find it acceptable. It was altogether too vague. There were no witnesses and no confirmations of time. Only the cook leaving by the back door could have been a witness but Ferguson said he had withdrawn into a doorway and couldn't be seen. Yet it smacked of the truth simply because of its wooliness. Anyone guilty would have cooked up a much more convincing tale. The stumblings and slips were more characteristic of an embarrassed, lovesick fool than a determined murderer. Besides, Ferguson had not budged from his story. The solicitor had often grimaced at the stumblings and the corrections but he was essentially content with his client's account. But then, that was what he was paid for, wasn't it?

Johnson had one card left in his hand.

"If, as you say, you left the house at 6.15, where was Gerald Frimton at this time?"

"What do you mean?"

"Wasn't Gerald Frimton staying at your house at the time?"

"Yes he was. I thought he had gone out with my sister to The Players"

"Did you not see them go out?"

"No, I was upstairs at the time."

"What time did you get back that night?"

"I told you, it was about....8.30."

"And Gerald Frimton was not in the house?"

"They don't get back until after 9 as a rule."

"Did you speak to him when he got back?"

"No, I went up for a bath as soon as I got indoors."

"You needed a bath?"

"I was weary and stiff, I thought I may have caught a chill. I had a long soak and went to bed."

"So you saw none of your family that evening after you returned to the house?"

"No, I heard them talking downstairs as I was soaking and my mother spoke to me through the door. She asked me if I wanted a hot drink, that's all."

"You didn't have one?"

"No. I was too tired."

"What clothes were you wearing that night?"

"Clothes? I was wearing these, what I'm wearing now....I think."

"And you haven't had them cleaned?"

"I fail to see where this is leading, Inspector." The solicitor's voice intruded.

"If Mr.Ferguson did carry out the murder, he may have had bloodstains on his clothes. He went for a bath immediately he got home. No one saw him. Perhaps he needed that bath for other reasons than to fight a cold."

"Inspector, Mr.Duncombe has covered all this ground…."

"Has he Sir? It will do no harm to go over it, surely?"

Johnson thought that Ferguson had responded in such a way that the question was new to him.

"You wear these clothes for work, do you?"

"Yes."

"You don't usually change to go out?"

"Sometimes…."

"But not that night? You were hoping to meet the lady you loved yet you didn't change out of your work clothes?"

"I'm not sure, I might have done. I sometimes do, I sometimes don't…."

The solicitor leaned forward and whispered for several moments.

"My client was in a great hurry to go out that night, he hadn't time to change."

"What time did you get back from work?"

"It is usually 5.45.It wasn't any different that night."

"You ate at home?"

"Yes, I had just time for a quick bite."

If he had left at the time he said he did he would have had very little time to change. There were no witnesses, of course. Johnson had played his card but had not won the hand. It was time for another round and it was his Chief's turn.

"Before you go in, Sir, what about Frimton? It's funny that Ferguson didn't see Frimton in the house either before he went out or after he came back. Should we have Frimton in at the same time?"

"There is no harm in letting him wait. They haven't cooked up anything between them and they have had plenty of time. I think that one of them might hang the other if we give them enough time. Neither of them really has a motive as far as I can tell. It is all suspicion and

Ferguson's actions have been the most suspicions. Let's continue to apply some heat to Ferguson, see where it takes us.

We'll bring Frimton in tomorrow after Ferguson's situation has sunk in and see if there is collusion or corroboration. If Frimton is guilty he will be anxious to keep our attention on Ferguson. We shall see!"

CHAPTER THIRTY SIX

Henry's day had not been as difficult as he had anticipated. His newly acquired briskness was strange and unexpected to his typing pool. He had always been distant and aloof, quick to withdraw from embarrassment. His rapid retreats to his office sanctum had left plenty of room for mockery. Today, he showed no sign of being put out by his sojourn at the police station. Far from it, he strode among his ladies, eyes alert, missing nothing, a challenge in every step. He lingered occasionally to check some individual's progress in such a determined manner that he impressed the whole body, even the provocative Mrs.Sibley. When the official break came, he turned to his office and a murmur stole round the workroom. Henry was unabashed, they could say what they liked, it was their break. He was doing his job and carrying it through as never before. He didn't quite understand it and felt a little guilty that he should be so relaxed, but the work was being don and it was going well.

He was not troubled by Mr.Turnbull or the Senior Manager and he gave them little thought as the day went by. There was the usual Friday rush of correspondence and the new work schedules to arrange for Monday. Orders were up on last month and new orders coming in late had to be given urgent priority. Henry was not in the least flurried, he distributed the tasks with thoughtful efficiency immediately they arrived on his desk. Some he despatched himself with a light-heartedness that left him almost gasping. By the end of the afternoon he had a very strange feeling. He put on his coat and hat and walked to the gate, as he nodded to the commissionaire in his cabin, understanding suddenly came to him. He had enjoyed his work! He had had fun! He broke into a smile which so shocked one of the ladies standing nearby that she trembled all the way home and spoke of it with bated breath.

As he approached the hotel steps, he felt a palpable detachment. This respectable establishment had been a much-needed refuge for him for over five years. He had come to depend on it, its solid comfort, its worthy food, its routine, its quiet, even its hot water. What would he have done without it? Now he could begin to contemplate doing without it. Henry, the man of fixed habits, the man who fled from human contact, who would go out of his way to avoid the unfamiliar, was thinking so freely that he astonished himself.

By the time he entered his room, he had made up his mind to do something quite extraordinary. He would ask Elizabeth out for the evening. If things went well he would propose matrimony. Whether or not he would do so immediately would depend on Elizabeth's response to the evening. If she was not in a receptive mood, then, as a true gentleman, he would not press the matter, but he felt in a tremendously adventurous mood. Tonight would be the best opportunity. He uttered a loud "Hah!" and almost capered.

D.C.I.Duncombe went as far as possible to try to break Thomas Ferguson's story. He raised the hackles of the solicitor time and again but he managed to remain within legal bounds. Again and again he invited the muddled young man to rethink his visit to The Moorcroft hotel. Again and again, Ferguson, writhing in embarrassment at his own fumblings, rejected any suggestion that he was in the wrong. He had never been to the hotel before. He did not know where it was, he had simply guessed from Lucy Oxbury's conversation when she had visited their house. He admitted to having no witnesses to any of his activities between six in the evening and the following morning when he rose from his bed. Duncombe released him, warning him that he might be required for further questioning. As soon as he had gone, the D.C.I. sent for Johnson.

"Right, let's have Frimton in!"

"I thought you said you would wait until tomorrow, Sir?"

"I'm entitled to change my mind, aren't I? Ferguson told me that Frimton wasn't at their house last night. He'd made a quick visit to his parents. I think we should capitalise on that. If we have him in now, he won't know anything about Tom Ferguson's story. So…."

"Right, Sir, but what if he phoned her at lunch time?"

"We'll take a chance on that."

"Mr.Frimton, you said in your statement that you stayed at home, that is at 16 Mortimer Crescent last Friday night. You said that you weren't feeling well and that you stayed in while the others went out. Is that right?"

"Yes, that's right." Gerald Frimton was relaxed and smiling.

You didn't see Thomas Ferguson during that time?"

"Tom? No, didn't he go out with the others?"

"Did you not see everyone leave the house?"

"Well, Mr. and Mrs.Ferguson said they would give Sally a lift down to the theatre. She wanted to get there early for some reason and Tom left the room at the same time. I assumed that he had gone with them."

"You didn't ask where he was going?"

"No, we aren't close. We don't have much to say to each other."

"Why is that?"

"No particular reason. I think he just doesn't like me."

" Did you see Mr.Ferguson return to the house?"

"No, I was in the front room watching television when Sally came in. Her parents came in about half an hour later."

"You didn't ask what had become of Tom Ferguson?"

"No I didn't. He didn't always come back with them. I was surprised when Mrs.Ferguson said that Tom was in the bath. He must have gone straight up."

At this point, Sergeant Green put his head in to say that someone was asking to speak to Inspector Johnson. Johnson slipped out. To his surprise, it was Miss Stanley on the phone.

Inspector Johnson, we've made a discovery. One of my staff has had a good rummage round and has discovered the projects of some of the winners from the past in on of the office cupboards. Lucy Oxbury's project is here on my desk. What do you want me to do with it? Post it on?"

"That's excellent news! I wonder, if I send a constable through, would you give it to him? It would save time and would be much the safest way. I would have come myself but we are very busy at the moment. Thank you very much. It might be just what we are looking for. Thank you, Miss Stanley."

Johnson thought this an extraordinary piece of luck but he decided not to be too hopeful. He was aware of the disappointments that could follow upon too much expectation.

The interrogation of Gerald Frimton occupied the rest of the afternoon. Neither Johnson nor the D.C.I. were happy. Frimton had no witnesses to his presence on the Friday night, nor had Ferguson. While they were both suspicious about the way the two men had been in the house without being aware of each other, they knew that the prosecution would not be willing to proceed with a case built only on suspicion. There was still the matter of motive. Neither Ferguson nor Frimton had reason to kill Lucy Oxbury. Opportunity and in Ferguson's case a smokescreen of possible lies were hardly sufficient grounds for proceeding against them.

They let Frimton go and went into the D.C.I.'s office to commiserate with each other.

What about Sally Ferguson, Sir? She might be able to give us a clue as to the attitudes of either of them to

234

Lucy."

"Attitudes! I'm sick of attitudes. They don't tell a straight tale, either of them, yet the longer we were at them, the more I was convinced they didn't do it. Why should they? I thought that we might have shifted Ferguson. He might have given us some insight. No, he just got a little more sorry for himself. He is just a baby and not too bright. He wouldn't have the guts even if he had the cunning. Frimton was a smarter character and had the inside knowledge but he had even less reason than Ferguson."

"So we are back to square one? Yes, it would seem so. Well, I'm not lingering today. I've got a dinner with the rotary. We'll pick up the reins tomorrow. I hope our Lords and Masters are not getting too impatient. Goodnight, Trevor. Give yourself a night off. I'm sure we both deserve a break.

CHAPTER THIRTY SEVEN

Elizabeth Elmwood was charmed by Henry's invitation. They left about 7 o'clock in a taxi. In his present state of mind, Henry rather regretted that he had nothing flamboyant to wear but his Sunday suit was presentable and might remind Elizabeth of the last time he had worn it. Elizabeth was decked out in a simple but expensive looking dark grey suit with a dazzling white polo neck jersey and a blood red brooch near the throat. Her hair was radiant and, in the close confinement of the taxi, Henry was almost intoxicated by her exotic perfume.

She was light-hearted and, with just a little prompting from Henry, talked animatedly about how happy she had been in Maskerley. She told him about her job as secretary to one of the directors at Crompton's, it was both responsible and privileged. Henry gathered that she was something of a senior figure. Her salary was generous and she had always taken her annual holiday abroad, treating herself to good hotels. She thought that she had never enjoyed such a good standard of living. She liked The Moorcroft, it had suited her well, not too expensive but comfortable and genteel. She would miss it terribly.

"Does that mean that you are seriously thinking of leaving?"

"I think that we will all have to go, Henry. I don't know how Mrs.Ridgeway is going to survive all this."

"Mrs.Ridgeway is a strong character. I don't think she will give up easily."

"Well, I will wait for a day or two to see if this whole thing blows over, I wont do anything rash."

"Nor will I, Elizabeth."

Mrs.Elmwood roared with laughter. Henry found himself laughing too.

"Sorry, Henry, I couldn't quite see you doing anything

rash. I haven't offended you, have I?"

She took his arm and held herself close.

"I feel so secure when I'm with you, Henry."

"And I'm always relaxed in your company, Elizabeth...."

Henry was just about to launch into his daring proposal when the taxi pulled up outside The Granby, the restaurant they had visited only last Sunday. He was disconcerted, but only for a little while.

They were both a little dismayed to find that the atmosphere was not the same as that on Sunday. It wasn't quite so busy but the crowd was comparatively noisy and brash. However, they were taken to a table in a quiet corner well away from the entrance where the light wasn't too strong and where they could continue their conversation without being easily overheard. Service was much slower than on Sunday but Henry was not sorry about that, he would have more time to consider his proposal.

"Have you made any progress, Henry?"

"Progress, Elizabeth?" Henry was startled.

"With your investigations? I think you'll be interested in what I've found out. I've had a long talk with Christine - Mrs.Jervis. I asked her what had been upsetting her. She was very reluctant to tell me but it turns out that she has been seeing a gentleman she had met while researching in the library. She said it was an innocent friendship but, on Monday, she discovered that the gentleman's wife had placed a serious interpretation upon it and had threatened to make a complaint."

"A complaint! To Mr.Jervis, you mean?"

"No, to the education authority. Christine was certain that it would ruin her chances of promotion."

"She wasn't worried about her husband knowing?"

"No, she had already mentioned this friend to her husband. She insists that the friendship is innocent."

"Well, perhaps she shouldn't have been worried. Did

237

you believe her?"

"Yes, Henry. I think it may have been innocent on her part but who knows what the gentleman was thinking. Anyway, it could still mean trouble if the wife does complain."

"Yes, a very awkward situation."

"It could leave her open to blackmail."

"Blackmail? Yes, I suppose it could. Do you think that is what the wife is up to?"

"No....I was thinking of someone else."

Henry was aghast.

"You can't mean Lucy Oxbury? I couldn't believe that! Not Lucy!"

"Henry, you are an old-fashioned romantic!" She gave a little laugh.

"Yes, I suppose I must be...."

Here was a chance to steer the conversation but at that moment the waiter brought the wine and Henry was obliged to go through the ritual of tasting it and accepting it. They both sipped and murmured satisfaction but Henry was not quick enough to speak again.

"Tell me what you have written in your notebook recently."

Henry groaned inwardly. Elizabeth was being persistent. He topped up her glass, perhaps that would help to turn the conversation.

"Well, I have been thinking about the hotel, about those plants, about hiding things and losing things. For example, what became of your canvas bag, Elizabeth? You've never found it have you?"

Elizabeth gave him a sharp look.

"Do you know, I've almost forgotten that, so much has happened. I still miss it of course. I keep feeling for it."

"Yes, I've watched you when you sit down or stand up. You sense it isn't there, don't you?"

"Why, yes, that's it exactly, Henry. You are clever! What made you think of my bag?"

"Well, looking at those big ceramic pots at the end of the corridors...."

"The big blue and green ones?"

"Yes, those. It occurred to me that they are big enough to hide behind and big enough to hide things in."

"You couldn't hide my canvas bag in one of those - it's much too big."

She gave another little laugh. Henry also laughed. He was quick to ask her if she would like some more wine. She drained her glass instantly.

"That would be lovely, Henry, yes please. I feel a little reckless tonight."

Henry was more than delighted to hear that but as he was pouring, something nagged at him from the back of his mind. By the time he had filled his own glass, it had gone.

"I think Frimton has to be our man, Henry. I don't know why he should want to kill Lucy but he had the best chance of putting that box-spanner under your mattress. I agree with you that Lucy wouldn't have blackmailed Christine, she hardly knew her, that was silly of me."

She laid her hand on Henry's. Henry purred. If only she would stop talking about the murders. The waiter arrived with their first course and for a while they concentrated on eating. Their conversation turned to food. They agreed that the cooking at The Granby was excellent but they wondered if this meal could be as good as that they had eaten on Sunday. They laughed together then, suddenly, Elizabeth choked and coughed. Henry half rose from his seat in alarm but Elizabeth waved him back, clutching a handkerchief to her mouth. Smiling at him, she excused herself and said she would be back in a moment.

While she was away, the waiter cleared the first course. He was just bringing the second course when Elizabeth returned, patting her hair and smiling assurance that she had entirely recovered. Henry warmed to her

239

poise and charm. She was so easy and relaxed. He himself would have struggled to recover from such a bout of coughing at the table and would have caused embarrassment in doing so.

She was quite at ease and was considerate enough to help Henry to vegetables from the dish furthest away from him.

They ate for a while in silence.

"Remember, Henry, you promised to show me your notebook when you were ready."

"I might give up the notebook, Elizabeth."

"Oh, surely not, Henry, after all your efforts!"

"What use can it be? All those little things, they hardly amount to anything. It would be different if I knew what the police knew, then the little things might add up. What they got from Elliott and Baxter, for example..."

He stopped suddenly. That was the second time he had been niggled by a thought without being able to register what it was. He saw a puzzled expression on Elizabeth's face and hastened to continue.

"It's full of nonsense. You wont make much of it. I'll show you when it is all over."

"You mean when the murder is solved?"

"Yes."

Henry had some difficulty pouring some more wine and was obliged to mop up a small stain. The old Henry would have been mortified at this clumsiness, the new Henry took it all in his stride.

"What if it is never solved, Henry. Will you stay on?"

"At The Moorcroft? Yes, I suppose so. It will depend on many things. Have you never hankered after a home of your own, Elizabeth?"

"I couldn't bear the thought of being on my own again, Henry."

"But would you have to be on your own again?"

She stared at Henry, her eyes wide.

"What I mean is...Elizabeth...could you think of

marrying again?"

She continued to stare at him but with a softer expression.

"Elizabeth, you know what I am trying to say...is it possible that you could consider...."

"I think I know what you are trying to say, Henry. It is very sweet of you and I am honoured, believe me, truly honoured...but..."

There were tears in her eyes.

"It's too late, Henry."

Trevor Johnson met his messenger by the front desk just as he was about to leave for home. The project was well wrapped in brown paper but it seemed very small. He set it on his desk, took off his coat and undid the parcel. He hadn't known what to expect but he was disappointed, all the same.

Time had not been kind to it. Its cover was of a very thin card which was now sadly scuffed and battered. Its title, "Criminals and the Law", was in what must once have been very bold red letters, now they were badly faded. A group of four magazine photographs of famous criminals filled up most of the cover. Inside was a very clear table of contents. The handwriting was regular and neat but bedevilled by that curse of schoolgirl fists, the 'roly-poly' style - so much attention being given to the loops that verticals and horizontals were absorbed into the curves and several letters were lost altogether.

He smiled at the list of names - Crippen, Christie, Bentley, Ellis, Ley and Smith, among others. These were bloodthirsty subjects for a young girl to choose, a boy might be in his element, but a girl.... He turned the pages and realised that Lucy Oxbury had been seeking to make a point, naively perhaps, but with intelligence, given her years. She was trying to assess the weight and justice of the sentences. He quickly turned to the conclusion. Again there was youthful naivety, she had expressed sympathy with jurors for the immensity of their task and said how difficult it must have been considering her own experience at County Court when she had been allowed to observe the accused and had listened to the evidence. It had been "a very enlightening and chastening experience."

Those were rather mature words from a girl of only thirteen or fourteen. They must have been her own, she would have had no help from home, he felt sure. He acknowledged that Lucy was intelligent and in some ways very mature. Her teachers had thought well of her project and had awarded her a prize. There wasn't a great deal of research, it was entirely taken from popular magazines as far as he could see. Her teachers couldn't have been too happy about the subject, he imagined the shudders in the all female staff room. Presumably they had been impressed by the attitude Lucy had taken. There was a touching solemnity about the whole thing. He reflected that a boy of the same age would have made it a sensational blood and thunder project with no holds barred.

He turned to the last case, the case that Lucy had witnessed. It was vaguely familiar. It was a sad case of a long suffering wife who had taken a knife to her brutal husband. It had not been spectacular and had not reached the national headlines as far as he could remember. The name, Mary Telford, meant nothing to him. Lucy Oxbury had been fascinated by the figure in the dock, she had recorded her appearance, her mannerisms and gestures and her despair. She had noted the relief and gratitude on the accused's face when the verdict of manslaughter had been brought in. The sentence had been six years. Lucy had thought this harsh and had wondered about the power of counsel over juries. Why, she asked, should the fate of the person in the dock be determined by the ability of the advocate more than anything else? At that age she probably hadn't been fully aware of the powers of the judge, Johnson thought.

He closed the folder. There had been no photograph nor had there been any newspaper cuttings. Perhaps the case had cropped up rather late in Lucy's scheme of things and she had had to hurry to include this material. Was this what he had pinned his hopes on, this slim project with its schoolgirl wisdom? Was this Mary Telford relevant to the murder? If she was living in Maskerley, if she had met Lucy Oxbury, if they could possibly have recognised each other after nine years or whatever it was, could this possibly have triggered a murder? It was a very dubious prospect. Nevertheless he would delve into it. Another stone to be turned.

The journey back to The Moorcroft was a silent affair. Elizabeth sat close to Henry and held his hand but neither of them could find anything to say. Henry was not too disappointed by Elizabeth's gentle refusal, he had hopes of renewing his proposal in the near future, perhaps when the investigation was over. He didn't believe it was too late, as Elizabeth had said. Neither of them was too old. The trouble was that he was feeling tired. It was the combination of good food and wine. He wasn't used to it. He must adjust to it if he was to change his lifestyle as he intended.

He got out of the taxi and helped Elizabeth onto the pavement. As they went up the steps, a photographer's flash exploded violently in their faces. Elizabeth gave a wild cry and snatched at the offending camera. She flung it with all her might. It soared into the night sky and crashed into pieces on the other side of the street.

Before the stunned photographer could protest, she roundly abused him for his beastly intrusion. He had hounded the residents day and night, she had had enough, she would not have him destroy the few moments of peace that were available to her, how dare he, she would complain to the Press Council, what right did the press have over everyone else's right, they didn't favour freedom they favoured oppression or they would leave people alone. It was a torrent the photographer was never to forget. Before he could summon a word, Elizabeth had hurried through the door.

Henry gazed at her with admiration. She was flushed and trembling.

"Beastly man! I'm afraid he has ruined our lovely evening."

"Not at all, Elizabeth, I enjoyed it tremendously," a mischievous smile flitted across his face, "especially the last bit."

"Oh, Henry!"

She was near to tears. She pressed his hand and rushed upstairs.

CHAPTER THIRTY EIGHT

D.C.I.Duncombe was at something of a loss the next morning. The Ferguson and Frimton interrogations had provided excitement and hope, just as the Allingham interrogation had done. Now he had to find some other avenue. Before he could do so, he was called to see to other matters not connected with the murders. He popped his head round the Inspector's door and cheerfully told him he was leaving it all in his hands for the moment.

Trevor Johnson was quite happy about that. Systematically he set about a search through records. One of his men was put onto looking into Jenny Phillips' origins to see if there was a possible link there. Another was put onto looking up the case of Mary Telford. He, himself, would check through the membership of the Maskerley Players and the Choral Society. They were the organisations in which it was possible for Lucy Oxbury and Mary Telford to have met. The other place would have been the estate agent's but enquiries there would be fruitless without a photograph. Records would be able to provide one. He hoped that nine years wouldn't prove too much of an obstacle to recognition.

There wasn't time to get far. An urgent call came in from Mrs.Ridgeway to say that both Mrs.Elmwood and Mr.Allingham had been taken to hospital with suspected poisoning.

"Food poisoning was it, Mrs.Ridgeway?"

"The ambulance men didn't think so. They thought it much more serious. They are both very poorly. They've been taken to Broughton Hospital."

Inspector Johnson did not delay. He was at the hospital within three quarters of an hour. The doctor who admitted them drew him into his office.

"A very serious business, this. I've done what I could

245

but it might be too late for Mr.Allingham. The lady, Mrs.Elmwood, is quite ill but we should be able to save her."

"What was it, doctor?"

"We're not absolutely sure. It wasn't corrosive, we know. We've washed the stomachs out and given routine injections but we must wait until the lab has finished some analyses before we can do anything else."

"It was taken orally?"

"Almost certainly, Inspector. The symptoms are fairly general. It wasn't one of the more common poisons."

"If it wasn't a common poison, could it have been an accident?"

"I wouldn't like to say until we know more."

"What are their chances?"

"We will know when the lab tells us what the poison was. At the moment, the lady is holding her own. The gentleman is comatose."

"It's touch and go, then?"

"I'm afraid so."

Mrs.Ridgeway had always been tough, independent and sharp in thought and speech. When Inspector Johnson called on her later that morning, he found her pale, silent and fraught. She was more troubled by this last misfortune than by any of the others. It wasn't just a serious incident to add to the others, this one particularly reflected on her. She felt that people would associate poisoning with her establishment, either its food or its hygiene. The loss of two more of her residents under suspicious circumstances had almost undermined her determination to carry on.

After commiserating with her, Johnson asked her to go over the events leading up to the two being taken away in the ambulance. When they had not come down to breakfast she had been worried. She had gone up to Mr.Allingham's room and when he had not responded to her knock she had used her passkey to enter his room.

Mr.Allingham was lying rigid among a welter of bedclothes. She had felt his pulse and found it to be very rapid. His brow was very hot. He was still fully clothed so he must have fallen ill almost as soon as he had returned. Knowing that Mr.Allingham and Mrs.Elmwood had been out together last night she had feared for Mrs.Elmwood. She had shouted for Sarah to phone for an ambulance and had run upstairs to Mrs.Elmwood's room. Mrs.Elmwood was barely conscious. She too had had a very disturbed night. She too had a racing pulse and a temperature. That was all she could say. The ambulance men had been very quick and had whisked the two residents away immediately. She had no idea where the two had been that night, she only knew that they had left together and had said they would not be taking dinner.

Mrs.Ridgeway asked after them and Johnson told her all he knew, which was very little. He was careful to ask if they had eaten or drunk anything after they had returned to the hotel. Mrs.Ridgeway had not seen them after their return but she had tidied their rooms after they had gone and there had been no sign of eating or drinking, no cups or glasses by their beds.

The Brambles brothers confirmed that they had not been involved in the Mary Telford case. They could not help. Records could. The file was awaiting Johnson's return. He flipped it open and gazed at the police photograph. It didn't stir his memory. This kind of photograph seldom did. This one wasn't even very sharp.

Two dark eyes stared out of a very pale, thin face. Worry rather than defiance governed the expression. The hair was straight and lifeless, there were shadows around the eyes and nose and the mouth was drawn down. The bone structure indicated that the woman had lost weight, Johnson thought that the face would be more filled out now. He wondered why all photographs should not be in colour, considering the date, it was an unfortunate

247

economy. There was no indication of the true nature of the eyes, the hair or even the skin.

He read through the file. Mary Telford was a native of Sunderland. Her age was 32. Her occupation was given as housewife. Her husband's occupation was given as garage owner. He too had lived in Sunderland all his life. He was two years older than his wife. There had been one child, a daughter, who had died aged four. There were no further details of the family. The case was that the ten year old marriage had been a long struggle for the wife, the husband was often violent, sometimes but not always when he was drunk; there had been other women in the husband's life and he was careless with money; there had not been much to live on in spite of an apparently successful business; twice, the wife had been admitted to hospital with bruises and lacerations and suspected broken limbs; finally, she had been unable to stand any more and had turned on her husband with a kitchen knife. Only one wound was necessary to kill him, it had penetrated deep into his chest.

To Johnson, this was not an unusual crime. It followed a pattern that was not uncommon. Not all such crimes reached the headlines. It was very sad even in such bald outline, they all were. What had he to go on? He could check with the Sunderland police, they might be able to tell him more about this woman. She would have been out of prison for at least five years by now, maybe more, allowing for good behaviour. If she had stayed in the North East they may know what happened to her. It would be a great help if she could be eliminated.

The Sunderland Police were of little help. The garage had stood in the way of a new road system and had been demolished eight years ago. They did not know of any relations on either side. Mary Telford had been an only child, her parents had died long before the case. She had had no one to turn to, that was what had driven her to the extremity. She had served only three years. They had no idea where she lived now but they believed that she had left the district.

"This is beyond a joke! What is going to happen next at that bloody hotel?"

The D.C.I. was enraged at the new development.

"Now the whole heirarchy will be down on us before you can say dogsbody! You'd better tell me everything, that phone will be red hot before ten minutes are out."

He listened very patiently to Johnson's account.

"They took neither food nor drink at back at the hotel?"

"No Sir, there's no evidence of it. They went out to eat, last night, they could have taken the poison there, wherever it was."

"And the hospital doesn't know what the poison was?"

"Not yet, Sir. it was something unusual. They were hoping the lab could tell them within an hour or two."

"This was no accident! It stinks! It has to be deliberate. Damn! Damn! Damn! I don't suppose it could be suicide, could it? It would save an awful lot of bother if it was."

"Hardly, Sir, two of them."

"It could have been a pact. What if they had both been involved in these murders? They were the only ones who claim to have seen Jenny Phillips on the Saturday, they returned to the hotel together that day. They go out to dinner to celebrate or to say farewell, to wind it up. It could be...."

"It just doesn't ring true, Sir. Allingham wasn't the type to commit suicide." Johnson shook his head, "wouldn't murder be more logical in this instance?"

D.C.I.Duncombe looked cooly at his Inspector.

"You keep supporting Allingham. Your instinct again, I suppose? I hope you will not regret it. Well, I've got to leave it with you a little longer. Good luck to you! Keep me informed even if it's only a note on my desk."

The D.C.I. was between meetings, he rushed off before

Johnson could tell him about Mary Telford. The Inspector thought it wise to leave that particular file on his Chief's desk.

It was time for more checks. Everyone with any connection with the case was questioned as to what they were doing on the previous evening. The day was a very exhausting one and Johnson could only hope that it wasn't fruitless. He phoned the Broughton Hospital before he went home. There was a slight improvement in Mrs.Elmwood's condition, none in Mr.Allingham's.

From time to time, Henry was aware of a great internal struggle. Wave after wave of nausea and accompanying dull pain seemed to be sweeping through him. There was a sensation of heat and numbness and heaviness and thirst and blackness. Sudden cramps seemed to grip his stomach. When they receded he was aware of a soothing warmth then another wave of nausea then blackness. It seemed to happen again and again. There was a thudding in his chest then in his head. The blackness would turn to a great red glow then there was nothing then the cramps again. He longed for rest, a long, long rest. If only the blackness would be steady. But it wasn't, there were swirling patterns in his head, more cramps, another wave of dull heavy pain, then blackness. It would help if he could get his mind clear.

Out of the turbulence, the heat and numbness, a voice nagged at him. He couldn't make out what it said. Then Elizabeth's fine grey-green eyes spun round and round and she looked distant and troubled. Tears ran down her face. Box-spanner. Another wave of pain submerged him. The blackness gave way to red again and once more Elizabeth swum across his vision. She was so gentle and lovely. She was sitting in the easy chair. The swirling wouldn't stop. Blackness and pain and nausea and numbness and red and heat, it was endless. Mrs.Jervis at his bedside, swirling round his bed. Gerald Frimton standing there. What did he want? It was endless, endless. Mrs.Sibley sneering then laughing, Ormesby-Phelps squinting at him, all pomposity and primness, breaking into obscene laughter, swirling into the blackness. The Chief Inspector bullying and bullying, his voice rising then trailing away. Denzil Elliott at the bathroom door, knocking at an open door, wide open, running away, his sneer trailing into nothing. He must know what it was, he must find out, he must struggle. He must! Where was Elizabeth? For a moment he confused her with Miss Catesby. Miss Catesby who was whirling about in her blue dress. He had lost her that day as he did now. Blue dress, where was the blue dress? The blue dress gave way to green. Elizabeth had a green dress. Where was Elizabeth? She was there, there in the easy chair with her canvas bag. That was it! That was what he had to tell Inspector Johnson.

"There's a young woman to see you, Inspector."

Trevor Johnson had had a troubled night. He was not refreshed and he wasn't ready for surprises. The young lady waiting for him was a nervous girl of about eighteen, mousy haired, plump, snub nosed and pink cheeked. Quite a country girl, was Johnson's first impression.

"It's about Jenny, Jenny Phillips, I knew Jenny at the orphanage, for years, we left at the same time, well, I didn't know where she had gone but we were friends and it was ever such a surprise when we saw each other outside the pictures and we arranged to go again when we had time off and so we went once or twice...."

"Hang on! You are much too fast. Take your time and let me understand what you are saying...."

"Well, I was so shocked about what happened to poor Jenny, I was ill. I was ill in bed for days. You see, it could have been my fault. I didn't know anything would happen to her did I...?"

"Wait, wait! You must take your time! Now, how could it have been your fault?"

"Well, I got permission to invite Jenny that Saturday. I gave Jenny my number at Mrs.Lee's...."

"Who is Mrs.Lee?"

"That's the lady I work for at Langton. She's very nice and she said invite Jenny through. Jenny was so upset, you see...."

"Jenny was upset?"

"Yes." The girl looked at Johnson with some astonishment, were all policemen so slow? "She phoned me that morning and said she needed to talk to me, there was no one else she cold talk to. She was worried sick, I could tell. So I said come through and have tea. Mrs.Lee said so, as I was talking to Jenny, it was all proper. So I told her where to come, the address like, and said I would expect her. Well, we waited all afternoon and she didn't come. Mrs.Lee was a bit put out, I think she thought we were a bit unreliable like. I said I was sorry and I would have phoned Jenny but she never said exactly where she worked. She only said that it was a place in Ruthven Street. We only talked about the people, she never said where it was, the name I mean."

Johnson was quick to take advantage of the pause.

"Your name is?"

"Paula Thwaites. We grew up together in the orphanage. We got on well, better than most, it wasn't a friendly place for pals really. We were good friends, Jenny and me. Mind, we knew that we would lose sight of each other when we got jobs. I was a year ahead of Jenny, well, something like that, and I got a job first and I never knew where Jenny had gone. It was great when we met again, it was such a surprise, outside the pictures. Jenny said she was very happy and that her boss was very kind, but when she phoned she sounded very frightened. She wouldn't say what it was, she said could we meet. Well, I couldn't, I asked Mrs.Lee and she says ask Jenny here.

252

Jenny said she'd come. I told her the number 22 and where to get off and everything but she never came. We waited all afternoon. Mrs.Lee laid on a special tea and she never came. I didn't know what to think. I didn't know what to say to Mrs.Lee either. Well, Mrs.Lee saw it in the paper on Monday and told me. We were both....shattered. I was ill and had to go to bed. I've had a temperature and Mrs.Lee thought she should call a doctor. I'd not long recovered from flu and I wasn't right. When I got better, Mrs.Lee said I must come and tell somebody."

Paula Thwaites talked with the speed of a machine gun. Fortunately, her voice was sharp and clear, much to the Inspector's relief. Here was the explanation for Jenny Phillips catching that particular bus. Sadly, it did not explain why she got off again. Johnson asked a few more questions but he knew that Paula Thwaites couldn't help any further. She had no idea why Jenny should be frightened, Jenny had said very little on the phone.

"Do you know where Jenny phoned from?"

"No, it was a call box, I know, because Jenny said she hadn't much change and couldn't wait."

"What time was it when she phoned?"

"We were having our dinners, well, lunches then, I always call them dinner but Mrs.Lee says I should call them lunch. It must have been about half past twelve."

After Paula Thwaites had gone, Johnson thought about the frightened girl walking about town for several hours. Jenny had been very unlucky. Half an hour later she might have told her story and have been safe at Mrs.Lee's house at Langton. He also reflected on the fact that no one had thought to question Jenny on the night of the murder simply because she had been downstairs at the time. He needed to ask Mrs.Ridgeway for a more detailed account of Jenny's whereabouts that evening. Perhaps she had left the kitchen at some time and had seen someone coming out of the bathroom.

As soon as he was free to do so, Inspector Johnson contacted the firm of solicitors who had represented Mary Telford. They were able to tell him that the sale of the garage had brought her a tidy sum. It had been invested for her while she was in prison. When she came out she asked for the investment to be realised. She had not asked them for advice of any kind. She had simply thanked them and had left. Their account had been settled quickly. They understood that she had left the area. When asked their opinion of Mary Telford, they thought she had not been brutalised by her stay in prison but had come out determined to make a new start. They were rather sorry for her and disappointed that they hadn't been able to help her more.

Another stone turned. What next?

The phone rang. The officer on duty at the hospital wished to inform the Inspectorthat Mrs.Elmwood had regained consciousness. Johnson hurried out.

CHAPTER THIRTY NINE

Trevor Johnson was shocked at the change in Mrs.Elmwood. In her hospital nightdress, she looked quite shrunken. Her fine light-brown hair was brushed rather straighter than he remembered and her face looked different. It was wan and damp with perspiration. There was no make up to soften the pallor, nor perfume to take away the lingering smell of bile. Her eyes seemed not quite focussed yet she was aware of his presence at the bedside. Johnson turned to the nurse and asked if it was alright to speak.

"I can hear you, Inspector, don't worry, I think I'm a lot better."

Elizabeth Elmwood's voice was low but steady.

"Careful now, Mrs. Elmwood, you've been very ill, you know. You mustn't tire her Inspector."

"I expect you will want to ask a lot of questions, Inspector."

"Yes, Mrs. Elmwood, but if you don't feel up to it, do say and we'll wait until you are."

"Carry on, I'll tell you if I can't go on."

"Where did you and Mr.Allingham go to eat last night?"

"Oh, The Granby in Beresford Road. We went there last Sunday and had a splended meal. We thought we would try it again. It must have been something we ate. How is Mr.Allingham by the way?"

"He is very ill, I'm afraid. What did you have to eat?"

"We both had the same. Garlic mushrooms then steak au poivre. Could it have been the mushrooms, do you think? I'm never certain about mushrooms but I can't resist them."

"We don't know yet, when did you first feel ill?"

"We were both sleepy by the time we got back to the

hotel. I went straight to bed but I woke in the middle of the night with a fearful headache and dizziness. My mouth was dry and I had a raging thirst but I couldn't get out of bed. I was terribly hot and restless. I don't remember anything more until the morning when I thought I heard Mrs.Ridgeway's voice. That's all, really."

"You were unconscious when the ambulance came?"

"I don't remember the ambulance I'm afraid."

The doctor met Inspector Johnson in the corridor and took him back to his office.

"The poison turns out to be one of the digitalis type. That means it is highly unlikely that the intake was accidental. Now that we know what it is we can go ahead with treatment but there is still some doubt about the condition of Mr.Allingham."

"Would this substance have a strong taste?"

"Most of the digitalis type medicines are quite bitter so whatever this substance was it would be similar in taste. In tablet form they are usually swallowed whole."

"One could not swallow a tablet accidentally, doctor, so I presume that this substance must have been in powder form when taken?"

"Yes, it could be taken with liquid but it wouldn't be solluble."

"Would this substance be in the form of a prescribed drug?"

"These medicines are usually prescribed for heart problems, as stimulants. There is little margin between safe dosage and toxic quantity. You wouldn't be able to buy any of them over the counter."

"You think that only a small quantity of this substance would be fatal and that it would almost certainly have been mixed with food?"

"Yes, food rather than drink. It is more likely to have been noticeable in drink. In a highly flavoured food it would hardly be noticed at all."

"Just one more thing, doctor, would this poison not take effect straight away? Both your patients had time to get home and into bed before they became ill."

"Well, it is possible that it could take up to an hour to take effect, maybe more under special circumstances."

"Presumably, the person who administered this poison knew what he or she was doing."

"I would say it was highly likely."

Johnson asked whether he could look at Henry Allingham. The doctor thought it pointless but, as it would do no harm, he took the Inspector into the side ward where Henry lay and left him. Henry was a large man and, unlike Mrs.Elmwood, he had lost none of his stature for being in a hospital bed. He was frighteningly still. A nurse hovered, checking on a green electronic signal pulsing in a machine at the side of the bed and fussing with a tangle of plastic tubes feeding into both arms.

As Johnson drew close, he could see small twitches about Henry's mouth and the slightest occasional flicker of the eyelids. He was also aware of variations in the signal on the screen. He sensed a struggle going on in that solid frame. He felt that, somehow, Henry was going to pull through. This was no frail, suicidal wimp, someone who couldn't face living. He remembered his first impression of this man, the clear, unfaltering statement, the straightforward simplicity of him. No, this Henry Allingham was not going without a struggle. There seemed no reason why he should die.

He looked about the room and caught sight of Henry's overcoat on a hanger next to a hanging wardrobe. He remembered that Mrs.Ridgeway had said that Henry had been lying on his bed fully clothed. He wondered if there could be anything in the pockets to tell him more about the evening out. He signalled quietly to the nurse to indicate his intentions, she gave him a slight nod. He began with the jacket and trousers. Loose change and keys, wallet and handkerchieves, no bus tickets, no souvenir menu. The wallet revealed nothing. Henry's lifestyle didn't seem one to attract clutter. There were no scraps of paper, no bills or receipts, not even for the last meal he had taken, presumably that had been left with the tip. Johnson took down the overcoat, there was nothing in the right hand pocket but in the left, almost caught up in the stitching at the bottom was a scrap of thin card. Johnson peered at it. It was a part of a small carton, part of the flap and body of the carton, torn off haphazardly. The lettering in the corner read "Digoxin is a regulated...."

Sadly, the Inspector folded the overcoat and took it and the rest of the clothes with him.

Trevor Johnson was stunned. All the way back to Maskerley he kept saying to himself that it couldn't be true. He had gone back to speak to Mrs.Elmwood and had learned that she had left the table and had been away for three or four minutes, time enough for the plates to be tampered with. It was a simple conclusion and one his Chief would immediately seize upon. Henry Allingham had committed suicide and had tried to murder Mrs.Elmwood at the same time. The doctor had verified that Digoxin was a digitalis medicine and most probably the substance that had been ingested. Johnson couldn't believe it, his every instinct denied the possibility. What else could have happened? If Henry Allingham died, there would be no hope of reconstructing that evening with any other interpretation.

What could have been Henry's motives for the killings? The D.C.I. was certain to trot out his theory about an oddball for the killing of Lucy Oxbury and the killing of Jenny Phillips would be due to her observing something; Henry's own death would be suicide because he saw no escape, but where did Mrs.Elmwood come in? Had she seen something too? If so, why hadn't he made sure she had died. Clearly she had taken a smaller dose, was that accidental? Had she eaten less of one of the dishes at that meal? It didn't add up to Johnson but he felt sure that his Chief would make it add up as would a coroner or a judge.

Henry Allingham had to live. That was imperative. Johnson didn't know whether he stood in any danger but he had posted a constable outside the ward with two instructions. The first was that nobody other than a doctor or a member of the hospital staff was to be allowed in. The second was that the constable was to phone in the moment that Henry showed any sign of life.

The first thing was to get the overcoat to the lab, the second was to enquire at The Granby and the third was to speak to Mrs.Ridgeway again.

It didn't take long for Johnson to reach The Granby. The waiter who served them remembered the couple clearly, they had left him a susbstantial tip. They had been very pleasant and had enjoyed their meal. When pressed, he remembered that the lady had left the table, she had not been there when he removed the plates from their first course but she returned just as he was bringing the second. She would have been away for maybe three minutes or so. They had not lingered after their meal nor did they go into the lounge for a drink as many customers do. They had left by taxi because he had heard them talking about it. The manager confirmed this and also was quick to state that no one else had been taken ill as far as he was aware. He dipped into a box by his desk and drew out a small pocket notebook. One of the staff had found it in the cloakroom at the end of the evening. The name on the inside was the same as the person who had reserved the table they had been talking about.

Johnson flipped the cover and saw the name H.C.W.Allingham. This was the notebook Henry Allingham had showed him at the time of his interview at the station. This must have fallen out of his pocket when he was taking his coat off or putting it on. If he was genuinely playing at detectives as he claimed, he could not have been the murderer. There would have been no point - unless, as the D.C.I. had said, it was part of an elaborate smoke screen. Johnson shook his head, he still believed Henry incapable of such guile. He thanked the manager and left, taking Henry's notebook with him.

CHAPTER FORTY

Mrs.Ridgeway was out when Inspector Johnson called again at The Moorcroft. Sarah Lucas showed him down into the kitchen where Mrs.Hammond was busy preparing the next meal. She was a cheerful woman with a shrewd eye that missed little. She said he could ask away so long as he didn't get in her road. It was lunchtime and they had to eat before they could get on with the dinner for that evening. He was welcome to stay and share it, Mrs.Ridgeway wouldn't mind, she was sure.

Johnson sat down on the chair Sarah Lucas had brought from the rest room next door. He felt he would get better answers from them in this informal setting, talking would come naturally to them in the kitchen. He asked them about Jenny Phillips.

"Eeeh she was a good little worker! What a treasure that girl was. Such a delicate little slip of a thing, weren't she Sarah?"

"She was, Mrs.Hammond. So shy, it took her a week or two before she spoke."

"Yes, and a bit old-fashioned as well. Ever so nervous she was when she first came, dropped a pot or two, I must say, but Mrs.Ridgeway was very patient with her."

"Yes, she was, Mrs.Hammond, I'm sure I wouldn't have got away with it, she'd have had plenty to say to me if I'd dropped anything." Sarah Lucas laughed.

"Well, the girl was so quiet and well behaved, you couldn't help but like her. When we got to know her she would smile, just smile, she was very gentle like. Not like lots you see nowadays. She never answered back or anything like that. She would just look and listen and get on with things."

"She was happy here, then?" Johnson prodded gently.

"Oh yes, I'm sure she was. Of course, you knew she

261

came from an orphanage, didn't you? Mrs.Ridgeway's been asked to take girls from there before, you know. The first was a long time ago, not long after she started here. I was new myself then. Eeeh the trouble she had with that firstun! What a trouble that girl was! She didn't want to be here and that's the truth. It was row, row, row every minute of the day - pass me the sugar, Sarah, will you, thanks - so naturally she weren't keen to take on another and I don't blame her. The trouble is that these girls aren't trained for anything. I don't know what they do with them there but half of them don't want to do anything when they leave. Mind you, you can't but be sorry for them as they've never had parents - the big pan, Sarah, that's a good girl - or haven't known them like. So it's a case of charity, isn't it, but as Mrs.Ridgeway says, she couldn't keep a girl here out of charity, especially if she upsets the customers, and she did, you know, that she did, so she had to go." Mrs.Hammond paused for breath. "Eeeh I remember how peaceful it was after that one left. Anyway, you can understand how nervous we were of having a new one. Well, it turned out so well that Mrs.Ridgeway took that girl to her heart. To her heart she did. I'm sure she would have done anything for that girl, wouldn't she Sarah?"

"Yes, you're right...."

"Well, to tell you the truth, we all did, didn't we? We've missed her something terrible. It's not just that we have more to do, we miss her cheerful ways, we miss having her here in the kitchen...."

"She spent most of her time down here in the kitchen, did she?" Johnson had to be quick.

"Oh yes, it was warmer down here than up there in the attic. I would think she found it very lonely up there in that attic. I wouldn't like to be up there on my own, would you, Sarah? I would have hated to be up in that attic, myself. No, she liked to be down here, taking notice. If there was nothing for her to do she would sit quiet in the rest room, but she was mostly busy. She liked being busy, didn't she, Sarah? She would do anything for you...."

"I think it was for the company, don't you, Mrs.Hammond?"

"Yes, Sarah, you're right. She needed the company, I think. When she was in the rest room we hardly knew she was there she was so quiet. She would sit reading one of her story papers...."

"You would only hear her if she sniffed. She was a terrible sniffer, wasn't she, Mrs.Hammond?"

"Eeeh yes, poor lass, she was always catching colds, well she was no size at all, she needed building up. She had no appetite at all when she came here. I had to persuade her. I used to tell her that if she didn't eat, the wind would blow her over. Mrs.Ridgeway said she should take cod liver oil but whether she did or not I couldn't tell you. Anyway, Mrs.Ridgeway couldn't have her sniffing when she was serving and carrying food so she laid down some rules. I used to hear her telling her, brush your hair back, straighten your pinny and blow your nose before you go into the dining room. She would repeat, brush, straighten, blow. Brush, straighten, blow. We had many a laugh over it."

"Mrs.Ridgeway was strict with her, was she?"

"Oh yes, well she was strict with all of us, she ran this place very well, you know. Never a single complaint. But she wasn't harsh, not with Jenny, anyway. She would say quietly, 'have you got your hanky, Jenny?' and Jenny would take it out to show her or she would run upstairs to get a new one...."

"Do you remember if she did that on that Friday night?"

"Eeeh, I've gone over that day in my mind dozens of times, I'll never forget it. But, you know I was out and gone by the time all the fuss began. I finished at half past seven and went straight home....."

"But you were there when dinner began. Was Jenny

down here with Mrs.Ridgeway before dinner?"

"Yes, they were all ready and waiting as usual. You were on, that night, weren't you, Sarah? Sarah will tell you."

"Yes, I did the serving that night, but I went off early with you, Mrs.Hammond."

"Was Jenny down here as well?"

"Yes, she was standing by the Aga, waiting to have something to do, as always. Then Mrs.Ridgeway turned and said 'Got your hankie, Jenny?' I think she meant it as a joke. Jenny took it out and made a face. She had another cold, you see. Well, off she went and fetched a clean one. I know because I saw her show it."

"What time was that?"

"It must have been about twenty past six, it was before Mrs.Ridgeway went up. She always goes up about twenty five past. She takes the first order and starts us off, you see."

"Jenny wasn't serving that night?"

"No she was washing up. She was a good washer up, she was conscientious in everything she did, that girl...."

"So she never left the kitchen after dinner started?"

"No, she was still at the sink when I left."

It seemed that Miss Catesby had misled them. Lucy Oxbury could have been going to the bathroom earlier when she had seen her. Because at 8 o'clock she had said that she had seen her "an hour or so ago", they had all assumed that it had been when she went upstairs after dinner. If Miss Catesby had seen Lucy earlier, say on her way down to watch the T.V. before dinner, then it could be that Jenny had seen the murderer coming out of the third floor bathroom when she went to replace her handkerchief. She would not think anything of it until much later and even then she might have been more puzzled than frightened. The more she thought and the more she heard, the more frightened she would have become until, the next morning, she could not stand any more and had to tell someone, someone from outside the hotel.

The trouble was, Johnson realised, the retiming did nothing to help Henry Allingham. In fact, it gave him a better opportunity to commit the crime. He returned to the station quite depressed and seized the first paper in his in-tray with impatience. It was a copy of the lab report on the trousers Henry Allingham had left at the cleaner's. The particles still clinging to the fibres were not related to human blood. They were traces of vegetable and animal protein and acetic acid. He was amazed at what could be discovered from articles after they had been submitted to the scourging of the dry-cleaning process.

This, at least, was one small crumb of support for Henry. He had been telling the truth about his trousers. Johnson couldn't wait, he phoned the lab immediately. He was delighted with what he was told - no trace of powder of any kind had been found in the overcoat pocket where the fragment of card had been. The lab technicians were mystified. If tablets had been carried in that pocket, they would have expected to find some evidence of them by way of debris of some sort. Even the piece of card was clean. They were continuing their examination.

CHAPTER FORTY ONE

Henry could get no rest. He was worried. It wasn't just that the heat and the heaviness and the stomach cramps weren't stopping, he sensed that he was weakening. He seemed to be floating away. He was a long way off but he knew he had to get nearer. He had something to do. Suddenly the thumping in his chest made him spin. He felt his arm stretching out further and further as if seeking to touch or to hold. There was nothing but blackness, then, slowly, a golden light came to fill the horizon. Trails of red and black swam through the golden light. He reached towards it but felt himself failing. He hadn't the strength. The golden light changed to a brassy green, a harsh, bright colour. It spun and flowed and in it there was a face, a pale elfin face with small red lips and soft brown eyes, open and pleading. It floated into the blackness under the bridge and there was a figure walking endlessly ahead of him then a flock of birds in the distance and children's voices and a hand with a piece of bread looming up close, "Go on, mister, it's only bread!" A small round face brushed close and Henry flinched. Then the blackness and pain and heat, only not so near. He felt himself slipping back. His desk wasn't where he had left it. He floated through the office, tables and files and machines moved past and beyond him, nothing was still. He too must keep moving. Noises and heaviness and cramp but an urgency, there was an urgency, there was something he had to do. He couldn't rest, he couldn't float, he couldn't let it go. He owed it. He owed it to someone.

Mrs.Ridgeway brought him a plate and floated away. There were faces eating and smiling then Mrs.Jervis laughing and choking and rising from the table in that way of hers. Mr.Baxter rose in a panic and rushed out and Elliott sneered and sneered and changed into Miss

Catesby who touched her eyebrows with the tips of her fingers and pursed her lips but wouldn't speak and pushed against the very pale face of Jackson who shook his fist and roared but Henry couldn't hear because he was drifting away again. Numbness and heat welled up again and darkness but not so dark. He was slipping. Slipping.

If only...if only...a strange door looming up and a dull light in the hall. Where was she? A small round figure with a fat neck and a gash of a mouth...but she didn't belong. She had gone, there was a space, he couldn't remember. There was Elizabeth, Elizabeth and her scent bottles and the warmth of her room and her smile. "You are clever, Henry." she had said...what had she said, but how could she have known? He felt the taxi gliding slowly and smoothly. Elizabeth, relaxed and comforting. Floating towards him, smiling and reaching for his arm, holding him tight. Too old, too old, too old, too late, too late. She whirled and whirled and her arm flung out and the door opened and they were home and safe and everything was drifting. He mustn't drift. He must try, he must try, must try once more. Must. Another face, faint yet insisting, struggling to emerge from the mist, the dim. He must speak to this face, he had something to tell him. He owed it to him.

The D.C.I. was back at his desk, his diversionary business had been concluded and he was eager to get on with the investigation. He glanced again at the note Trevor Johnson had left him - Digoxin, a digitalis type drug, normally given for heart problems. He picked up the file on Mary Telford and read it through, not at all sure why his Inspector had interested himself in it. He was sorry that Johnson wasn't back yet, he needed to be brought up to date. That was the trouble with interruptions, they left you feeling way behind. He found Henry Allingham's notebook next to the file and read it through with growing interest. Then, with great determination, he read through

267

the statements made by the residents concerning their movements on the previous evening and concentrated on them. Soon he growled and reached for the phone.

"Could I speak to your Mr.Frimton, please. Yes. Detective Chief Inspector Duncombe here. Mr.Frimton, I wanted to check on your last statement. You said you dined out with Miss Ferguson but you did not say exactly where you dined, you simply said a restaurant in Beresford Road. Ah, The Granby. You didn't happen to see Mr.Allingham or Mrs.Elmwood during the course of the evening? Yes, they were there. You saw who? Mrs.Jervis! When was that? 8.30. In the bar? You are absolutely certain? She didn't see you? What time did you leave The Granby? You sat in the lounge, what time did you leave the dining room to move into the lounge? You didn't see Mr.Allingham and Mrs.Elmwood leave? You couldn't see either the dining room or the bar from where you were sitting? I see. Did you have occasion to go to the bar yourself? Waiter, I see. Now, please think very carefully about my next question, I don't want to come back to you again. Did you ever leave Miss Ferguson's side between 7.30 and 9? Thank you Mr.Frimton, I'm afraid I must ask you to make another statement, it's a pity these details were left out."

Duncombe pulled out Mrs.Jervis's statement. It was suspiciously vague. She was upset about something and had decided to go for a walk to clear her mind. She had walked all evening without being sure where she was going. She had left The Moorcroft at 7.20, after dinner and had arrived back at about 9.15. She had made no mention of visiting The Granby. She had not seen anyone she knew on her walk.

The D.C.I. growled again and telephoned Mrs.Ridgeway to check that Mrs.Jervis wasn't at the hotel then he despatched a constable to find her at the public library. He studied Mrs.Jervis's other statements then read Johnson's file on her. There was nothing obviously amiss.

She had been in town on Saturday 28th, she had visited the library but times weren't exact, there was time for her to have killed Jenny Phillips. It would have been difficult for her to have killed Lucy Oxbury given the time she entered the dining room that night, but not impossible since the time of death wasn't exact. He must dig further to unearth a motive.

Further telephone calls failed to enlighten him. Mrs.Jervis led a well organised existence, married to a man who was a pillar of his community, the couple were well known and generally approved of. Christine Jervis was ambitious and affected a superior manner. It was likely that she would gain the promotion she desired. Her sister knew of nothing that might have upset her, Christine had been quiet and self absorbed since childhood. She had not wanted children, she had wanted security and an interesting career. He enquired after Mr.Jervis's health. Mr.Jervis suffered from an irregular heartbeat and had medication for it. That last piece of information was particularly interesting. Duncombe wondered if it could be Digoxin. Unfortunately, he was unable to speak to Mr.Jervis, he had no record of his employers. There were many firms of accountants in the phonebook and none of them had the name Jervis in the titles. He may have been working for a large company as its own accountant. He would have to wait until the evening.

The phone rang. The constable he had despatched to find Mrs.Jervis had phoned in to the station to say that Mrs.Jervis had not been into the library today. The librarian had expected her but she had not turned up. Duncombe sat up. Mrs.Jervis had not been a prime suspect until now. It seemed that things were beginning to gell rapidly. Immediately he needed to be out and about. First, he would put out an alarm for Christine Jervis. He phoned for D.S.Green only to be told he was with Inspector Johnson. He stalked down the corridor.

"What's this?" He roared. "I thought you were still

out?"

"I came in ten minutes ago, I thought you were still out."

"Never mind all that, I've got news for you. Christine Jervis was at The Granby last night. Your note said that was where Elmwood and Allingham were. Frimton didn't say which restaurant he dined at so I checked with him and found out it had been The Granby. He didn't see our two victims but he did see Jervis in the bar there at 8.30. Now, Jervis hasn't been at work today and, guess what? Mr.Jervis has a heart condition. I think we have a case brewing."

Johnson was quick to tell his Chief about his discovery and the lab's report on it.

"A plant? A piece of box and no contents? Very interesting and very well planned, it seems. Let us trace our Mrs.Jervis, if her husband's medication turns out to be Digoxin it will look bad for her. But how could she get the stuff into their food without being seen?"

"Perhaps she was seen. We don't know whether the two victims saw her, perhaps she stopped to speak to them at their table. They've not had a chance to tell us the whole story yet."

While the search for Mrs.Jervis was going on the two senior detectives thought they would visit the hospital together. D.C.I.Duncombe wanted to get out of the station and Inspector Johnson wanted to enquire about Henry Allingham. First, they called upon the constable who had been posted outside the ward. He reported that there had been a visitor, most anxious to see the gentleman, a woman, dark hair, early forties, wouldn't leave her name but enquired most urgently after the patient. Duncombe and Johnson exchanged looks. It had to be Mrs.Jervis. The constable had no idea where she had gone. He was sent to seek assistance and to search the rest of the hospital in case she was still in the building.

They looked from the doorway to the side ward at Henry Allingham and saw him lying rigid as before. The nurse by his bed shook her head to indicate no change and to discourage their approach. They crossed the ward and looked for Mrs.Elmwood. They were admitted to her small side ward. Johnson saw at once that she looked much brighter. She was still very fatigued but her hair looked more silky and her face bore signs of delicate make-up. She greeted them with a wan smile. The nurse was quick to say that she was still weak and should not be bothered too much as yet.

Duncomb immediately took charge.

"We think you can be of further help to us, Mrs.Elmwood. Did you or Mr.Allingham see anyone you knew while you were dining at The Granby the other night?"

"No, I don't think we did. At least, I didn't."

"No one stopped at your table for a chat?"

"No one. Why do you ask?"

Johnson bit his lip. Clearly, Mrs.Jervis was not going to be in the running. Whatever she was doing at The Granby that night she could not have interfered with the food. The pointer was still firmly in Henry's direction.

"Inspector Johnson tells me that you left the table for a while during the meal. Could anyone have stopped by while you were away?"

"I should think it was perfectly possible but Mr.Allingham didn't mention it when I got back."

"You do realise that your meal had been tampered with? What we are trying to establish is how and when it could have happened."

Mrs.Elmwood passed her hand swiftly across her hair, looked solemnly into Duncombe's eyes and shook her head.

"I have no idea...it is all a mystery."

Duncombe left the room in silence. He wasn't listening to

Johnson when he said he would stay to enquire about Henry Allingham. He hardly troubled when the constable rushed up to say that Mrs.Jervis had been found in the hospital's main waiting room.

"Oh, have her brought down to the station, will you. I'll have a word with her later. But I want you back on that door."

"I'm going to make a few enquiries, myself. I'm going to work on a private hunch. Do you remember your rule book?"

Johnson was accustomed to enigmatic questions from his Chief and it wasn't the first time that the D.C.I. had disappeared on solitary missions. He recognised the determination on his face and knew that it would be totally wrong to ask what it was all about. He would get no answer. He was intrigued with what he saw as his Chief's sudden loss of interest in Christine Jervis. It was all stop, go, stop, go with D.C.I.Duncombe but he had to admit that the man got results.

When he re-entered Henry's side ward he found the nurse there in a state of excitement. She beamed at him and invited him to look at the green signal in the box by the bed. It looked different but he couldn't say the same for Henry. He lay, as before, absolutely still except for the tiny movements round the mouth and eyelids he had seen before.

"Is that good?"

"Oh yes, that's a very good sign. I'll have to get the doctor to have a look at him. Please wait outside."

There was a great flurry. A senior sister rushed along followed by the doctor who had spoken to Johnson earlier and another figure in a white coat. They brushed past and disappeared into the ward. After quite some time, they emerged looking pleased.

"It looks as though your Mr.Allingham has begun to turn the corner at last, Inspector.

"When do you think he will regain consciousness,

doctor?"

"I couldn't tell you, it could be hours, it could be minutes."

"Would it be safe to talk to him when he comes round?"

"Oh, you mean would it be a shock for him? It might be. Would he know you? It might be better if the first person he sees is someone he knows."

"I fear Mr.Allingham doesn't know many people. He probably knows me as well as any anybody. Is it alright if I stay here for a while?"

"I'm not too happy about disturbing him. If he were to ask for you it would be different."

"The nurse can keep an eye on me. I promise to do exactly as she tells me. If she sees that my presence is in any way disturbing him, I'll immediately withdraw. Is that reasonable?"

"Alright, under those circumstances, I agree."

CHAPTER FORTY TWO

Henry had had a good rest. The cramps had abated, the heat, the dull pain and heaviness seemed to have left him. There were no swirling visions, just a numbness and a thirst and a sourness. He wanted to move. He needed to stretch. The darkness did not hang so heavily as it had seemed to do. He thought he could hear a distant sound. A soft, regular signal to his left. Curious! He roused himself to listen and encountered light. He blinked. Just out of the corner of his eye he saw a face. It was a familiar face, one he had seen just recently. It was the face he wished to talk to. He struggled to remember and the nurse rushed over to calm him.

"The canvas bag!"

Henry's voice was strained and distant.

"The canvas bag! That was how."

"Take it easy, Mr.Allingham, just rest." The nurse helped Henry to a glass of water.

"How did she know? I didn't tell her, but she knew what it was."

Henry was desperately thirsty and desperately anxious to tell the Inspector what he knew. The nurse was not happy that he should be so restless.

"He mustn't get excited like this, Inspector, you'd better go."

"No, no, not yet! It was carried out in the canvas bag...."

"Inspector!"

"And the box-spanner. She knew what it was."

The nurse pulled Johnson towards the door. He was obliged to leave.

Trevor Johnson couldn't think what Henry Allingham had meant. Canvas bag had no significance for him. He was thinking of the meal at The Granby, he thought Henry was refering to the poison. Who could have taken the poison out in a canvas bag, Mrs.Jervis? A waiter? What sort of bag was a canvas bag? And who had known about the box-spanner? He was puzzled that the knowledge of it was so important to Henry, perhaps he was just wandering as he emerged from his coma.

He arrived back at the station guessing, rightly, that his next job would be to interrogate Mrs.Jervis. He did not relish this prospect, he remembered that she seemed formidable at their first meeting, besides, the only things he knew that might give him teeth in this interview were that she had not mentioned visiting The Granby on Thursday night and her husband was on medication which might turn out to be Digoxin. He found Mrs.Jervis rather angry at having been brought to the police station. She demanded to know why.

"You didn't mention in your last statement that you called at The Granby on Thursday evening?"

"The Granby? What...Oh, you mean....I simply needed to sit down. I went for a long walk, as I said. There have been one or two things on my mind that I wanted to get clear. I didn't notice where I was going, I didn't know that part of town, I suddenly realised I needed a rest. There was this hotel, very respectable looking, I went in and had a brandy to pick myself up. I didn't stay more than twenty minutes. I'm not in the habit of going into public houses on my own...."

"Did you know where Mr.Allingham and Mrs Elmwood had gone to eat that night?"

"No, I didn't even know they had gone out together until Mrs.Ridgeway told me the next morning."

"Did you see anyone at The Granby you knew?"

"No. As I said, I didn't linger and I didn't know the place. I wouldn't expect to know anyone there."

"What time did you get there and what time did you leave?"

"What are all these questions for? Why have you brought me here?"

"Just answer my questions, please, Mrs.Jervis."

"You can't think I can have had anything to do with what happened to Mr.Allingham and poor Elizabeth?"

"What time did you arrive...."

"I didn't notice the time I arrived there but I left at twenty to nine. I suddenly realised that I would have to hurry back. I always phone my husband between nine and quarter past. I walked part of the way back then took a bus...but it's all in my statement."

"Unfortunately, you never mentioned your visit to The Granby in your statement."

"Didn't I? Well, it isn't very important...."

"Everything is important when you are making a statement, Mrs.Jervis. It so happens that The Granby is the restaurant where Mr.Allingham and Mrs.Elmwood ate and where they were poisoned."

Mrs.Jervis paled. There was a silence.

"Why didn't you go to the library today, Mrs.Jervis?"

"I couldn't face research today. I went up onto the moors for some fresh air and pulled myself together. When I got back I realised I had been very selfish so I thought I would make amends. I went out to Broughton to visit the hospital. I went to the ward where Mr.Allingham was and they turned me away, I gather it was the same for Mrs.Elmwood. They didn't say what the reason was so I went down to the waiting room for a cup of tea. I was going to try again later."

Johnson pressed her hard on the reason for her walks but she said that her worries were personal, to do with her work and her chances of promotion. She refused to enlarge on that and she insisted that she had arrived at The Granby by chance. She had not seen Henry and Mrs.Elmwood return to the hotel. She did not think it odd that she should try to visit them in hospital.

Johnson then asked her about her health and the health

of her husband. This was something Mrs.Jervis was happy to talk about. Her own health was very sound but her husband suffered from an irregular heartbeat. Without prompting, she talked about his symptoms and his medication. He had been prescribed various things over the years. His most recent prescription was of the digitalis type. When asked about dosage she claimed that at this time the dosage was very low, their doctor was only trying it out. Her husband had only shown her the new tablets last week when he visited the hotel. Johnson asked if anyone else at the hotel had seen these tablets. Mrs.Jervis was surprised at the question but she thought that anyone in the sitting room at the time could have seen them. She was curious as to why the Inspector had asked. Johnson told her that the two victims had been poisoned by just such a medicine. For the second time, Mrs.Jervis grew pale and was silent.

Trevor Johnson returned to his office. The woman had been straightforward, there had been no deception. Had she mentioned The Granby in her statement they may not have troubled to bring her in. He had looked into her background himself only the other day. There was nothing to connect her with Lucy Oxbury. She was too tall to be Mary Telford. There were no gaps in her history. Nothing suspicious. He had taken it on himself to let her go. If the D.C.I. wanted to see her he would have to bring her back, but he had sensed his lack of interest and was fairly certain he would not want to speak to her again.

The Inspector found himself, temporarily, at a loss. Unconsciously, he was waiting for Henry Allingham to tell him what he needed to know so that he could proceed. Without a statement from Henry, he was stuck. He would have to wait with as much patience as possible. He thought of the murders from the beginning, trying to get away from personalities and motives and to turn his mind to practicalities. He suddenly thought about the bathroom and the lack of steam. This was what Henry Allingham had noticed. Why had the extractor fan been switched off? Who had switched it off, Lucy or her murderer? It was a small bathroom, it would quickly become steamy. Would Lucy Oxbury want the extractor off while she bathed? That didn't seem likely, it would not have been considerate of the people who would follow her. Why should the murderer want to switch it off? Would he or she have wanted the room to cool more slowly?

Johnson decided to do some testing. There was a fan in the washroom just down the corridor. It hadn't been used very often, it wasn't automatic and the washroom wasn't used so very much. He looked at it and wondered how quickly it would clear a room nearly twice the size of the washroom. There was nothing to do but try it. It started reluctantly but by the time it got into it's stride, Johnson knew why the extractor at the hotel had been switched off. The noise. Someone had wanted to talk to Lucy, someone she knew and would not be too troubled about seeing her in the bath. That person, it had to be a female of course, had gained entry by turning the bolt, had excused herself, they had spoken briefly, the extractor had been switched off, the conversation had resumed and, in the middle of it, the visitor had struck. It was all perfectly clear. He guessed that the murderer was in too much of a hurry to think of switching the extractor on again.

He needed to know just one thing. Mrs.Ridgeway would be able to tell him if the extractor was still working.

Duncombe had left the hospital very uneasy. Both his experience and his instinct had told him to distrust disparity in recovery rates. He was hard headed enough to distrust the sort of evidence that passed quickly before his eyes but he remembered the jottings of two entirely different people he had read only an hour or two ago. Now he must do some research to back up his new idea.

278

He settled to the telephone as soon as he got back to his office. After further reading of the papers on his desk and a series of difficult telephone calls over long intervals, he felt ready to make an arrest.

As he came out of his office, he saw Trevor Johnson beckoning him from the far end of the corridor.

"Not another damned disappearance, I hope?" he roared mischievously.

"Sir, I know how it was done...."

"You do, do you?"

Johnson looked around then drew his Chief into his office. Duncombe grinned, took off his hat and coat and sat down rather like a Rajah waiting to be amused.

"We know there was no steam in the bathroom when it was broken into, the extractor fan was switched off. I asked myself why it was switched off in a hotel where residents follow each other and it is important to keep everybody happy. The answer is because of the noise...."

"The noise?" The D.C.I. guffawed but Johnson took no notice.

"The murderer got into the bathroom by manipulating the lock as we know and spoke to Lucy Oxbury. In order to have a brief conversation, she, it has to be a she, switched off the fan. Lucy Oxbury continued to see to the taps and the murderer struck."

"Excellent! My congratulations, Inspector! Fine reasoning, it will finish the business off nicely. Between us we have done very well."

Johnson looked at his Chief suspiciously. "Between us," indeed!

"Yes. Between us. I know who the murderer is."

CHAPTER FORTY THREE

The doctors were well pleased with Henry's recovery. They were still concerned with the effect the poison may have had on his kidneys and other organs but they were relieved that he had emerged from his coma in relatively good shape mentally. Henry was rather embarrassed by all the attention he was receiving after he had roused himself the second time. Doctors and nurses alike referred to him as though he was a long lost friend or relation, seeming to vie with each other to make the most humourous quip. One in particular, the ward sister he gathered, took a distinctly proprietorial attitude towards him. The old Henry would have boiled within at this but the new Henry rather liked it.

The fact that he had no relations triggered a further wave of sympathy and attention and soon his locker top was crowded with small gifts from the staff. Fruit, sweets and fluffy mascots predominated. Henry could hardly look at them without a blush. He realised that there had been a time when none of them would have been welcome, his embarrassment would have been too extreme. Now it was entirely different, he could accept them all with true gratitude.

When the fuss had subsided and his tests were over, Henry lay back. He was still weak and in some discomfort but he was happily relaxed, thinking only of the friendliness of everyone at the hospital. Inevitably, after a while, he began to think about how he came to be in hospital. His memory was still not at its most vigorous, he had to make an effort, but he began to remember Elizabeth and their meal together. She had been so attractive in her grey suit and white pullover with the gorgeous red jewel at the throat. Suddenly, he wondered what had happened to her. He struggled to sit up and immediately a nurse approached the bed.

"Mrs.Elmwood, Mrs.Elmwood, what happened to Mrs.Elmwood?"

His voice was not yet strong. The nurse had to stoop to listen.

"Mrs.Elmwood? Oh, she's in the ward, on the other side. She's making good progress. It shouldn't be long before she's out."

"Good, good!" Henry didn't quite understand.

"She can come and have a word with you later, if you feel up to it."

Henry smiled, remembering how Elizabeth had snuggled up to him in the taxi on the way back.

"Yes, that will be nice." He whispered and sank back.

When he awoke again, she was there, sitting beside his bed, but she was different. He stared at the severe looking woman near him. He recognised the hair then the eyes and the mouth but the face was thinner and there were shadows under the eyes and the cheeks.

"Hello Henry!" Elizabeth spoke simply and smiled. It wasn't the radiant smile he remembered from their evening out. Somehow, she had suffered.

"Have you been ill, Elizabeth?"

"Yes, Henry, but I'm getting better. You too have been very ill, can you remember?"

"I remember our evening out, Elizabeth. Do you?"

"Henry, listen! You remember you had a notebook? You were keeping a record of everything that happened."

"Notebook?" Henry made a great effort. "Notebook...yes, it's coming back. The hotel... everybody waiting in the sitting room....Lucy Oxbury....."

"Yes, Henry, think! You kept a record, didn't you?"

"Jenny, that was cruel. They were both cruel deaths...."

"What did you do with it, Henry?"

"Do with it, why I kept it in my overcoat."

"Are you sure?"

"I always kept it in my overcoat except for

mealtimes...."

"But you didn't have it when you went to The Granby, did you?"

"Yes, Elizabeth, I did. It was in my overcoat when I took it off, I remember I nearly put it in my jacket pocket then changed my mind."

"But...but...."

"I nearly went to fetch it when you asked to see it again but I didn't want to spoil such a lovely evening."

There was a long pause. Elizabeth looked rather put out.

"What's wrong, Elizabeth? That notebook is hardly worth worrying about, I was going to throw it away anyway."

"Henry, I want you to do something for me. Don't ask me why. Just...out of the regard you have for me. I have a note here. Will you write something on it for me?"

"If I can, Elizabeth. I'm not in the best position."

"I'll help you Henry. Quick, before the nurse comes back! Here's the pen, just print if it's easier. I want it as a souvenir of our wonderful night out. Say: 'you are the only one for me, Elizabeth, sorry'. You are sorry, aren't you Henry? Sorry that I couldn't marry you, I mean."

Henry stared at her. This wasn't like the Elizabeth he knew. She was pale and trembling.

"Please, Henry, it means so much to me."

She had become very agitated. Henry thought there was no harm in humouring her in this way. He leaned forward and took the pen. He was shaky but he managed to scribble down the words Elizabeth had dictated. She snatched up the note with a little cry. They had been quick. No nurse had disturbed them.

"Goodbye, Henry, you are a good soul. I'll always remember you. Go back to sleep now."

It wasn't long after this visit that Elizabeth had visitors of her own. She had been wearied by her effort to secure

Henry's note and was lying propped up but half asleep when D.C.I.Duncombe and Inspector Johnson arrived at her bedside.

"Mrs.Elmwood, the doctor tells me you are fully capable of understanding what I am saying to you, is that correct?"

"Yes, what is it? Is it Henry? What has happened to him?"

"Nothing we know of, Mrs.Elmwood. Should anything have happened to him?"

"Er...I don't know, he has been so very ill, you see."

"Yes, he has...."

"Are you sure he's alright? I looked in to speak to him a few minutes ago and he did not look well at all."

"No, I'm sure he didn't, but he's going to pull through. Then he should be able to talk to us...."

"You mustn't be too hard on him, Chief Inspector. He's had a hard time, under so much strain. He didn't know what he was doing. He asked me to forgive him, look, here's the note he wrote me."

Elizabeth brought the note out from under her pillow. Duncombe looked at it and smiled grimly.

"Excuse us a moment, Mrs.Elmwood, we'd better take a look."

He and Johnson left the bedside and crossed the ward to Henry's little room. Henry was sound asleep. The Sister was at his locker changing his water jug.

"Excuse me, Sister, is Mr.Allingham alright? His condition hasn't suddenly changed?"

The sister bridled and colour rose in her cheeks. She took this as a challenge. She put down the jug she was holding, glared at the intruders, thought better of a protest and took up Henry's wrist in a brisk movement. At the same time she raised the watch pinned to her tunic. After a few seconds, she felt Henry's brow then turned up one of his eyelids. Henry stirred.

"Try this, Mr.Allingham."

Quickly, the Sister popped a thermometer into Henry's half open mouth. Henry's eyes opened wide. It was the old Henry who resented this rude awakening but he was not allowed to speak. Two minutes later, the sister studied the thermometer and checked her reading of it with the chart at the foot of the bed. Then, taking a deep breath, she turned imperiously to her questioners.

"I can declare quite clearly that Mr.Allingham's condition has not changed. Is that all you wanted to know? Because if it's...."

"Just a moment, Sister, is that Mr.Allingham's water jug?"

Johnson took up the jug from Henry's locker.

"That's the new one. I change them every day - when I get the chance!"

She glared at them more fiercely.

"And that's the old one? There's not much left...."

"Mr.Allingham has to drink as much as possible to clear his...."

"And there's something in the bottom, too. Look, Sister, see for yourself. I think we should have this tested, sir."

They returned to Mrs.Elmwood's bedside.

"Is everything alright?"

Elizabeth Elmwood was most solicitous.

"I think so, Mrs.Elmwood."

"I have to tell you, Chief Inspector, that Henry told me everything. He had decided to end it all. He waited until I had left the table, I had a coughing spell and had to go to the cloakroom to recover. While I was away he put this poison into the food. He said he didn't really mean to hurt me but he did want to do away with himself, you see...."

"Mrs.Elmwood, how did Mr.Allingham manage to do that?"

"Do what, Inspector?"

"Put the poison into your food while you were away

from the table?"

"Why...I suppose...he must have sprinkled it or something. I didn't taste it."

"But the waiter told us that while you were away he took the first course dishes away and he was just bringing the second course when you came back."

Elizabeth was dumb. Her mind was spinning.

"Well, that is what he said."

"Just now?"

"Yes, when I was speaking to him a little while ago."

"Ah well, no doubt he will confirm that in due course."

"Why can't you respect his last wishes, Chief Inspector? He said he only wanted to die in peace."

"I think he will, eventually, if he is left to do so."

Elizabeth looked puzzled.

"Mrs.Elmwood, what was the nature of your late husband's illness?"

"Parkinson's disease. I'm afraid he had a long struggle."

"And what was his medication?"

"Oh, I can't remember. It was five years ago, you know."

"It was Digoxin, wasn't it? It was, Mrs.Elmwood, I checked with your doctor in Leeds, earlier today."

"Well, if you say so...."

"Before you married William Elmwood, your name was Mary Telford, wasn't it?"

A terrible change came over Elizabeth's face. Her eyes and mouth seemed to sink and her cheeks went slack. She shut her eyes and was completely still.

"Lucy Oxbury recognised a mannerism of yours. She had seen you in court when you were charged with killing your first husband. Did she tell you that? I can't imagine that she was much of a threat to you. Why did you kill her?"

Mrs.Elmwood kept her eyes shut. Her voice seemed to come from far away.

"I worked hard for a new life. I nursed my second husband through a long illness and when he died I came to Maskerley. I came for a new life. I thought I was free. I only wanted freedom and security."

"But why did you kill her. Was she blackmailing you?"

"Oh no! No! No!" She shook her head slowly. There was a long silence.

"Why did you kill Jenny Phillips?" Duncombe's voice was soft but insistent.

"Jenny saw me coming out of the bathroom just before dinner. She saw me relocking the door. She didn't understand what I was doing but I couldn't let her be a witness. I didn't want her to be interviewed by the police. I asked her to come into town that morning to get her away from the hotel. I didn't know what to do with her so I said meet me in the Coffee Shop and have a chat. I wanted to know exactly what she had seen and what she thought of it. She saw that I wasn't alone and wandered off. It was just luck that I saw her on that bus. I waved...she must have trusted me...she got off and we went for a walk along the tow path. It was very dark and quiet on account of the rain. I asked her what was troubling her and....when she wasn't looking I strangled her and pushed her into the water...."

She seemed in a trance. She spoke softly and slowly, almost mechanically, her eyes still closed.

"And Mr.Allingham?"

"Ah, poor Henry...I needed to find a scapegoat before your enquiries turned up my past. I thought of it when he said he had seen Jenny in town."

"You never gave any of them a thought, did you?"

"Did you know what sort of life I had? Do you have any idea what it is to struggle for years with pain and guilt, do you know what three and a half years in gaol with hardened criminals is like?" Mrs.Elmwood was suddenly animated.

286

"None of them did you any harm, did they?"

Tears streamed from Mrs.Elmwood's closed eyelids.

"Oh, you cannot understand......you cannot possibly understand...."

There was a silence, the whole hospital seemed to be waiting.

"I thought the past was dead...I was shocked...I recognised a birthmark just by her left wrist, when she moved her watch...I couldn't believe it. I couldn't believe that life could be so cruel....Lucy was my daughter, my first husband's child. I arranged for her to be adopted when she was very young after my husband became violent. He was jealous and threatened to abuse her...I was so shocked, I couldn't bear her to know.... to live with the knowledge....."

There was another long pause.

"Mary Elizabeth Elmwood, I am arresting you for the murders of Lucy Oxbury and Jenny Phillips and the attempted murder of Henry Allingham. You are not obliged to say anything but anything you do say will be taken down in writing and may be given in evidence against you."

CHAPTER FORTY FOUR

Several days later, Henry was allowed to leave hospital. He was delighted to arrive back at The Moorcroft. Mrs.Ridgeway was delighted to have him back. Much seemed to have changed. Henry was astonished to find that he was the only member of the original group left. Mrs.Jervis had completed her studies and had gone home. Miss Catesby had suddenly become more fragile and a distant relative had taken her away. Mr.Jackson had recovered his licence and had gone back to his flat in Wakeham. Mr.Frimton had gone to stay with his fiancee's family permanently. Baxter and Elliott were detained at Her Majesty's pleasure. Mrs. Elmwood was awaiting trial.

Mrs.Ridgeway had kept Henry's room for him and he was thankful that at least that was constant. To his mingled fear and delight there were four new boarders and Mrs.Ridgeway told him with distinct pride that another was expected at the weekend. She declared that the future of The Moorcroft was assured once again. For a while after Mrs.Elmwood's arrest, there had been a sudden rush of customers. She claimed that they were almost certainly ghouls or journalists writing copy "From the Inside" but they were welcome from the financial point of view. Her reputation had not suffered. Her present customers were a mixture of long and short term residents. They had all come to her on recommendation and she was proud and grateful for that.

Henry noticed at once that new locks and catches had been fitted to the bathrooms. On his tour of inspection, he noticed a small button near each door. Just below it was an engraved notice. "For use in Emergencies Only". He smiled grimly, thinking first of poor Lucy Oxbury then of his own situation; what would his tormentor, Denzil Elliott, have made of that?

A light step on the stair made him vacate the bathroom. A young woman, tall and dark, passed him and gave him a shy smile. With only the slightest hesitation, Henry greeted her pleasantly. She introduced herself as Mary Coulson, she had only been at the hotel two days, was Henry new? They walked down to the sitting room together, where, for the very first time, Henry sat and talked for no other reason than a pleasant wish to do so.

Before dinner, he had a visitor. Inspector Johnson called to see him. Henry was honoured but apprehensive. He wasn't sure that he wanted anything more to do with the case. He knew that Elizabeth, the soft, warm, friendly woman of his recent dreams had sought to kill him. He knew, now, that she had killed Lucy Oxbury and Jenny Phillips but he could hardly bring himself to believe it. There had been a flurry of publicity from which he had been protected by the vigilance of the hospital staff. They had said that he should try to put it all from his mind, but with so little to occupy him, he had found it very hard to do so. There had been black moments when the hurt and the numbness had returned. He did not want them to return if it was at all possible.

"I wanted to congratulate you on your recovery, Mr.Allingham. You must be relieved to be back. I hope that you will have a little more time to take it easy before you have to go back to work."

Work! Henry had never given it a thought.

"I have to warn you that you will be required to give evidence at the trial in a few weeks time. I'm not sure when exactly it will be, it depends upon the prosecution."

"Must I?" Henry was dismayed at the thought.

"I'm afraid so. You will be one of the principal witnesses. It won't be easy of course."

"Humph! It would be so nice if it were all over."

"I agree Oh, by the way, we're hanging on to your notebook. It will be vital to the prosecution. You will get it back in due course...."

"Oh, I don't think I want to see that again."

"It was extremely useful, sir. I have to apologise, I remember saying that amateur detectives never pay and often obsruct. You proved to be the exception and I'm only sorry we didn't look at your notebook sooner."

Henry was amazed but he had lost interest.

"You were right about the canvas bag, Mrs.Elmwood had the murder weapon in it all evening. She hung it outside her window when she went to bed. Later, when it was thoroughly dry, she cut it up and took it away in her handbag. And the box-spanner, she couldn't have known what it was unless she had put it under your bed herself. The third thing was the extractor fan. You were the first to realise that it had been switched off."

Henry smiled and nodded, it seemed not so important now.

"Finally, your notes about the personal mannerisms. I don't suppose you ever guessed how significant they were to be?"

"No, but none of it matters now. It's almost dinner time, Inspector, would you excuse me?"

The Inspector was most amused.

"Certainly, Mr.Allingham. Thanks for all your help. Goodbye!"

Henry enjoyed his dinner but he enjoyed the company of the strangers in the dining room even more. Never had he been more relaxed and interested. He resisted talk of the murders and only acknowledged his involvement as a fellow resident. At the end of the meal he decided he would take a short walk. He put on his coat and hat and opened the front door ready for a small adventure. Immediately there was a flurry of movement. Reporters had been told by someone at the hospital's reception desk that Henry had been discharged. They had descended upon The Moorcroft in force and before he could retreat, Henry was photographed and bludgeoned with questions from all sides. He pulled a face and backed through the door. It took all of his strength to shut the door against the howling mob.

He wasn't unduly troubled. He'd survived two weeks of it before he went into hospital. He could do it again. He didn't have to return to work for a few days yet, he would remain indoors and frustrate the press.

The next morning, he suffered two blows. First, a letter arrived from his firm to tell him that, due to re-organisation, he was to be assigned to a new post in South Yorkshire. Starting from the beginning of January, subject to his acceptance, he would be in charge of a small despatch depot with a modest rise in salary. Should he not be willing to accept this move, he would be retired on full salary for one month followed by half salary for two months. In that time he was expected to have found alternative employment. After that, his firm would no longer be responsible for him.

The second blow was deeper. Inspector Johnson telephoned to tell him that Elizabeth Elmwood had committed suicide during the night. Henry might be required to attend the coroner's enquiry but there would not be a trial. He did not care to ask the Inspector for details. The newspapers gave full accounts the next day. She had slit her wrists with a narrow penknife before she went to bed. No one had suspected what she had done until they found her dead the next morning. There was no note.

Henry Allingham had long experience in enduring hurt. He had rarely understood it, he had simply bypassed it. He was always stunned but his subconscious absorbed the hurt and he was able to survive behind a barrier of cold reserve. The new Henry struggled to prod him towards company and cheerfulness but the old Henry had never disappeared. Now, the hurt was such that the old Henry took over. Behind his reserve, Henry was less happy but also less vulnerable. He gave up his plan to stay indoors, fought his way through the newsmen and went on a long walk over the moors. He went down to dinner early as had been his wont, spoke to no one, ate silently and bade no one goodnight. The next morning found him silent at his usual table, his eyes averted from the newcomers as they came in. After he had eaten, he rose silently, nodded distantly and withdrew without ceremony. Mrs.Ridgeway was quick to recognise the Mr.Allingham of old and sighed to herself.

Henry eschewed the extention of his recouperation period and returned to work immediately. The office ladies saw at once that C.W. had returned to normal. They were rather relieved. The new Henry had been almost too much for them. They had a well established pattern of work under the old Henry and had no wish to change.

That evening, Henry had difficulty in obtaining entrance to the bathroom at his usual time. It was necessary for him to speak to Mrs.Ridgeway about it. She said it would take time for the newcomers to acknowledge Mr.Allingham's routine. In time, all would be well.

In time, all would not be well. The need to move would see to that. Henry remembered his hopes of a new life, warmth and scent bottles, pictures and magazines...but that would never be! Tomorrow was Saturday, he would take a bus to Fernhead and walk back over the moors. He would be back at five at the latest for a good soak. He would think about his new job and his next lodging. He, himself, did not have to change. He would quickly establish a new routine, a new orderly existence. After all, he had done so on more than one occasion.